ARCHMAGE

A Montague & Strong Detective Novel

ORLANDO A. SANCHEZ

ABOUT THE STORY

When faced with overwhelming odds, there's only one option…overwhelming power.

When Monty and Simon emerged from Hell, they did so possessing the first of the five arcane runes—Mu.

Divided between the two of them, the rune is the only way to stand against and defeat a Keeper of the Arcana.

Keeper Gault has only one purpose now: the obliteration of Montague and Strong. After his second, Tellus, failed to capture the rune, Gault finds himself forced to take extreme measures. In order to increase his power and recover the elder rune, he must erase Monty and Simon from existence.

Now, Monty and Simon must find a way to harness and control the power of the first rune before it's too late. Their only chance of defeating Gault is using the energy contained within the elder rune.

There's only one small problem.

The rune possesses too much power for them. Any attempt to use it would destroy them both. To access the elder rune, they need the power of an Archmage.

To achieve this power, they need to cause a runic shift in Monty.

A shift he isn't ready for.

A shift that will kill him on his way to becoming an Archmage.

"Nearly all men can stand adversity, but if you want to test a man's character, give him power."
—Abraham Lincoln

People speak of hope as if it is this delicate, ephemeral thing made of whispers and spider's webs.
It's not.
Hope has dirt on her face, blood on her knuckles, the grit of the cobblestones in her hair, and just spat out a tooth as she rises for another go.
—Matthew @Crowsfault

The best way to keep a prisoner from escaping is to make sure he never knows he's in prison.
—Fyodor Dostoevsky

DEDICATION

To the escapists, the ones who squeeze in just one more chapter, the ones who begin in the early evening, then turn around bleary-eyed to greet the new dawn; to those going through dark times, but are able to find some light in these stories.

This story is for you.

For Zella

ONE

Peace is an illusion.

I sat in the shade on a massive stone bench in a large courtyard, my eyes closed, enjoying the brief tranquility.

Beside me on the ground, my hellhound slept. Chainsawing snores interrupted the silence every few minutes, causing me to smile as he kicked his legs in his sleep.

I wondered what he was chasing in his dream.

The bench faced an open plaza surrounded by tall trees. In the center of the courtyard—if I focused hard enough—I could see the faint outlines of a large runic circle. It pulsed rhythmically with latent energy, each pulse turning the symbols in the circle a different color.

I looked away and reflected on the last few days.

Considering I was, literally, in Hell not too long ago, this was a nice change. The best part was no one was actively trying to end my existence. It was surprisingly tranquil being able to just sit and do nothing. In the back of my mind, that small voice advised me: *Enjoy this while you can. You know your life. You'll be running from something trying to maim or kill you soon enough.*

I sighed and shook my head free of the voice.

Just then an energy spike caught my attention, causing me to look around—but aside from my hellhound, I was alone.

Not that I expected a threat in Dex's School of Battle Magic, previously known as the Golden Circle before Dex pulled a hostile takeover and borrowed the entire sect to create his school of battle magic.

I would assume a move like that would piss off some of the more proper mages that believed relocating an entire sect was against the rules somewhere.

Not that Dex was big on following rules. Except, as I gave it thought, he did follow some rules—those that worked to his benefit, usually.

Another energy spike had me resting my hand on the holster of Grim Whisper. Peaches looked up at me and chuffed.

<*Can you tell who it is? Are they a threat?*>
<*The Nut Girl. I like her. She is friends with the Cold Girl.*>
<*The Nut Girl?*>
<*She is close.*>

He opened his massive jaws in a gaping yawn, chuffed again, and then, promptly fell back asleep. So much for my Hellhound Early Warning Threat Detection System.

I slowly moved my hand from Grim Whisper. If he wasn't bothered, then I had no reason to be.

Another energy spike, this one closer, had me scanning my surroundings. I turned to the entrance of the courtyard, sensing her energy signature before she came into view.

I looked at the young girl approaching me.

The energy signature was impressive. She had to be around Cece's age, and gave me a short wave as she entered the expansive space. I watched her as she skipped from one stone to the next, with a grace and fluidity only gifted to the young.

Her jet-black hair was pulled back in a ponytail which bounced with each skip as her bare feet barely touched the stones. She wore a white T-shirt that read: *If you gaze too long into an abyss, the abyss also gazes into you.*

Beneath the quote it read: *Nietzsche was a coward.*

I let out a small chuckle.

"Nice shirt," I said. "Make it yourself?"

"I did," she said, looking down at her shirt when she finally reached the bench. "I can make you one. Would you like one?" She looked around the empty courtyard. "What are you doing here?"

"Enjoying the peace and quiet," I said, with a small smile. "I don't get much of either often."

She nodded sagely.

"The Sanctuary is really quiet, especially at night," she said. "You're Mr. Strong, right?"

"Simon is good," I said. "Hi, um... I don't really know what to call you. Is your name really—?"

"Peanut," she finished. "Yes, it is."

"Peanut?"

"That's what my mom used to call me, and that's the name I chose for me."

"Fair enough," I said with a nod. "Miss Peanut it is."

She shook her head.

"Just Peanut. No 'miss,'" she corrected. "Uncle Dex says titles are overrated."

"I agree with him on that. Peanut, then. How do you like it here?"

"I love it," she said, with barely controlled excitement. "Uncle Dex lets me explore anywhere. Well, *almost* anywhere. The lab rooms are off-limits after the last time."

"What did you do?" I asked, sensing a trend with magic users and destruction. "And how bad was it?"

"I'm still learning how to use my abilities, Aunt Morrigan

said." She climbed up on the bench and crossed her legs, facing me. "Mistakes can and will happen."

"Sounds like it was pretty bad."

She gave me a solemn nod as she thought on the incident and looked off into the distance. She wore an expression that was about thirty years too old for her young face. She shook herself out of her reverie and smiled at me.

It was a mischievous smile, full of secrets and knowing. A sense of familiar unease fell over me. For the briefest of moments, I looked around to make sure the Morrigan wasn't nearby.

"Uncle Dex turned red and did lots of screaming," Peanut continued. "Then he used a bunch of words I've never heard, but they sounded like the kind of words I would get in trouble for, if I said them out loud."

I smiled despite myself.

"Sounds like your Uncle Dex. I've made him curse a few times too."

"Really? How?" she asked. "No offense, but you don't seem very powerful. Your dog is cute, though. Can I pet him?"

"Give me a second," I said. "Let me ask him."

"You can speak to him?" she asked, her voice filled with awe. "That is amazing."

"The conversations usually revolve around meat," I said, raising a finger. "Hold on."

<Can she pet you?>

<She is very strong. Yes, she can rub the special place behind my ears. I like that.>

"He says you can rub him here," I said, showing her where my ham of a hound enjoyed having his ears rubbed. "He really likes that."

She scooted off the bench and proceeded to rub his ears

as he rumbled his satisfaction. When she was done, she jumped back up on the bench and stared at me.

"Why did Uncle Dex get mad with you? What did *you* do? Did you destroy a lab too?"

"That would be too long a list to go into, trust me," I said, shaking my head. "Most of the time I get into destructive situations because people have felt the need to remind me that I'm not a mage."

"So? Me neither. I think you get to decide what you are. Don't you?"

"I've realized that the world of magic has more than just mages," I said. "I'm going to choose to be something more than a mage. How about you?"

She nodded, giving it thought.

"Uncle Dex says he doesn't know what I am yet, but that I have power."

"That means you have to learn how to use it, especially when you're a non-mage."

"Even if you aren't a mage, so what? You have power, and you have to use it to help people who don't have power," she said. "That's what Uncle Dex says."

"Do you agree?" I asked. "Sounds like a big responsibility."

She took a few moments to think in silence. I could see the wheels in her young mind turn as she considered her answer. A frown flitted across her face before she smiled with a nod.

"Some bad people were going to take my power away."

Dex had briefly shared her history with me, but I wanted to hear her side of the story.

"Why?"

"I blew up a building and they thought I was too dangerous."

"Are you?"

She formed a small sun in the palm of her hand; the orb hovered above her hand, a bright blue-white. The energy around it was more than impressive, which concerned me. It was nearly as powerful as the orbs Monty formed—the only difference being that Monty was over two hundred years old, and this child was, well, a child.

She let it float for a few seconds, admiring it as it attempted to blind me, before she closed her hand into a fist, absorbing the orb and the power it released.

"Yes," she said, no pause in her answer this time. "I'm very dangerous...to bad people."

"How do you know who's bad?"

She cocked her head to one side and placed her hands on her hips as she looked at me.

"Oh, that's not hard," she explained. "Bad people want to hurt those who are weaker than them: those who don't have power, or those who can't protect themselves."

"Did you learn that from Dex too?"

"No, I learned that by living through it."

"You're wise for your years, Peanut," I said. "I'm glad I could learn from you today."

"I'm smart like that," she answered. "Uncle Dex says I'm too smart for my own good, but I don't think there's such a thing. Do you?

"I don't. I think you should try to be smarter than everyone."

She paused, smiled, and nodded her head. The next moment, she looked up suddenly and narrowed her eyes.

"I have to go," she said, quickly scooting off the bench. "I'm supposed to be doing my chores."

"Why aren't you?" I asked, smiling despite myself.

"Are you kidding?" she asked, incredulously and looked around the courtyard. "I'm living in a castle fortress. Who wants to do chores when I could be exploring?"

"Good point."

"Say hi to Uncle Dex for me!" she said, running off with a wave and disappearing around a corner. "Bye!"

Dex materialized behind me a second later, then walked around the bench and sat down heavily next to me.

TWO

"She just left, didn't she?" he asked, with a tired sigh.

"You just missed her," I replied, smiling. "She seems like a handful."

"Ach," he said, with a short nod before running a hand through his hair, which he wore loose this morning. "That sprite will be the death of me."

He formed an enormous sausage and placed it in front of my ever-ravenous hellhound, who promptly vacuumed it up into his massive jaws, devouring the meat in seconds.

"That's a good boy," Dex continued, patting Peaches' massive head. "You need to keep him fed. Have you learned how to make him meat yet?"

"The last time I tried that it was a danger to the tri-state area," I said. "Maybe I should just walk around with a crate of sausages."

"Don't be daft, boy," he said. "Learn the cast—it's easy and will help him grow into the hellhound he needs to become."

"Why does that sound scary?"

"Because it is," he said, with a smile. "Hellhounds are meant to be scary."

"How did Peanut know you were coming?" I asked, changing the subject from scary hellhounds. I wasn't quite ready to go there yet. "Is she that skilled?"

"She can sense me without even trying," he said, sitting on the bench next to me. "Do I need to explain how rare that is? Me—she can sense *me*. She is beyond her years in skill."

"Seems like a good skill to have when you should be doing chores and need to escape the authorities."

"Authority," he corrected. "She's Mo's favorite, which is why she gets away with murder. Being favored by a death goddess is not a good thing. As you are learning, very few manage to walk away with their lives intact."

I nodded my understanding.

Being the favorite of a goddess of death had a tendency to make life...interesting, if not downright deadly. I wasn't Kali's favorite, not by a long shot, and my life had gone from normal to catastrophic in the span of one curse. If Peanut was favored by the Morrigan, I could see her being steered into the business of death with little difficulty.

Something like that would radically alter who she became.

The only other person I knew who had managed to live her own life after serving a goddess of death was TK. According to the little I knew, her life under the Morrigan had been less than pleasant.

TK wasn't exactly known for her warm and welcoming demeanor. She was closer to petrifying and fearsome. I was fairly certain most of that came with the package, which was probably why the Morrigan chose her, but I had a feeling that it only became more pronounced after working with a goddess of death.

Being in close proximity with a goddess of Death changed a person—not always in a good way.

I didn't know if Peanut would become as powerful as TK, but if the orb she produced was any indication, she was well on her way to becoming scary strong and an easy candidate for the Morrigan's Death Squad, if the goddess had one.

That would be a bad thing.

"Would the Morrigan really recruit—?"

"No, not while I'm alive," Dex said, his voice firm. "Peanut will make her own choices as to what she wants to do with her life, but Mo is ancient and clever. It's why I love her, among other things." He gave me a wide grin, then grew serious again. "Mo won't have to ask her to join her. The sprite will do so willingly. That's what I'm afraid of."

"She's not a mage," I said. "Do you even know what she is?"

"Besides a major pain in my tuchus?" he asked, shaking his head. "I don't know what she is, but one thing is certain: she is not a mage."

"Tuchus? Really?"

"Too many years spent around Ezra," Dex grumbled, waving my words away. "Things rub off you know."

"How are you going to teach her?" I asked. "Is there a non-mage curriculum of study? A Magic for Dummies easy version?"

"I worry about you sometimes, boy," he said. He then gave me a look that said: *Do you ever stop to consider the words before they leave your lips?* "Mage, Archmage, sorcerer... Just words, and useless titles." He gave me another appraising look. "What do you think I am?"

"You mean besides scary and insane?" I asked. "No offense intended."

He laughed.

"None taken," he said, tapping my thigh with a chuckle. "Aye, I admit to both, but I meant in terms of power. How would you classify me?"

"Classify you?" I asked. "You're asking the wrong person."

"Try anyway," he said. "You can do it."

It wasn't a request.

This is where the scary part of Dex kicked in. Most of the time he appeared to be the crazy, fun uncle we all wished we had growing up.

Then I remembered his weapon, Nemain, and that he was currently the Harbinger of Death, involved in a relationship with the Morrigan, a triune Goddess of War and Death—and yes, her full title needed to be capitalized.

She was that fearsome.

Once that knowledge surfaced in my memory, Dex stopped being the fun uncle, and became the scary old mage that wielded a weapon designed to drive a person mad and managed to do so without any major side effects—at least none that I could see.

I cleared my throat and found my voice again.

"You're ancient and wield more power than my brain can process," I said. "I would say you're an Archmage, but you're also the Harbinger of Death, which to me requires you to possess more power than any Archmage I've met."

"Not bad," he said, rubbing his chin in a way that immediately brought Monty to mind. "You're observant, if not always prudent."

"Thanks," I said. "Is there something more powerful than Archmage?

"Aye, there is."

"Does that power level have an official name? Is it something like the Ultimate Supreme Grandmaster of Mageness?"

"Every time I think you have a grasp on the situation, you open your mouth and prove me wrong," he snapped. "What kind of nonsense is that?"

"It's not like *Archmage* is any better," I answered defensively. "Who thought that one up?"

"Occasionally, I forget you have no formal training," he said. "Archmage comes from the Latin *archmagus*. It just means first, or chief, mage. When it was first being used, it was not in relation to power, but position. That changed over time to include levels of power."

"So you're saying the Sorcerer Supreme is really just an Arch Sorcerer?"

He sighed.

"Did you happen to leave what little brain you had left in Hades?" he asked. "There is no such thing as a Sorcerer Supreme, outside of your imaginary doctor character."

"Just checking," I said. "Doctor Strange is a total badass, you know. So, no real name for something above an Archmage?"

"Not really," he said, pensive. "How do you feel when you hear you aren't a mage?"

"A little fed up, actually," I said, letting the frustration through. "Like, tell me something I don't know."

He nodded.

"The thing is, you need to shift your listening," he said, tapping his temple. "There is a part unsaid in that statement, *'You are not a mage.'*"

"So I'm beginning to understand," I said with a small nod. "I'm not a mage. I'm something else, with the potential to be something more."

He nodded again.

"Like the sprite," he admitted. "I have no idea what she is, but as I said, I do know she's not a mage. It doesn't lessen who she is, or the power she wields."

"She formed an orb that was impressive," I said, remembering the mini-sun she created without any gestures, or words of power. "A little more than impressive. It was scary how easily she created it, with no gestures or whispered words."

"Aye, you'd be wise to fear that power," he said, his voice grim. "Why do you think I'm here?"

"I thought you just enjoyed my company and wit."

"Boy, if I want to torture myself, I could have some words with Mo," he said, with a mischievous smile. "She can facilitate any torture I can think of, and many more I haven't imagined. In fact, just the other day—"

"No, thanks, really," I said, raising a hand in surrender. "I'm good on images of torture between you and the Morrigan."

I shuddered at the thought.

He laughed.

"You're saying you felt that orb she created?" I continued. "Not that I'm surprised. The energy it contained was off-the-charts."

"I sensed her cast across the sanctuary," he said, looking across the courtyard. "She's not to form any orbs without me or Mo present. Not that she always listens, as you've noticed."

"I noticed," I confirmed. "What was the orb she made?"

"She calls it a disintegrator," he said with a headshake. "It's a small cast, but it packs a punch. The last time she did something like that, she blew several holes in the outer walls. I came over to make sure she wasn't tearing the place apart."

"That would explain the hasty retreat," I said, gazing off where Peanut exited the courtyard. "She may not be a mage, but she seems to have the destruction part figured out."

"It's not in the title but the actions," he said. "Are you a dark immortal?"

"What?" I asked, taken by surprise. "I'm not a dark anything."

"You are according to Verity," he said with a small smile. "We are all villains in someone's story, boy. I'm making sure she doesn't fall into the trap of titles. Inflated egos can be a dangerous thing when one wields power."

I remembered Monty's position on titles. It made a bit more sense now.

"She has power, but doesn't fit into an easy classification, besides dangerous. And powerful."

"Aye, that she is," he said. "Much to Mo's delight. That woman is going to kill me one day."

"Except she's not really a woman, is she?" I asked. "She's the scary incarnation of war, death, battle, and more death, right?"

Dex looked to both sides before answering.

"You do realize she's a *goddess*?"

"Well, yes, I get *that* part," I said, confused. "I'm not understanding."

"That much is clear," Dex said with a small headshake. "She's a goddess, as in feminine. She may be a goddess, but she's all *woman* too."

"Oh," I said, still uncertain. "You're saying my words could probably get me blasted into little Simon particles, aren't you?"

"Good to see you're finally learning something," he answered. "There may be hope for you yet. In regards to the sprite, it's the same for you and my nephew. She needs to use—"

"She needs to use her power for good," I finished. "Not to become some scary being of insane power."

"Wrong," he said. "She can become an insane being of scary power. In fact she *must* become exactly that, or else she will either be exploited or killed."

"I don't follow," I said. "You *want* her to become scary?"

"Having power is not the same as abusing it," he clarified. "In order to do good, she must be as strong or stronger than those willing to do harm."

"You're saying having power doesn't mean being evil," I said. "Except, that my experience in this world of magic has shown me that in most cases, power or the seeking of it, is usually done by the twisted evil types."

"There's no denying that power can corrupt, which is why power on its own—"

"Can't be the goal," I said, getting a glimpse of understanding. "It has to be channeled toward something, something good and worthwhile."

He nodded approvingly.

"Exactly," he said, rubbing the side of his nose. "I've just spoken to my nephew."

"About?"

"The path you are both on."

"You mean the path where everyone wants us dead or erased?" I asked. "Do you know where this path leads?"

"I know where it could lead, but no, I don't know where it will end for the two of you," he said. "That's for you two to decide."

"How bad is it?"

He gave me a cheery smile.

"Not everyone wants you dead or erased, not yet," he said. "But they will."

"That sounds wonderful in a root-canal-without-anesthesia kind of way."

He chuckled and clapped me on the shoulder.

"It's going to get much worse before better is even on the horizon," he said, still chuckling. "Embrace it. Your life is going to get far more interesting."

"I had a feeling you were going to say something like that," I said. "I don't want an interesting life. I'd prefer a dull, boring life without regular lethal attacks. Can we arrange something like that?"

"I'm afraid not," he said. "It can't be helped, not now. Not with that rune you both hold."

"Monty said we can't give it back. Is he right? We're stuck with it?"

Dex nodded.

"For the foreseeable future, yes," he admitted. "Even if you could, no one in their right mind would take it off your hands unless they wanted to do massive damage to this world."

"It's been my experience those types are never in their right mind. It's usually the opposite."

"Precisely, which means you must learn to use it and find a way to acquire the others," he said, giving me a serious look. "It won't be easy."

"Use the power for good," I said. "That's what this is about, isn't it?"

"Yes. Even if it costs you everything."

"Everything," I repeated softly, and then the realization hit me. "That's why you're here, right now. You can't help us."

"Not directly, no. Not with this," he said, his voice grim. "This is your path to walk with Tristan. Those of us who care about the both of you will be close, but we can't walk it for you. No one can."

"So we're alone in this?"

"I never said you were alone," he said with a wicked smile. "I said we can't walk the path with you. I never said we were abandoning you."

"But that's what it sounded—"

"Ach, boy, you need to clean out those ears of yours," he said, getting up. "Some of us can't assist you directly, but there's nothing that says we can't help you indirectly. In fact, I'm sending you to some indirect help as soon as my nephew decides he's ready."

"Ready? Ready for what?"

"Why don't we go find out?" Dex said, pointing. "He's over in one of the training areas with his apprentice."

THREE

I headed over to the training area, following Dexter.

It was a smaller version of the courtyard I had been sitting in. The center of the space held a large runic circle with a group of symbols I couldn't decipher.

Even though the training area was smaller than the courtyard, the circle in its center was oversized compared to some of the circles I had seen in the past. This one was easily forty feet wide and sat on a slightly raised platform, giving the impression of a stage of sorts.

In the center of the circle stood Monty. Several feet away, facing him, stood Cece, looking determined. The outer ring of the circle flared a deep blue, and if I angled my head just so, I could see the wall of energy that enclosed them in the circle.

"What's going on?" I asked. "This looks serious."

"It is," Dex answered. "Cecelia has asked to ascend—to be shifted."

"Shifted?" I asked. "As in going up in power? You can *ask* for that?"

"At the lower levels, yes," Dex said with a nod. "I would imagine her exposure to Peanut has sparked a healthy rivalry. She wants to be as strong as the sprite."

"Is she?"

Dex shook his head.

"Cecelia is a Jotnar mage," Dex said. "She's powerful for one so young, and one day she will be as strong as the sprite, but not today, and not for a very long time. Peanut is not a mage; her power scales differently. Its source is... Well, I have theories. Cecelia still has a long way to go. This is the lesson Tristan must be ready to impart, without losing her."

"Losing her? You mean she can die from this ascendance test?"

"Stop being so daft, boy," he said, giving me a sidelong glance. "Losing her as in losing her as his apprentice. If he handles this poorly, she will turn away from the teaching. Whether she goes rogue depends on what he does today."

"Monty doesn't exactly have a great track record with children," I said, keeping my voice low. "Was he ever a child? Because honestly, communicating with anyone younger than a century seems to be a challenge for him."

Dex smiled.

"That's why having an apprentice is good for him," Dex said. "Keeps him grounded and out of his head."

"Out of his mind is probably closer to the truth," I said. "I'm serious. His idea of encouragement is pointing out everything she did wrong. You should've seen his reaction when she blew a hole in the Moscow."

"She blew a hole in the Moscow?" Dex asked, approvingly as he glanced at me. "How large was it? Was the building in danger of collapsing?"

I stared at him for a few seconds. What was it with mages and destruction?

"It was large enough that Monty needed to repair it," I said, recalling the incident. "He was not pleased. Olga was even less so. She kept shooting ice daggers at me."

"Why you?" Dex asked. "You didn't blast a hole in the building."

"I may have encouraged Cece to cut loose by testing the dawnward."

"Testing it how, exactly?"

"I told her to try and blast through it," I admitted. "I told her to unleash the beast."

"Unleash the beast?" Dex asked, with a small smile. "Those were your words?"

I nodded.

"She hit the dawnward hard," I said. "It didn't go through, but her blast bounced off the shield and into the side of the Moscow, punching a hole in it."

"Did Olga see that?"

"No," I said. "It was just Cece and me outside. There was no way Olga could've seen it happen. I barely saw it happen, and the blast was directed at me."

He nodded and rubbed his chin.

"Where was my nephew when all of this happened?"

"He was on his way downstairs," I said. "I think his reaction was a little over the top, if you ask me."

"It usually is, but this is a special case."

"How so?"

"Everything Cecelia does, or doesn't do, points back to him."

"You mean it makes him look bad if she demolishes a building?" I asked. "I guess that makes sense."

"No, it's more than that," Dex said. "As her instructor, he is responsible for every action she takes. He is accountable for *everything* she does."

"That would explain his initial reluctance," I said. "It doesn't explain him blowing things out of proportion. Do you know how much property damage he has unleashed? Property damage I get blamed for because I happen to be in the area?"

"Aye, I'm familiar," he said. "He's a bit high strung, that nephew of mine. Having her in his life is good for him. His apprentice adds some much needed disorder to his life—as all children do."

"Have you met Monty?" I asked. "The last thing he needs is more disorder in his life. He gets twisted if his jacket gets the wrong kinds of wrinkles, much less destroyed—which happens regularly."

"Aye," Dex said, with a nod. "You'd think he'd be over that by now. What with the enemies you two keep making. Ruined suits are the least of his worries. He always was a tad fastidious, even as a child."

I had no trouble imagining Monty as a fastidious and proper child. He was probably the type of boy that had his clothes sorted by color, fabric, and expected use, along with which day of the week said item would be worn.

"So he was well behaved?"

"Well behaved?" Dex asked, with a snort. "He's a Montague—I doubt it's even possible. No, that lad was a terror of the first order, even before he learned to manipulate energy. There's a reason I was called in to reinforce his studies. He was an unruly, difficult, arrogant little snot of a child, who felt he knew more than his instructors, and had no reservations about voicing his opinions."

"That sounds like a problem."

"It was," Dex said, with a mischievous smile. "Only because he was usually right and did know more than most of his instructors. The boy was a prodigy, mastering casts that took years in a matter of weeks. It turned him into an arrogant prig. So the Circle called me."

"What did you do?" I asked. "Was it an ascendance like this?"

"Not at first, no," Dex said. "He wasn't strong enough to request one from me when I took over his instruction. We just had a *conversation*. I had to let him know where he stood in the order of things."

"A conversation?"

Dex gestured forward with his chin.

"Something very similar to that, except I told him not to muck about with harmless casts," he said, his voice serious. "If he wanted to show me how serious he was, and how much he truly knew, he could use any cast he liked. The more lethal the better."

"What did he do?"

"He messed about and found out there's more to being a mage than being able to use energy and unleashing powerful casts. It was a lesson that I hope stayed with him, although I'm having my doubts these days."

"Me too," I said, looking at Monty and Cece. His recent trips into the darker side of things still nagged at me. Now, with this elder rune we shared, my concern only grew.

A thought occurred to me. "Wait, is that what—?"

"Relax, boy," Dex said, with a small chuckle. "Little Cecelia is not looking to break free of her instruction like he was. She just wants to know where she stands."

"This is the only way to do that?" I asked. "Can't they have a written test or something less, I don't know, violent?"

"No. This is the way it needs to be done," he said. "It is the way it has always been done. This is not a theoretical situation. It can't be discussed, it must be experienced. We can speak about energy, orbs, and casting all day, but nothing can replace the sensation of being struck in the face by an orb, can it?"

"Nothing comes close, except maybe an ogre fist punching you into next week."

He laughed.

"True, that does come close," he admitted, and then grew serious again. "This is a normal part of instruction. Tristan must give her the space and ability to unleash her power, and she must feel confident enough to do so."

"Sounds dangerous...for both of them."

"It is. More for him than the lass...but aye, it's dangerous."

I returned my focus to Monty and Cece in the center of the training area. For the moment, everything appeared calm, but I knew looks could be deceiving.

In the far corner of the training area, I saw Rags standing guard, focused completely on Cece. Peaches rumbled at my side and proceeded to make his way over to where she sat.

<*You sure that's a good idea? She's focused on Cece right now.*>

<*I will help her keep guard. It will show her I have a mighty focus.*>

<*I wouldn't get my hopes up, but good luck with that.*>

He rumbled again and padded off.

"Her Guardian won't choose your pup as a mate, at least not until he matures and can protect her and her charge," Dex continued with a smile. "That won't be for some time. He still has much growing up to do."

"I tried telling him not to get his hopes up," I said, watching my hellhound join Rags. "He wants to show her how mighty he is."

"Right now, he's mostly mighty at eating," Dex said with a small laugh. "He's not quite where he needs to be such that a Guardian of her stature would consider him as a mate."

"I'll try explaining that to him," I said. "Maybe a few sausages during the conversation to get him to pay attention."

"It will happen eventually," Dex said. "If she wasn't interested you'd know, boy. Trust me."

"Really? How?" I asked, thoroughly confused about the courtship rituals of hellhounds and Guardians. "All she does is give him the cold shoulder. It doesn't seem like she's the least bit interested."

"If she weren't, or felt he was a threat, they'd be locked in battle," he said. "Hellhounds are nearly indestructible, but her class of Guardian is a close second. He wouldn't walk away from *that* fight unscathed."

"Oh," I said, impressed. "I had no idea Guardians were *that* strong."

"Most aren't, but she's a Jotnar Guardian—just think Fenrir on a smaller scale."

"Oh, isn't Fenrir a god-killer?"

"Supposed to kill the All-Father himself, if you believe the stories of Ragnarok," he said, gazing over at the pair of canines. "I shudder to think of what kind of pups those two would create."

"*That* is a scary thought," I said, refocusing on Monty and Cece. "I'm not seeing much activity here. Is this some kind of high-level mage-staring contest?"

"This is testing before the practical," he said. "Pay attention. They're about to start."

"The testing before the practical?" I asked. "What does that mean exactly?"

"She requested a shift," he explained. "As his rightful apprentice, he must honor her request, according to the discipline she is being instructed in."

"Which is?"

"What kind of mage is Tristan, boy?"

"You mean besides the 'annoying, scary, and prone to massive amounts of destruction' kind?"

"Yes, besides that."

"Oh," I said, as it dawned on me. "He's a battle mage. Wait, are you saying he's teaching Cece to be a battle mage?"

"I thought that was clear," Dex said. "What did you think he was teaching her to be? How to make sausage for your hound?"

"I wouldn't go that far, but isn't she a little young to be on the path of battle magic?"

"She's Jotnar," he said, as if that explained it all. "It's practically in her blood."

He must've seen the look of confusion on my face.

"She's predisposed to battle magic," he continued. "Jotnar mages are some of the fiercest mages you can ever face. Most of the time, you only face them once, and never live to tell the story."

"Whoa," I said, remembering our visit to the Jotnar. "Is that what Cece is going to be?"

"With my nephew instructing her, no," Dex said, shaking his head then smiling again. "She will be more powerful than any Jotnar mage currently living. It is a concerning thought, don't you think?"

"More than a little concerning," I said. "So what is this 'testing'?"

"She needs to make the formal request, which she did," Dex said. "Now the parameters of the testing are being established."

"What happens to the padawan after the parameters are set?"

"The *what?*" Dex asked. "What is a padawan?"

"You know Jedi Masters and their padawans?" I said. "She is learning from Monty. That makes her his padawan."

"She is his *apprentice,*" Dex said, his voice firm. "Not some paddy—whatever you called her."

"Actually, now that I think of it, with all that skirting around darkness, Monty is probably closer to a Sith these days," I said. "Apprentice does fit."

"How long exactly were you out there sitting in the sun?"

"Not too long," I said. "I was in the shade, by the way."

"From the sound of it, you were out there too long," he said, looking at Monty and Cece. "Now, truly, pay attention, boy. It's starting."

FOUR

The circle Monty and Cece stood in flashed white for a brief second.

"Do you understand the rules?" Monty asked, looking at Cece. "If you step out of the circle, your request will be null and void, and instruction will continue as usual."

"I understand," Cece said, her voice serious. "What if I hurt you?"

Monty nearly smiled at her words.

"If you do manage to cause me injury, then I was clearly not paying attention and deserve any injury I incur," he said. "I will not underestimate your ability, Cecelia. I expect you to do your best."

"*Can* she hurt him?" I asked. "I know she's strong, but is she *that* strong?"

"It's not just a matter of her strength," Dex said. "He answered truthfully. If she does hurt him, he wasn't paying attention. The burden of this all rests on him. He has to encourage her, and at the same time demonstrate she still has so much to learn."

"Did Monty ever ask you for ascendance?"

"Aye," Dex said as his expression darkened for a moment. "I was too harsh with him when he did. I believed he needed to be taught in the old ways—the hard ways. The way I was taught. Connor showed me different. I guess even old dogs like me can learn. I did manage to avoid killing him."

"You almost killed him?"

Dex nodded.

"The old ways are unforgiving," he said. "There was no room for compassion or understanding. The request for ascendance in my time usually resulted in a death—either the apprentice made a fatal error, or the instructor underestimated the pupil and paid for the error with their life."

"Is that still done in the sects?"

"Not to my knowledge, no, but it's possible some of the more obscure, ancient sects still adhere to the old ways," he said. "It's not the norm any longer."

"Why didn't Connor—I mean, Monty's father—help him with the ascendance?" I asked. "He had the skill and power. Why not ask his dad?"

"The request for ascendance can't be made to a parent," Dex said, shaking his head. "What parent would refuse their own child? No, it must be made to someone who can refuse the request. Someone with no vested interest in the outcome."

"That was you?"

"Aye," he said. "There's a reason the Golden Circle requested I leave the premises—well, many reasons. I had been the Harbinger actively for too long. It exacts a price, a steep one. I cared for no one. How could I? I was the Harbinger of Death. There was no room for compassion, much less sentiment, for family or friends. Now, hush. You're distracting me."

"You are to use any cast available to you," Monty continued, "without fear of reprisals or negative consequences. If you step out of the circle, your petition for ascendance ends. If I force you out of the circle, the same outcome applies. Do you understand?"

"I do," Cece replied. "What if I force you out of the circle?"

"Then you will ascend to a level of instruction commensurate to the level of power displayed," he said. "Are you ready?"

She nodded and shook out her hands in a very Monty-esque manner.

"You may want to step back a bit, boy," Dex said, glancing behind me. "That barrier around the circle isn't meant to stop anything; it's only to register if one of them steps outside the circle. This is actually too close, if we want to avoid any stray projectiles."

"Projectiles?" I said, as we backed up. "What kind of proj—?"

"Ice, boy," Dex said, moving faster. "She's a Jotnar mage. What do you think she's going to cast? Orbs of destruction? The lass is going to use what she knows: ice."

We moved to the edge of the training area. Dex whispered some words and waved a hand, creating a transparent, green shield in front and above us.

I tapped the shield, concerned about the warning of ice projectiles. My hand passed right through the shield with little to no resistance.

"Is this shield strong enough?" I asked, worried. "I mean my hand just—"

"Expert on shields, are you now?" Dex asked with a raised eyebrow. "The shields will hold, just make sure you stay behind them."

I glanced over at Peaches and Rags for a second.

"Will they be okay?"

"Who? Your indestructible pup and the Guardian?" Dex asked. "Aye, boy, they'll be just fine. No need to worry about them. The only one in any potential danger here is you. Now focus."

FIVE

They moved apart from each other, with Cece stepping near the edge of the circle.

"Ready?" Monty asked.

Cece nodded with a look of determination on her face. The fact that she could stand in front of Monty and challenge him was impressive. I chalked it up to her never seeing Monty fight in a life-or-death situation. I think if she had witnessed Monty in action as a battlemage, she would have reconsidered her petition.

Or, knowing her, it could have spurred her to make the petition earlier—she was a Jotnar, after all. My memory of them did not include any instance of them being shy about wielding their power.

Still, if Monty as a battlemage was a scary thought, it was even scarier to witness in person.

"Begin," Monty said, with a nod.

With an exhalation and a wave of her hand, a storm of ice formed around Cece. Shards of ice formed in the air around her, slightly obscured by a frost cloud, as a chill crossed the circle, filling the training area with a biting wind.

I use the word storm in a loose sense—what it really looked like was a swirling mass of ice and power around her small body. I managed to glimpse the massive shards of ice floating around her, in the swirl of blue energy that raced around the circle.

The shards were easily two feet long.

They were jagged pieces of dark blue ice, the end of each piece coming to a nasty point that seemed focused on Monty. If I had been standing in the center of that, my first and only thought would have been to escape.

Monty stood calmly in the circle and focused on Cece. He paid no mind to the ice floating lazily around her, nor the energy that filled the circle. If the sudden drop in temperature was affecting him, I couldn't tell by his expression. It appeared he was waiting for something, but I didn't know what it was.

"I didn't…I didn't realize she could do that," I said, focused on Cece. "She's strong."

"Aye," Dex said, with an approving nod. "Seems she's coming into her own as a Jotnar. Her power is growing."

"What is he waiting for?" I asked. "She's going to try and skewer him into a mage-kebab with all that ice."

"Aye, I believe that's her plan," Dex said, looking on with interest. "Let's see if he lets her."

In that moment, I realized a few things.

Even though it was Cece who was undergoing the petition for ascendance, it seemed Dex was conducting a test of his own. It appeared he was more focused on what Monty was going to do than the lethal shards of ice pointed his way.

If I had to guess, he was scrutinizing how Monty was handling this situation. There was more happening here than just Cece's petition for ascendance.

"How is he going to shut down all that power?"

"Shutting it down is not the issue, boy," Dex said, his

voice low as he kept his eyes on Monty. "Shutting it down without hurting the lass—that is the key. He has to neutralize her attack without injuring her, physically or psychologically."

"Psychologically?" I asked, confused. "What do you mean?"

Dex glanced at me for a second.

"There are three components to casting. Has my nephew mentioned them to you?"

"If he did, I wasn't paying attention, or he was trying to share this information while something was trying to shred us," I said. "He does his best explaining in the middle of life-and-death situations."

"His explaining is similar to your humor," Dex said. "Or lack thereof. It's how he deals with the stress of facing death. The explanation isn't for you."

"You mean he's explaining it to himself? Doesn't he already know what he's trying to explain?"

"A good question," Dex said, turning to glance at Monty and Cece. "Do you know that your responses heighten the risk of your death? Especially when speaking to beings who possess enough power to erase you with a thought?"

"Well, when you put it that way…"

"There's no other way to put it," Dex replied. "Yet you still allow the words to escape your mouth. Why is that?"

"I'm not going to let them see I'm scared," I said, after a few moments of thought. "Even if I'm on the verge of shitting bricks, I'm not going to let them see me quaking."

"Exactly," Dex said, rubbing a finger on the side of his nose. "Tristan does the same thing with his explanations. That is how he copes with his fear. You do it by being a smartass, while he does it by slipping into his professor mode."

"He feels fear?" I asked. "He never comes across as scared, and we have faced some truly horrific creatures. He always seems so calm and collected."

"He's a Montague and, more importantly, he's a battlemage," Dex said. "Fear can be useful, especially if you're the one instilling it. On a battlefield, it can get you killed."

"Makes sense," I said, thinking back to the times Monty appeared fearless. I knew he felt fear, but I also knew he had the uncanny ability to take that same fear and move it to one side while he did what needed to be done in the moment. "I never considered his professor mode as a coping strategy."

"You were probably dealing with your own fear at that moment," he said. "Hush now and pay attention. If I'm right, she's about to unleash her attack. This should be good."

All he needed was a bucket of popcorn. His enthusiasm at the impending attack could be heard in his voice. I was more on the concerned end of the spectrum. What if he hurt her—or worse, she hurt him?

I sensed a shift in the energy coming from the circle; the ice shards went from floating lazily in the air near Cece, to frozen in place around her, even as the energy in the circle continued to swirl.

As Dex predicted, Cece made the first move.

She raised both arms and brought them down rapidly in a slashing motion, unleashing a barrage of ice spears at Monty.

Monty stepped forward, blading his body and avoiding the initial barrage by the barest of margins. The first barrage was followed by another volley of deadly ice. He deflected the second group with a wave of his hand, shattering them into crystals around them both, filling the circle with an icy mist.

He raised an eyebrow, remaining motionless as he observed the crystals floating around him. At first, I thought the icy mist was the harmless effect of his shattering the barrage of shards. I didn't think it was dangerous until I looked at the expression on Cece's face.

She had planned for his counter to her shards. She raised a

hand and closed it into a fist. The cloud of crystals stopped falling and hovered in the air around Monty.

He nodded in approval, forming a golden orb in his hand. It gave off enough light and energy to obscure everything in the circle, blinding me as it hovered in his hand.

I looked away and heard the sound of water evaporating into steam. Monty was obscured by the steam cloud as Cece smiled.

She gestured and clapped her hands together.

"She's a clever one," Dex said, with a nod. "Ice, steam, and water are all under her control. She expected his reactions and acted accordingly. Not bad for an apprentice."

"She beat him?" I asked incredulously. "Really?"

"I said she was *clever*," Dex replied. "I never said anything about beating him. Clever only gets you so far. Watch."

The steam cloud solidified around Monty, flash freezing him into his best impression of a carbonite mage. Monty, still holding the glowing orb in one hand, was frozen in place.

Cece nodded with satisfaction and approached the ice block that was formerly her instructor. She tapped its surface a few times to make sure it was completely solid, then went up on her tiptoes to look into Monty's face.

"I can't believe she froze him," I said, my voice low. "Why would he let her do that?"

"He didn't," Dex said, matching the volume of my voice. "Look, but don't use your eyes."

I focused and used my inner sight and saw the frozen Monty. His energy signature was weakening with each passing second.

"We have to help him," I said, my voice tight with urgency. "He's in trouble."

Dex shook his head.

"Look again, closer this time."

I focused again and saw two energy signatures. The weakening one inside the ice, and one blazing with power, standing next to Cece. The Ice-Monty was an illusion, a trap designed to misdirect and lure Cece in close.

Dex smiled at me as my eyes widened with the realization of what had happened.

Cece pumped a fist in the air and then quickly composed herself. She looked very satisfied with herself.

Until Monty materialized next to her.

"What?" she stammered, stumbling back from the block of ice as Monty gestured, detonating the orb being held by his illusion. "How?"

He stepped to the side as a blast of golden energy raced at Cece. The blast originated from the orb and rushed forward as a solid column of power. Cece raised a shield of energy in a last-second attempt to deflect the blast, but it was too little too late. The golden blast punched through her shield effortlessly and continued into her body.

For a split-second, time slowed, allowing me to see the expression of surprise on her face as the blast enveloped her like an enormous fist. The next second, she was airborne.

The blast launched her out of the circle. She landed a few feet past the edge. I winced for her as she landed hard enough to hurt, but not break. She rolled to a stop with a groan. It took her a few seconds, but she slowly got to her feet.

Monty remained waiting for her in the center of the circle.

She walked back into the circle her expression serious, and then once inside, she smiled at Monty who returned the smile with a nod.

"I almost got you!"

Monty sighed and nodded.

"It was close," he admitted, but I knew better. It hadn't

been close at all. "Thank you for not holding back. Your control has improved."

"Where did I mess up?" she asked. "I thought I trapped you."

"You tell me," Monty said. "What was the first error?"

I noticed he didn't ask her what was *her* first error. He didn't make it about her, but rather the casting. It was a small difference, but it was important. Maybe there was hope for him yet.

Cece scrunched up her face and gave it thought. I could see her walking through the exchange of attacks.

"I overcommitted to my attacks," she said. "I should have impaled you first?"

"That certainly would have hampered my ability to mount an effective counter," Monty said. "What was the foundational error?"

Cece shook her head as if just remembering the lesson.

"Rooting," she said, frustrated. "I stayed in one place when I should've been moving around, making it hard for you to hit me with that blast."

Monty nodded approvingly.

"You are not a tree," he said. "In a battle, staying still can cost you your life. You must be mobile and able to move at a moment's notice. One mage against greater numbers must employ...?"

"Guerrilla tactics," she finished. "But I was only facing you. How was I supposed to use guerrilla tactics? It was one on one."

"When a weaker force meets a greater force?"

"The attack must be indirect to compensate for the difference in power," she answered, looking down. "I thought I had you. You were standing in the middle of my mist. I thought it was over."

"What did we discuss about appearances?"

"Never rely on one source of input," she said. "I should have scanned the circle for extra energy signatures. Would I have found you then?"

"No," he said, shaking his head, "but it would have been the right step to take. After my illusion was frozen, your first thought should have been what?"

"It was too easy," she said, narrowing her eyes at him. "You baited me into the blast; why didn't it hurt?"

"You were allowed to use any cast," he said. "The same did not apply to me. *You* needed to learn the lesson without being harmed."

"Use only enough power to accomplish the mission," she said, mostly to herself. "Is that what you did? Use just enough power to bounce me out of the circle?"

"Precisely. At the very least, you are paying attention during the laws of battle," he said. "Now, all you need to do is to implement the knowledge you possess. You did well for your first petition." He glanced over at Dex. "Much better than I did during my first petition."

"Really?" she asked, her face lighting up. "Or are you just saying that to make me feel better?"

"Really," Monty said, his voice serious. "On my word as a Montague and a mage."

She nodded solemnly, accepting his words.

"How did you do that illusion of yourself?" she asked, her voice laced with curiosity. "I've never seen that before. Can you teach me how to do that?"

"I can show you," Monty said, "if you will continue your training under my tutelage. Do you wish to continue as my apprentice?"

She paused for a few seconds and gave it some thought before nodding.

"Yes," she said. "I still have so much to learn, don't I?"

"We all do," Monty said. "What did *you* learn today?"

"Theory and practice," she said, with a smile, "are two *very* different things."

"Indeed," Monty said. "The petition is over. I believe you have some other pressing matters to attend to today? Something to do with a certain young Peanut?"

"I do," she said, excited. "Can I go find her? I need to tell her I almost froze you."

"If she's free," Monty said. "I hear she's been avoiding chores lately. Go see if she's available...after you practice your steam-to-ice conversion...fifty times."

"Fifty times?" she said, with a groan. "That will take hours."

"Then you should start as soon as possible."

"Yes, sir," she said, dejectedly. "I'll start right now."

"Perhaps," Monty said, pensively as he raised a finger to tap his chin, "you can have Peanut help you with the process. That should prove informative for the both of you."

"Really? She can help?" Cece asked, her voice hopeful. "Really?"

"I don't see why not," Monty said. "As long as my uncle approves."

Monty turned to face Dex.

"Aye," Dex said, with mock seriousness. "On one condition: you help her with her chores, and she helps you with your conversions. Sounds like the best of both worlds to me."

"Sounds like a sneaky way of getting us to practice and do chores to me," Cece said. "Not that I'm complaining."

"Well," Monty said. "You could always stay here with me, and we can work on the conversions now. I'm sure—"

"No, thanks!" she said, quickly, making her way out of the training circle. She paused at the edge of the circle and faced Monty, giving him a low bow which he returned. "Thank you for honoring my petition. If it's okay, I'll go find Peanut now."

"Enjoy the rest of your day," Monty said. "No destruction of property. That applies to the both of you."

She ran out of the training area with Rags in tow, before Monty could change his mind. Peaches chuffed and headed over to me, following Monty as he crossed the circle to where Dex and I stood.

SIX

Dex dissolved the shield that was around us.

"What did *you* learn today?" Dex asked, with a chuckle as Monty made his way over to us. "*That* certainly brings back memories."

"I nearly missed the illusion cast," Monty said, with a headshake as he glanced back at the training circle. "A few seconds later, and it would have been me trapped in the ice, not an illusion."

"She did freeze that mist fast," I said. "Did you know she could do that?"

"I knew the potential was there," Monty said. "I should have expected it given her facility with ice. It nearly cost me."

"Stop being so dramatic," Dex said with a wave of his hand. "The lass is strong, I'll give her that much, but she still has much to learn. The mist trap was a nice touch, though—that your doing?"

Monty nodded, still looking at the training circle.

"A variation on the lattice trap you showed me when I was about her age," Monty said, looking off into the past. "Do you think she should be taught in the old ways? I need to make sure she's prepared."

"Prepared?" I asked. "Prepared for what?"

"She's a mage and a Jotnar," Monty said. "Once she comes of age, she will be challenged. It's not a regular mage test like this."

"This was a regular test?"

"The test she will receive at the hands of the Jotnar will be life or death," Monty said, his voice grim. "If she fails, she dies."

"Harsh," I said. "She's still a kid—are they seriously going to give her a potentially fatal test?"

"She won't be a child for *that* test, which is why I was thinking of using the old ways," Monty replied, looking at Dex. "What do you think, Uncle?"

Dex, his expression pensive, remained silent for a few seconds.

"Do you think the old ways will serve her?" Dex asked, his voice hard. "Are you willing to break her will?"

"No," Monty said. "The same way you didn't break mine."

Dex nodded.

"The old ways have their use, but not at this stage or at her age," Dex said, after a few more moments of silence. "They usually do more harm than good. Any instruction I gave you under that method was tempered by Connor, thankfully. He made sure there was no lasting damage."

"You both did well," Monty said. "I will have to find a way to incorporate the teachings without doing damage to her psyche. I only hope I can live up to your level of instruction."

"Ach, you'll do better than a pair of crusty old mages," Dex said. "Though, I did worry for a moment there when she surrounded you with that mist. It *was* close."

"Yes, yes it was," Monty said, with a short nod. "The orb was the key."

"You allowed it to mimic your energy signature and laced it with a detonation component—devious and deceptive," Dex said. "She won't fall for that one again, I think."

"No, she won't," Monty agreed. "I'll have to be more creative in the future. Her next petition won't be for some time, though."

"It'll be here sooner than you like," Dex said. "I would have liked to see her be more aware of her surroundings. She goes in like a raging bull—you need to teach her some finesse and patience."

"Finesse," Monty said quietly. "She currently has two settings: volatile and destructive. The mist, however, showed promise. I can coax her in the use of misdirection and restraint."

"Are there really two settings, though?" I asked. "Isn't more like one general setting of mayhem and destruction?"

Monty gave me a look.

"Having the power doesn't mean she needs to use it all in one go," Dex said. "She could have created pockets of mist, preventing your use of the illusion."

"That would have been a substantial challenge."

"Aye, she *is* the apprentice of a Mage Montague," Dex said, "with all that entails."

"Is that a big deal?" I asked. "Being an apprentice to a Mage Montague? Is that like having bragging rights that you can destroy things with style and panache?"

"It sets an expectation," Monty said. "Not bragging rights so much as a declaration of a particular pedigree."

"It means you better know how to kick arse," Dex said. "Montagues are battle mages. Once it's known she is your apprentice, the challenges will come. She better be ready, lad."

"Challenges?" I asked. "Who is going to challenge her? She lives in the Moscow with Olga, our scary landlord and resident ice queen. Who is crazy enough to attempt that gauntlet?"

"The challenges will come," Dex said, his voice certain. "Not now—she's too young—but give her a few years. Some will be formal, but others, the dangerous ones, will be informal. Those are the ones she must be ready for: the ones that come unbidden when she least expects them."

"Sounds like Kali and her successors," I said, with a grumble. "It's like walking around with a target on your back."

"Aye," Dex said. "It will keep her sharp and ready."

"This is why I never wanted an apprentice," Monty complained. "I can't keep an eye on her every minute of every day."

"Train her properly and you won't have to," Dex said. "Besides, she has Olga and, more importantly, her Guardian. I wouldn't worry too much about her right now."

"I can't believe I was ever *that* difficult," Monty said. "I, at least, listened."

Dex stared at Monty for a good three seconds before breaking out in laughter. Monty gave him a glare.

"I'm sorry," Dex said, trying to speak in between chuckles. "You weren't being serious. Were you being serious?"

"Of course I was being serious," Monty said, indignantly. "I recall being an exemplary student. I listened and applied all of my lessons."

"Really?" I asked. "Were you the straight-A, honors nerd?"

"Aye," Dex added, with another laugh. "He listened and applied all of his lessons…to the destruction of the main dining hall, among other buildings, if I recall correctly. You applied that disintegration lesson with uncanny precision. The kitchens were completely obliterated."

"Elder Timu exaggerated the damage," Monty said. "I didn't destroy the entire hall."

"No, of course not," Dex said, trying hard to keep a

straight face. "Just the part of the hall that contained the kitchens."

"In my defense, the food was a crime against humanity. The destruction of the kitchens was an act of mercy and goodwill to my fellow mages."

"*You* were more of a threat at that age than your apprentice is now. In fact, I don't think she will approach your level of destructive ability for many years to come."

"I certainly hope not," Monty said. "She did manage to wreak some minor havoc on the Moscow, much to Olga's displeasure."

"She blew a hole in the Moscow," I volunteered. "It was impressive."

"Not helping," Monty said. "How am I supposed to teach her subtlety when she wants to blast everything into its component parts?"

"That pretty much sounds like every mage I know, present company included," I said. "Maybe have her use her ability to create something small but fragile? Something that will take major concentration to create?"

"Not a bad idea, boy," Dex said, looking at Monty. "In any case, that will have to wait. We have other pressing matters to attend to."

"The lost runes," Monty said. "Or rather, the harnessing of them."

"Not lost, hidden," Dex said. "That, and finding a way to get you strong enough to deal with the rest of them before Keeper Gault acts."

"You know of an accelerated path to shift to Archmage?"

"No, but I know the next best thing."

"An Archmage."

"Several, in fact, but you need one who will be willing to help you," Dex said, "in defiance of the Keepers. Gault has issued a decree against giving you any kind of support or assistance."

"He's trying to isolate us," Monty said. "How punitive is this decree?"

"No self-respecting mage or sect is going to officially offer either of you help during this," Dex said. "The cost would be too high."

"Meaning we're on our own...as usual?"

"Meaning you need help from some mages who don't necessarily adhere to the decrees issued by the Keepers of the Arcana."

"That sounds difficult," I said. "Are there any mages strong enough who would be willing to supercharge Monty?"

"Supercharge?" Monty said. "I am not some kind of sports car. Shifting to Archmage takes several shifts. Rushing the process can prove fatal."

"Agreed, it takes centuries and several shifts to achieve," Dex said. "Consider this the crash course. You aren't becoming an Archmage, we're going to get you as close as possible, without catastrophic damage."

"Catastrophic damage?" I asked. "Why is there catastrophic damage?"

"Accelerating mage shifts can be lethal," Monty said. "Especially the closer you get to Archmage."

"That's why I'm sending you to an Archmage you know," Dex said. "He said he knows of a way to simulate your shifting to Archmage, and he operates on the fringe of things."

"Who *exactly* is this Archmage," Monty asked, narrowing his eyes at Dex, "that he would be willing to defy the Keepers? Archmages on the whole prefer to avoid conflicts. This one would be actively seeking it out."

"I'm sending you to the Foundry," Dex said, letting the

words hang in the air. "It's your best, and, at this point, only chance."

"There must be someone else," Monty protested. "Someone from one of the other sects?"

"Two things," Dex said, holding up two fingers. "You pissed off a Keeper. Not some ordinary mage—a Keeper. Second, my actions with the Golden Circle may be partly to blame for your exclusion."

"How?" I asked. "I mean, you're starting a school of battle magic. Isn't that a good thing?"

"Yes," Dex said, "and no. At least not according to the Elders of the Golden Circle. That's why I'm sending you to the Foundry.

"*The* Foundry?" I asked. "Seriously?"

"It's the last place the sects will expect you to go for assistance."

"The last place I expected as well," Monty said. "Are the Elders planning to move against you?"

"You could say that," Dex said, with a wicked smile. "They're not keen on the idea of my appropriating the sect our family founded. They feel I've become a clear and present danger, and will take the appropriate actions to make me accountable—or at least that's what their letter said."

"They're going to attack you?"

"In a word, yes," Dex said. "Seems this group of Elders doesn't know much about me except what Connor and the records informed them."

"I'm sure my father didn't share much about you or why you were invited to leave the Golden Circle."

Dex laughed, but this time it was a low and dangerous sound. It sent chills down my back, causing my brain to reflexively want me to run away.

"Only your parents and Mo know about my role as the

Harbinger," Dex said. "If they pay us a visit, I will have to educate them."

"That is why you are sending us to the Foundry," Monty said. "You want to eliminate any fallout for our association with you."

"We're family," Dex said. "They will hold that against you while you're still breathing. There's no need to compound the issue by having you here when they arrive. They will think—"

"We are acting against them," Monty finished. "That will cause a sect-wide exile."

"One they won't violate," Dex said. "Right now it's a Keeper decree, which they will observe but not enforce completely. If they see you fighting against the Elders, however—"

"They will declare us enemies of the sects."

"Why does that sound like a bad thing?" I asked. "That is a bad thing, right?"

"It is," Monty said. "Think Verity, but organized across every major sect with some of the most accomplished mages coming after us. It would be a death sentence."

"For them," Dex said, his voice ominous. "That's why you're going to the Foundry."

"The Foundry," I mumbled. "Really?"

"Is there another Foundry I don't know about?" Dex asked. "Yes, the Foundry. Don't be dense, boy. Haven't you been paying attention?"

"I have. It's just that we didn't leave on the best terms the last time we were there," I said, glancing at Monty. "You think Julien is still pissed we wrecked his home the last time paid him a visit?"

"That wasn't us," Monty said. "If you recall, that was Arbiter Macintyre, sent by the Golden Circle to apprehend me."

"In any case, I spoke to my contacts in the Fleur de Lis

Elders," Dex said. "Julien may be an Archmage and sovereign of the Foundry, but he must abide by their orders—and they have ordered him to assist you in this matter."

"Oh, he's going to be overjoyed to see us again, especially if he's being forced to by his sect," I said. "What could possibly go wrong with this scenario?"

"I think I'm more concerned about the fact that you have contacts inside the Fleur de Lis," Monty said, looking at Dex. "You've never mentioned this in the past."

"Because that's exactly what it is—the past," Dex answered. "Julien will extend you every courtesy as a representative of the Fleur de Lis. He will help you or lose the Foundry."

"This Elder you contacted—he has that much authority?" Monty asked. "Enough to dissolve Julien's sovereignty?"

"He does," Dex said with a smile. "And he owes me his life, several times over. When things become difficult, sometimes enemies make the best allies."

I looked at Monty.

"Tell me he's kidding," I said. "He's kidding, right?"

"I'm afraid not."

"There is no way this is going to end well."

"Get ready," Dex said, leaving the training area. "You leave within the hour. I have news that we will be receiving some unwanted guests."

We walked out of the small courtyard, leaving the training circle behind.

SEVEN

"Unwanted guests?" I asked as we walked. "Who is suicidal enough to willingly come here and choose violence? They do know the Morrigan is here with you, right?"

"Not yet, they don't." Another wicked smile. "But they'll soon find out the error of their ways."

"It's the Golden Circle Elders, isn't it?" Monty said. "They're going to try and reclaim the sect."

"The sect hasn't gone anywhere," Dex said with a huff. "I may have just altered the access a bit."

"I don't understand," I said, looking around at the Sanctuary buildings around us. "How exactly do you *take* a sect?"

"I didn't," Dex said. "It's like a house. If you change the locks and install window guards, you haven't moved the house—you just made it difficult for anyone who doesn't have the new key to get into said house."

"You didn't make it difficult," Monty corrected. "You made it impossible."

"They allowed Oliver to take control," Dex said, his voice dangerous. "It happened on *their* watch. The whole point of the body of Elders is to prevent something like that from happening. They failed. They failed to keep this place safe. That incompetence is why Connor—my brother—is no longer with us. They deserved so much worse than what I did."

Monty nodded, remaining silent as he looked away.

"Killing the Elders would have caused the other sects to rise up against you and the Golden Circle," Monty said. "I'm quite surprised they haven't acted yet."

"They've sent emissaries to inquire as to my intentions," Dex said with a crooked smile. "They've had a hard time getting past the defenses ever since I changed the entry sequences."

"You changed the locks on the sect?" I asked. "All of them?"

Dex nodded.

"He did more than that," Monty said. "You remember the process to enter the sect now—do you recall?"

"I do," I said with a shudder. "Not fun on so many levels."

"What my uncle neglected to mention was that the defenses run deeper than that vetting process or merely changing the locks," Monty said, giving a Dex a sidelong glance. "Without being invited, access to the Golden Circle is now impossible."

"You can do that?" I asked, looking at Dex. "What happened to the people who were here? This place is huge. You kicked them all out?"

"*They* still have access," Dex said. "I'm not a monster. I only evicted the Elders who had become complacent, believing in their own grandeur—the fops. Everyone else is currently on leave until the school is open and operational. A place this large can't be run by one person. Not even one as gifted as me."

"The Elders have probably filed a formal claim with the

Council of Sects at this point," Monty said. "Do they have standing?"

I was barely following what Monty was asking, but whatever Dex was, he wasn't insane—well, not *entirely* insane. If he kicked the Elders out, he had to have known they would come back or else go to the main Council. He had to have some kind of plan in place to deal with them, one that didn't involve wholesale slaughter.

At least I hoped so.

He was the Harbinger, after all.

"It's not theirs to claim," Dex said, stopping near one of the buildings. He waved a hand and a tall, rune-covered obelisk made of black marble materialized. Dex pointed to the tall column of stone. "Read that."

Monty stepped close to the impressive obelisk. It stood nearly thirty feet tall and was close to eight feet wide at its base, tapering to half that near the top. Monty slowly walked around it, examining the symbols. After a few minutes, he shook his head.

"Uncle, this is beyond proto-runes," he said. "I can't read this. Nothing on this column of stone is even vaguely familiar to me."

"Ach, lad, my apologies," Dex said with small smile. "I sometimes forget you're still a pup. Still, you should keep up with your studies. These runes are important to our family, and eventually, you should know this alphabet."

"This is Old Montaguean?" Monty asked. "I've never seen it depicted like this."

"Aye, it's an ancient form," Dex said, nodding. "One moment."

Dex stepped away from us and moved close to the column of stone, pressing certain areas in sequence. I saw the stone shimmer a deep violet and glow green in the places he touched. Some of the symbols shifted and rearranged themselves as he walked around the obelisk, focusing on specific runes on each face.

"Your family has its *own* alphabet?" I asked surprised. "Since when?"

"Not an alphabet per se, more a series of codes usually only used within the family," Monty answered, keeping an eye on Dex. "Every mage family has a variation of the same. They were designed to keep certain casts secret from rival families long ago."

"Why don't you know it?"

"My family is old," Monty said, "much older than even my uncle. Some of the traditions date to a time when he was a child or before. Change, as you know, is difficult to implement once ideas become entrenched—especially with mages."

"A major case of, 'We've always done it this way'?"

"Indeed. Some things in my family are *still* kept from me," Monty said. "I had heard of the family code, but to see it written, much less learn it, would require more knowledge and power than I currently possess."

"You're not strong enough to read your own family code?" I asked. "Seriously? No one will teach you?"

He nodded.

"That and my association with Uncle Dex," he said. "My closeness to him hasn't won me any points in the good graces department. Most of the Montagues have shunned him—and me, by default."

"Why?" I asked. "I mean, yes, he has his issues, and there's the whole Harbinger thing, but he's family. Doesn't that count for anything?"

"I think that's the only thing preventing the family from rising up en masse and trying to remove him from this plane," Monty said. "Not that some haven't tried in the past."

"What happened to them?"

"They were relegated to the long-lost-relative list," Monty said. "No one knows where they are—well, no one besides my uncle, and he's not sharing."

"I think the threat of being punted off-plane is a good deterrent," I said. "But they still shun him...and you?"

"Don't forget who he's involved with," Monty said. "To be frank, it comes down to fear. They fear him and he does nothing to assuage that fear. I think he actively encourages it, not that it takes much on his part. As a mage, he is quite fearsome. As the consort of the Morrigan, he is mind-numbingly horrifying."

The memory of Dex confronting me with Nemain in his hand chilled me into silence as I nodded.

"That much I know," I said. "Is there anyone else in the Montagues strong enough to confront him?"

"There was. My father," Monty said. "My father could always get my uncle to see reason or refrain from violence. Now, I think the only person who holds that kind of sway over him is the Morrigan."

"That is one scary thought," I said. "Is that why they never taught you Montaguean? You're too close to the spine-chilling horror that is Dex?"

Monty shook his head.

"It's also considered a security measure to prevent the younger members of the family from abusing casts they're not ready for," Monty said. "It would appear this obelisk dates back to the formation of the Golden Circle, many generations before I was born."

"Okay, lad," Dex said as he walked back to us. "This should work to clarify the language for you. It's either going to do that, or explode wonderfully. You two better step back."

"Why is there always a danger of things exploding around mages?" I asked, stepping back from the obelisk and looking at Monty. "Aren't there any non-exploding casts mages can use?"

"Of course," Monty said. "When I know them, I'll be certain to share them with you."

"Hilarious, really."

Dex waved his hand and the symbols on the stone tower shifted and changed even more. Now even I, with my limited knowledge of runes, could make out some of the symbols and words.

"Go read," Dex said to Monty. "You have about five minutes before it reverts back to its original form."

Monty walked around the obelisk, pausing here and there to read and re-read some of the runes. He crouched down on one side of the column, and got up on his toes on another face of the obelisk to get to all the text. When he stepped away, his expression was one of surprise mixed with anger.

"Do the Elders know what is written on this?" Monty asked, pointing to the obelisk. "Have they read this?"

"Of course they have," Dex said. "Every sect has some variation of this obelisk. It shows who founded the sect, and its discipline. This one is slightly different from the ones found in all the other sects. Can you tell me why?"

"The detail."

"Elaborate, lad."

"The other obelisks I have seen only describe the sect and its discipline," Monty said, slipping into professor mode. "They are not covered in runes like this one, and possess merely a minor amount of detail. This obelisk is the opposite."

"How so?" Dex asked. "What did you learn?"

"It lists the Montagues and related families dating back hundreds, if not thousands of years, as the sole successors of this sect of battle magic," Monty said. "This sect was created by the Montagues?"

"Aye, Montagues have always been battle mages, along with the Fairchilds and Treadwells," Dex explained. "Those three families have always formed the pillars of the Golden Circle. All three are important, but the Montagues are the reason the Golden Circle exists in the first place. Over time, the Treadwells and the Montagues became one family by marriage."

"I never knew this," Monty said. "Nor of this particular obelisk. Why was this kept from me?"

"You're too young," Dex said. "This...this was to be Connor's privilege and duty. He was supposed to explain the lineage and heritage of the Golden Circle to prepare you for—"

Dex's voice suddenly choked up.

"He was supposed to prepare me to take his position," Monty said. "I was to take his place?"

"Not for a few centuries yet," Dex said, composing himself. "Then Oliver... Well, you know the rest. When I asked the Elders what had happened, I realized the mistake that had been made. They had stopped teaching battle magic and had settled for *studying* it. Two different things, as you know."

"Oliver exploited the lack of accomplished battle mages in the sect," Monty said. "It's what allowed him to take over."

Dex nodded.

"That, and he was strong in his own right," Dex added. "There was a time when any one Elder would have quashed his attempted takeover. Your father was a powerful battle mage, but the violence had changed him. He wanted peace above everything else, and thought surrendering to the Elders' wishes was for the greater good of the sect."

"He was wrong," Monty said. "It created an opening for Oliver to take control of the sect."

"Aye, and sadly he realized it too late," Dex said. "*I* won't make that mistake. The Golden Circle is for the training and creation of battle mages. That was its original purpose. Theory and practice must go hand in hand. Somewhere along the line they forgot that. I'm here to remind them."

"They will try to stop you," Monty said as we kept walking. "What will you do?"

"Not your concern right now," Dex said, leading us to a large teleportation circle. "You have other business to deal with, along with preventing a Keeper from tipping the balance of magic to Chaos."

I noticed he used the word like a name, not the current state of my life as I knew it. I could practically see the capital letter on Chaos.

"Can't you help us?" I asked, once I heard the name of the old god. "I mean, keeping the balance of magic seems like more of a priority than maintaining a sect of battle magic. If you help us—"

"We may lose the only place that will be able to stand against an enemy, should you fail," Dex finished. "I'm not thinking of today, I'm thinking of centuries from now, boy. We all have our parts to play. Yours is to confront Keeper Gault and stop him."

"Not kill him?"

"Kill him?" Dex asked, his expression going dark. "I seriously doubt you three can manage that feat. He's a Keeper, with all that entails."

"So we just *stop* him. Any idea on how that's supposed to happen?"

"Not a clue," Dex said with a smile. "But I am eagerly awaiting to see what you come up with."

I stared at him and took a deep breath, preparing myself to be blasted to little bits.

"While we're off facing with the Keeper who wants to

obliterate everything," I said, "what exactly are you going to be doing?"

"Simon..." Monty warned me.

"No," I said, holding my voice firm even though I realized I was standing in front of someone who could erase me with a flick of his fingers without even breaking a sweat. "I want—no, I *need* to know. Because every time something like this happens, I keep hearing how everyone was on the same page working toward the same goal, except that when it all hits the fan, and I look around, I only see Monty and my hellhound. Everyone else has mysteriously left the building." I turned to Dex. "So what *exactly* will you be doing while *we* try to stop Gault, and not die in the process?"

Monty shook his head.

"My apologies, Uncle."

"None needed," Dex said, looking at me. "I understand the frustration, boy. Truly I do. I don't envy what you must do, but do it you must. While you are keeping magic in balance, my role is to prepare for what comes after."

"What comes after?"

"My role is to find and help create the last ones."

"The last ones?" I asked, looking around. "The last ones of what?"

Monty cleared his throat before answering.

"In a group of one hundred mages engaged in battle," Monty began, slipping into professor mode with ease, "ten of them should have never entered the conflict to begin with, eighty of them will perish, nine of them will lead the battle, and the last one...the last one will be a warrior."

Dex nodded approvingly.

"Good to see you were paying attention."

"Training battle mages is a long, arduous process, Uncle," Monty said. "Not to mention, that finding the right candidates is nearly impossible. I'm still only at the inception of my journey. You mean to raise an army of battle mages?"

"There was a time when *everyone* in the Golden Circle was a battle mage, no matter their position," Dex said. "We've lost that, and we need it now more than ever."

"You can't do this alone," Monty said. "I've studied the texts. It took several groups of at least three Elders decades to locate the proper candidates for the Golden Circle. You need at least a Tribus to get started."

"Aye. That is *my* concern," Dex said. "I never said anything about doing this alone. I'll have help to find and train the last ones. With enough of them, we can face any threat on this plane. We've already begun with Peanut."

"Peanut?" Monty asked. "You think *she's* a candidate?"

"You don't?" Dex answered with an edge. "I'll ask her to show you where she is in her use of power the next time you visit. I'm certain she'll convince you, if she doesn't destroy the place first."

"You *loathe* teaching," Monty said, shaking his head. "You only tolerated my instruction because we're family."

"*And* you were in danger of getting expelled from the Golden Circle," Dex said with a tight smile. "Don't forget that little detail."

"And I was in danger of getting expelled," Monty admitted. "Still, you abhor teaching."

"Is that what you thought?" Dex asked, his smile fading. "I hated teaching you?"

"I knew you didn't like it," Monty said. "I assumed it was because of what I had done."

"Tristan, it's true, that I didn't enjoy teaching, and still don't, but it had nothing to do with you or what you had done," Dex said, his voice serious. "It had everything to do with what I had become. To expose you to the darker aspects of what I was at that time was unjust to you."

"I don't understand," Monty said. "What had you become?"

"When I received the summons to instruct my wayward nephew, I was in the thick of my Harbinger duties," Dex said. "Death hung about me like a second skin. No one should be exposed to that much death."

"I understand that feeling," Monty said, looking away to some memory I was sure held Albert in it. "It's not...pleasant."

"No, it isn't," Dex agreed. "I needed to maintain distance, not for me, but for you. I enjoyed *every* moment of teaching *you* and I'm proud to be your kin, in case it bears repeating. But in order to do that, I needed to pause my duties as Harbinger. *That* didn't go over too well."

Monty nodded and looked away.

"Thank you, Uncle."

"Now, enough dallying," Dex said. "I'll do what I can to give you a small window, but it comes with certain risks."

"A small window for what?" I asked. "Why do we need a window?"

"Are you daft, boy?" Dex said with a wry grin. "The moment you step out of this place, everyone will be looking for you. You two just *stole* an elder rune from a Keeper."

"Stole?" I said as the breath left my lungs in shock. "What are you talking about, *stole*? We didn't steal anything! Keeper Evergreen was the one who told us to do it."

Dex looked around.

"Hmm, I'm not seeing Keeper Evergreen anywhere to confirm your story," Dex said, waving an arm around. "Seems like there's no one here to lend credence to your words."

"But you *know* it's the truth," I said. "How could we ever take an elder rune from a Keeper against his will?"

"You can't, but that won't matter, will it?"

"No," Monty said his voice somber. "I will be depicted as

a power-hungry mage in search of more power and turning to darkness to do it. Simon will be portrayed as my dark immortal accomplice with a menace of a hellhound in our bid to take over what, exactly? The world, the plane? All of existence?"

"Any of the above," Dex said. "Probably some combination of all three."

"You're joking," I said, looking from Dex to Monty. "No one is going to believe that—no one in their right mind, at least."

"There's the rub," Dex said, tapping his nose. "Most of the people coming after you have left their right minds long ago. Now hold still."

Dex gestured and white runic symbols drifted over to fall on me, Monty, and Peaches.

"What was that?"

"A trigger in two phases," Dex said. "First phase announces your location to everyone."

"Because we *want* everyone to find us?"

"Yes, at least at first," Dex said. "The second phase is activated the moment you enter the Foundry. Julien will trigger it and you'll disappear completely from every magical scan. It should last about three days."

"Three days?" I asked incredulously. "We're supposed to defeat Gault in three days?"

"Have you lost your mind?" Dex asked. "Of course not. Three days will give you enough time to learn how to access the elder rune and shift Tristan far enough to be able to manipulate it."

"Three days to shift to near Archmage?" Monty asked, shaking his head. "Impossible."

"Did the same brick hit you both in the head?" Dex asked, scowling at us. "I never said it was a true shift. It's enough of a shift to get you to unleash the power of the elder rune, not master it. You do it wrong and it will kill you...*both*."

"Does Julien know this?" I asked. "Because the last time we were there—"

"He will know by the time you get there," Dex said, waving my words away. "Use the time wisely. Julien is the only mage with enough power I trust to do this for you, other than myself."

"You know *several* powerful mages," Monty said. "Do they all fear the Keepers?"

"They fear the repercussions if you fail in facing down Gault," Dex said. "Make no mistake they are not, and will never become, your friends or allies. They are associates of convenience."

"But *Julien* you trust?" I asked. "Isn't he a criminal?"

"Everyone is a villain in someone's story," Dex said. "Julien I trust because his motives are simple and direct. No subterfuge. Also, he owes me several times over. He will do this because it's in his best interests, and I asked him."

"That's it? You just asked him and he says okay?"

"When I'm the one doing the asking...yes. That's all it takes. Now, get in the circle and get ready—I have guests incoming and you can't be here when they arrive."

"Get ready?" I asked as my intestines clenched in fear. "Why do we need to get ready?"

"This is a fixed circle," Dex explained. "It won't be as potent or secure as one I would create, but we're pressed for time. It should be perfectly safe. Just make sure to remain inside once the cast begins."

We walked over to the large circle.

"Should be?" I asked. "What's the danger?"

"Nothing major," Dex said, waving my words away. "Some minor course aberrations. You may end up slightly off target, but you should be within walking distance of the Foundry."

"That's all?" I asked, concerned. "Just slightly off target?"

"Worst case, you end up on a completely different plane, but that hasn't happened in decades," Dex assured me. "I wouldn't worry too much about that, though. You'll be fine. Have I ever steered you wrong?"

"Five words," I said. "Magic missile on a plane."

"You really should get that cast under control," he said with a wicked smile. "I hope you've been practicing."

I stared at him as he motioned for us to get in the circle. It pulsed a soft green which brightened as we got closer. Distinct memories of the magic-missile lesson he conducted on a plane mid-flight came to mind as I stared at the symbols in the circle.

"Wait, if you're sending us to the Foundry, what happens to Cece and Peanut?" I asked. "Aren't they too young to be involved in this conflict? If something happens to Cece, Olga will freeze us, shatter us into little bits, then defrost us and kill us again. If she's feeling merciful."

"I'm certain my uncle has planned accordingly," Monty said, turning to Dex. "You *have* planned accordingly?"

"Cece is not ready," Dex said, glancing behind him. "Mo will make sure she is safe. Peanut, on the other hand, is fast on her way to becoming a decent battle mage. She reminds me of you at that age. She will stand by me as we welcome our guests."

"Is that wise?" Monty said. "She is still a child."

"I almost feel sorry for whoever is coming to convince me to turn the sect over. Almost," Dex said with a small chuckle. "Peanut is safe with me. I can't say the same for those Elders coming to pay us a visit."

He materialized Nemain, and immediately the air around us became charged with an oppressive power.

Peanut came running around a corner to our right, then came to a stop near Dex.

If she felt any fear due to the presence of Nemain, it was absent from her face. In fact, she looked eager to get into a fight. Whatever she was becoming, I was really glad she was on our side.

"Are they here?" she asked, her voice laced with anticipation. "Did they come?"

"She sensed Nemain?" Monty asked as we stepped into the teleportation circle. "Her level of awareness is that acute?"

"That would be Mo's doing," Dex said, turning to Peanut. "No, lass, they're not here yet, but they're coming. I thought you would like to say goodbye"—Dex motioned to us with Nemain—"and assure them of what we are doing here."

She nodded, her childlike face suddenly serious. She stepped into the circle next to us, rubbing Peaches one more time behind the ears as he rumbled his approval. She stood and faced us as she stepped out of the circle. Her childlike demeanor was replaced with a gravity that had been absent earlier.

"Don't worry," she said, her voice older than her years. "No one is taking our home. I do hope you come visit us again soon. Uncle Dex says we'll have more students before long."

Monty stepped close, remaining in the circle, and bowed.

"I have every confidence in your ability to keep our home safe," he said. "In battle…"

"First to strike," she finished.

"In defeat…" he continued.

"Last to fall," she said, returning Monty's bow. "Except we are Montagues. We don't fall in battle."

Peanut extended a hand to her side and formed a blazing white orb. The power coming off of it was nearly equal to anything Monty had created. She gestured and the orb split into three, which circled around her slowly in erratic orbits.

Each orb began increasing in power, taking on a green tinge as she whispered some words under her breath.

Monty raised an eyebrow and looked at Dex, who nodded in response.

"Remember the two phases," Dex said as he began gesturing with one hand. "Once you arrive, you will be a beacon to anyone who is looking for you."

"Which means everyone," I said. "This should be fun."

"Expect to be attacked shortly after you arrive," Dex said with a nod. "Your signatures have been heightened to pinpoint your location even before you arrive."

"Because hiding us on the way to the Foundry would be boring?"

"Where's the fun in that?" Dex said. "Because the cast works with two extremes. Once you disappear, it will be as if you no longer exist, but first everyone must know where you are."

"I'm not a fan of this cast," I said to Monty. "Dira is still out there, looking to take my place as the Marked of Kali—by removing me from existence, if at all possible."

"I think in light of the current situation, your successor is the least of our concerns. Verity and the Arcanists, including Keeper Gault, should probably be at the top of our list."

"Right," I said. "You think there are more besides them?"

"There are always more," Monty said. "Especially now." He turned to Dex. "Take care of yourself, Uncle. Thank you."

"Will you be okay?" I asked, looking at Dex. "I know it sounds impossible, but do they stand a chance against you and the Morrigan?"

Peanut, standing next to Dex, gave me a look.

"And the fierce Peanut?"

She nodded and gave me a scary Morrigan smile.

"They don't. Don't worry about us—we'll be fine," Dex said. "Go see Julien. You can thank me by stopping Gault."

EIGHT

The world flashed green and the Montague School for Battle Magic, formerly known as the sect of the Golden Circle, vanished. When I could see again, Peaches was gone, and we were standing in a small park near a large lake, around sunset.

"Monty? What happened? Where's Peaches?" I asked, trying to keep my voice calm as I looked around for my hellhound. "Where are we?"

"You are in the custody of the Verity Blades," a voice behind us said. "My name is Agent Terrance Davies. If you surrender peacefully, we will make this as painless as possible."

I whirled on the voice and took stock of the situation.

The small park we stood in was filled with Verity agents. I easily counted between ten and fifteen of them. All had weapons drawn, and about half of them had orbs hovering around their bodies.

"Well, shit," I said under my breath. "They look determined."

"This is a Blade Recovery Team. Their presence may have

something to do with our last encounter at the Cloisters," Monty said, matching my tone. "Where *is* your creature?"

"I thought *you* would know," I hissed. "I don't sense him anywhere nearby. Do you think they—?"

"No," Monty said. "Verity is skilled, but this is still the rank and file. I don't sense anyone with that caliber of power among this group. This must have something to do with the circle my uncle used."

"And that crazy trigger he hit us with."

"That, too," Monty agreed. "It would be the only way they could pinpoint our location so accurately. There must be a stasis component to the School; It would take time to assemble and dispatch this team. Time must flow slower at the School."

"Are we even close to our target?" I asked. "Or are we going to get the welcome committee to end all welcome committees?"

"The Foundry is close," Monty said. "I can sense it."

I managed to glance over at the sign near the entrance which read *Margaret L. Kempner Playground*. That meant the body of water directly across from us was the Jacqueline Kennedy Onassis Reservoir. I oriented myself in my mental map.

Behind the park where we stood was 5th Avenue, and in front of us sprawled Central Park. The Foundry, our original target, was about five blocks south of where we stood.

"I'm going to go out on a limb and say the port didn't go as planned," I said under my breath to Monty. "You think they had something to do with our detour?"

"Suspects located," another Verity agent said into a phone. "We have them contained and surrounded. They won't escape this time."

"Agent Davies," Monty said, focusing on the lead agent who spoke. "I'm certain we can come to some kind of understanding. We are currently in the midst of some urgent business, and time is of the essence."

Agent Davies stood in the center of the group with a gun pointed directly at Monty.

"Tristan Montague and Simon Strong, you are hereby ordered to surrender for summary erasure," Davies said. "If you refuse to comply, the use of deadly force has been authorized."

"Erasure?" I asked, looking around the park. "Right here? Out in the open?"

Davies gave me a slight nod without dropping his gun.

"We're not returning you to HQ without dealing with your abilities first," Davies answered. "Choice is yours: erasure, then come with us to answer for your crimes, or we eliminate you here and now."

"Since when does Verity do the whole Judge, Jury, and Executioner thing?" I asked under my breath to Monty. "They seem awfully twitchy."

"Probably since Edith and the Cloisters," Monty replied, gazing at the Blades surrounding us. "They do seem somewhat nervous. Do we really appear so fearsome?"

"I don't know about you, but I get all *my* fearsome from Peaches," I said. "Without him, I'm downright harmless."

"I doubt even you believe those lies."

"Hell, it was worth a shot."

"Weren't there three of them on the order?" another agent said. "I swore I saw three names listed. That one"—the agent pointed at me— "is supposed to have some kind of dangerous animal familiar."

"Look around," another agent said in response. "It probably couldn't handle the shunt. It's most likely unconscious somewhere in the park."

"What kind of rounds are you carrying?" Monty asked me, keeping his voice low. "We shouldn't kill them."

"Persuaders," I said. "Is this our new version of diplomacy?"

"Killing them will only complicate matters," Monty said, holding his hands out in front of him. Several of the agents jumped back at the move, training their weapons on him. "Who is leading this group now? Who would I speak to? I'm only inquiring due to the fact that both Edith and Tana have recently retired."

"Retired?" Davies scoffed. "You *killed* them. You're a cold-blooded murderer, and I'm going to enjoy witnessing your execution."

"You seem to be misinformed," Monty said, keeping his voice calm and even. "*I* did not kill Tana. That would be my associate here, who eliminated your supposed second-in-command. After she tried to dispatch him with a poisoned blade, I might add."

I stared at Monty for a few seconds.

"How is *that* supposed to help anything?"

"Just making sure the details are correct," he answered. "It's all in the details, you know."

"We're getting off on the wrong foot," I said, slowly holding up a hand, since they all seemed to be extra twitchy. "Why don't we start again? Who is in charge of the Blades—I mean now, after Edith and Tana are no longer with us?"

"You *killed* them," Davies repeated. "We don't owe you an explanation. We don't owe you anything, except a quick death. Surrender or die. Those are your only options. Choose. Now."

"They seem fixated on the whole Edith and Tana thing," I said. "Maybe we should just reach out to Cain? See if we can get him to call them off?"

"I don't think Cain would listen," Monty said. "I doubt we're in his good graces after Nana neutralized his abilities."

"That's just it: that was Nana, not us," I said. "Maybe he's cooled down by now?"

Monty looked out at the angry agents around us and shook his head.

"Unlikely," he said. "Cain is probably angrier than ever."

At the mention of Cain, Davies' eyes widened, and a flicker of doubt crossed his expression.

"You know Cain?" Davies asked. "How do you know Cain? Did you try to kill him too?"

"Funny you should say that..." I started.

Then I sensed my hellhound, and he was coming in hot. He blinked in, crashing into Davies, and the park erupted in gunfire and magic.

"Next time, a little warning perhaps?" Monty called out as he gestured, avoiding several orbs in the process.

"Not my fault," I said, running for cover. "I barely felt him before he crashed into Davies. Is he still alive?"

"For now," Monty said as his hands gave off a golden glow. "Get behind cover."

"Great idea, thanks!"

I drew Grim Whisper as I dove behind a low wall. Monty slashed the air with a hand, launching a barrage of small white orbs at the Blades, while throwing up a small golden shield and creating a large orange lattice.

The orbs punched a group of agents in the chest, sending them flying in several directions. Peaches blinked in and out of sight, pouncing on unsuspecting agents and slamming his massive head into their sides and backs.

A few of the agents got the extra-special hellhound treatment of having Peaches clamp down on their leg or arm, and slam them repeatedly on the ground like a chew toy until they lost consciousness.

I shot a few with Persuader rounds and watched as their bodies betrayed them, releasing the contents of their stomachs and bowels. It wasn't a pretty or fragrant sight, and the pungent smell soon filled the park, making me gag.

"I don't think using Persuaders were the call on this one," I said, stepping away from the apocalyptic concentration of odor. "This whole place is going to need to be incinerated and rebuilt after this…Wow, that's bad."

Monty had hit Davies with the orange lattice, which seemed to put the Verity Blade into stasis. The rest of the Blades were either unconscious or wished they were.

The entire conflict was over in five seconds.

I looked down at my hellhound as Monty approached Davies.

<Where did you go, boy?>

<In-between. Then you left.>

<I thought I lost you.>

<You are my bondmate. You can never lose me. I go where you go.>

<I know, but I didn't see you when we got here. I was worried something happened to you.>

<If you ate more meat, you would be able to smell me wherever I am. Then you would be stronger and not worry.>

Zen hellhound wisdom—everything was solved by eating more meat.

<I'll get right on increasing the meat in my diet.>

<Good. Can you ask the angry man to increase the meat in my stomach? I'm very hungry right now.>

<He's going to ask them some questions. Maybe after, when we're not being chased by angry mages.>

<We are always being chased by angry mages. I'll starve.>

<Keep it together. You'll get fed soon enough, boy. Come, step over here, and stop smiling! You're scaring the mages.>

Peaches rumbled and walked a few feet away, standing by my side and sitting on his haunches in a silent protest. Thankfully, he stopped baring his teeth in what he considered to be a smile—which, for everyone else who wasn't a hellhound, appeared to be the moment before he tore into a victim and shredded them to pieces.

Monty stepped close to Davies, dropping half the stasis and keeping Davies' legs trapped in the orange lattice of energy. Davies tried to move back and failed, ultimately falling on a bench, fear etched on his face.

"Stay away from me, you murderers!" Davies yelled. "You both deserve to die!"

"He seems a little high-strung," I said, taking a step forward with Grim Whisper in my hand. "You want me to *persuade* him?"

"Please don't," Monty said, holding up a hand. "I'd like to gather information without the mess."

"Suit yourself," I said, holstering my gun and moving away from Davies, but keeping him in my sights. Peaches followed me and rumbled next to my leg. "I don't think he's going to cooperate without some persuading, though. Let me know if you need an assist. I'm right here."

"Duly noted, but I think he'll cooperate," Monty said, turning to Davies. "Won't you?"

"You'll have to kill me first," Davies said, putting up a brave front. "I have nothing to say to you."

"I was hoping it wouldn't come to this, but very well. Death it is," Monty responded, forming a small black orb. "Do you know what this is, Agent Davies?"

"Whoa, Monty, really?"

Davies shook his head as fear contorted his features. It was the right reaction. The orb itself was potent. I could feel the energy coming off of it from where I stood. Even scarier, Monty was surrounded by a black aura of energy I had never seen before.

"Monty?" I asked. "Can we dial it back a bit from complete darkness to maybe some light grayness?"

"I don't see why," Monty said without looking away from Davies. "Isn't that what Verity has accused me of—going dark? Why not show them what true darkness is?"

"This is *not* a good idea," I said, worry lacing my voice. "Darkness tends to attract powerful beings of destruction. We don't want to do that, do we?"

"You hear the concern in my associate's voice?" Monty asked, still looking at Davies. "He sounds like that because he knows a long and horrific death is what awaits you."

"Monty, maybe it would be better if I just shot him?" I offered. "Your approach sounds cruel and unusual. Maybe we can let Peaches eat him?"

"Hmm," Monty mused, glancing at Peaches. "He really hasn't fed lately. Maybe we should feed him this agent, though I worry what it may do to his digestive system. You remember what happened after he ate those other Verity agents? The flatulence was unbearable."

"He ate…ate…other Verity agents?" Davies asked, paling further as he glanced at my hellhound with a horrified look. "You let him *eat* people?"

"Only if he behaves," I said, seeing where Monty was going with this—even though the orb did concern me. "And he has behaved so well today." I rubbed my hellhound's massive head. "Haven't you, boy?"

Peaches rumbled by my side and smiled at Davies.

"Don't let him eat me…*please*."

"If you answer my questions, I'll make sure you do not become dinner for the hellhound," Monty said. "Although, you do seem a little on the thin side. You'd be more of an aperitif than a proper meal."

"You're bluffing," Davies said, finding a false sense of bravado. "If you were going to kill me, you would've done it by now. This is all talk and no action."

Monty unleashed some more energy around him, and

even I took a step back. He was really going to sell Dark Monty this time.

"You *are* going to die," Monty continued, his gaze focused on Davies, "but it will take days, perhaps weeks for the end to arrive. No one will be able to help you once I unleash this cast. Each moment, every breath, will be inexplicable agony. You will beg and plead for your life to be over, but it won't be possible. This cast will keep you alive while it devours you from within."

Monty let the small black orb hover in his hand as Davies fixated on Monty's face. He tried to move back, but his immobilized legs prevented him from making much progress.

"I can't," Davies said in between gasps, finding his lost sense of self-preservation. "If I tell you, she'll kill me."

"What do you think he's going to do, lick your face?" Monty pressed, glancing at Peaches. "Who is *she*?"

Davies fought a mental battle as he came the conclusion that death by hellhound would be worse than what this mysterious woman could do. He raised a hand, catching his breath, and buying himself some time.

"I'll tell you," Davies said, resigning himself to his fate. "I'll tell you. Just keep that thing away from me."

The black orb of power floated between Monty and Davies, bobbing gently in the air. I figured the worst the Verity Blades would get for divulging information would be some kind of reprimand. They seemed strict in their rules, but I didn't think death was one of the punishments they used to keep the rank and file in line.

"How did you intercept our teleport?" Monty asked. "You're not nearly powerful enough to execute a shunt like that. How did you do it?"

"You can't hide," Davies said with bitter laugh. "Your energy signatures are too strong. Even *I* can sense you."

I cursed under my breath. Dex wasn't kidding when he

said everyone would be able to sense where we were. This had to be a result of the trigger that Dex had cast on us. The real question was, how long ago had he sensed us? Did Verity have enough time to mount a serious attack or were they reacting to our sudden appearance?

A few minutes could make all the difference.

Monty was unconvinced.

"Who directed you to this location?" Monty asked. "How long ago did you sense us?"

Monty must've been thinking the same thing I was. Dex's cast was strong. We were dead men walking if the alert had gone out to the whole city with enough notice to our enemies.

And we had plenty of those.

"You think you can hide from Korin?" Davies looked around before turning his eyes strangely upward. I followed his gaze and saw only the night sky. "She sees everything. We call her the Gray Shadow."

"The Gray Shadow?" I asked. "Who's Korin?"

Monty's face darkened as he ignored me.

"How did you do it?"

"I didn't... It wasn't...wasn't me," Davies stammered. "Here...this. She gave me this, and told me to wait here. That you would appear here."

Davies reached under his shirt and pulled out a dark gray stone medallion. It was about the size of a quarter and pulsed with violet light. Its surface was covered with a red runic symbol I couldn't understand. Monty's expression froze when he saw it.

The medallion looked innocent enough, but I could sense the dark intent behind it. It reminded me of a watered-down Nemain.

"Bloody hell," Monty said with a hiss as he stepped away

from the bench as if it was on fire and grabbed my arm. "Simon, we need to go. Now."

Monty released the lattice around Davies and backed away farther from Blade, leading us out of the small park fast, his jaw clenched as he gestured. White-gold symbols trailed us as we moved, and I got the distinct impression that something wicked was coming our way. I had never seen him react like this, which meant the danger was real...and lethal.

I felt a distant energy spike, which grabbed my attention, causing me to look up, but didn't think much of it, since it felt far away. That, in itself, should have told me everything.

We had just managed to get out of the small park, when a massive beam of violet energy slammed down into the center of the playground, reducing it and everyone within it to ash.

"Run!" Monty yelled. "Now!"

Peaches nudged me out of the park as we ran for our lives.

NINE

Two more beams hit the ground behind us, leaving craters in our wake as we ran. Monty stopped for a second and cast symbols to our right, leaving them to float off into the night. Moments later, three more beams struck the location where the symbols had been.

"That won't work for long," Monty said mostly to himself. "We need to move."

Behind us I heard another beam hit the ground, before the night became silent.

"What the hell just happened?" I asked as we ran. "What are those beams?"

"Not now," Monty said. "We have to move."

I risked a look back and saw the smoking crater that was once the Margaret L. Kempner Playground. All of the Verity Blades were gone—vaporized. The only thing that was left was the smoking molten slag that used to be playground equipment. It looked like the twisted sculptures of a demented surrealist.

"Monty, when I said the place needed to be incinerated, I wasn't being serious. What the actual fu—?"

"That wasn't me," he said in a rush as we ran. "No time to explain. We need to get to the Foundry. It's our best chance to avoid this."

"What exactly is *this*?" I asked. "Who is Korin?"

"Stay close," he said, increasing the pace even more. "I'll answer your questions once we get to relative safety."

We ran for several blocks until we reached the corner of the Foundry. I looked up to the sky, expecting another beam of purple death headed our way.

He slowed his pace and crossed the street from the Foundry, to stand in front of the Kahn House on 5th Avenue. I looked around—but mostly up—every few seconds.

"Was that beam Korin?" I asked, keeping my eyes on the sky. We stood near the stairs of the subway which led underground. A smart move to avoid a death beam from the sky. "More importantly, who is Korin? You know this person?"

"That beam," he said as he began gesturing, "was part of an elaborate trap. Those Verity Blades were the bait, and we... we were the prey."

"I'm getting that," I said. "What just happened?"

"One moment," he said as a twin Monty and me appeared across the street in front of the Foundry. "We need to be certain that the attack was tied to the area of the medallion, not to us specifically."

Our illusion twins stood on the corner for a few minutes, before slowly fading out of sight a few minutes later. There was no beam of ultimate destruction to blast the illusion to atoms.

Monty sighed, visibly relieved, but made no move to cross the street to the Foundry. I wasn't feeling eager to step out into the open either. It was one thing to know there was an impending attack headed our way—it was another thing entirely to not know where it was coming from.

"Does this Korin have a Watchtower in low orbit, capable

of unleashing purple beams of obliteration?" I asked. "What the hell was that?"

"I'm not familiar with what a Watchtower is."

"It's an orbital station—nevermind," I said. "Who is Korin?"

"The name Korin is unknown to me, but she must be the Gray Shadow," he said with a shake of his head. "This is bad. The Gray Shadow works for the High Tribunal."

"They're the same person?"

"It would appear so," Monty said, looking around. "This wasn't a targeted attack. It was triggered by Davies revealing the medallion. My best guess is that he was instructed to show it to us. That started the sequence."

"And this Gray Shadow?" I asked, still glancing up at the sky. "Do you know who she is?"

"I know *of* her, but I don't know her personally, no."

"She seems to know who we are."

"It's unlikely that she knows us," Monty said. "The more likely scenario is that we were designated as targets, and my uncle's trigger helped her locate us."

"We were designated as targets by Verity," I said. "That makes sense, but I didn't think they had this kind of firepower."

"They don't."

"Then who just tried to introduce us to a long-distance flambé?"

"The Gray Shadow is a High Tribunal Enforcer," Monty said. "She's reputed to be a mage of considerable power. I didn't think the High Tribunal would act this directly on the matter."

"She's not just Verity on steroids?"

Monty shook his head.

"In the hierarchy of the organization, she sits above Cain, but below the High Tribunal," Monty said. "She executes their commands—in many cases, from my understanding, quite literally. It would seem this situation has escalated considerably since our last encounter with Verity."

"You think?" I said. There may have been a hint of hysteria in my voice, not that I would ever admit to it. "What gave it away?"

"Be calm, and please take a deep breath, Simon," Monty said. "We're out of danger—for now."

"I just witnessed a beam of death disintegrate a group of Verity Blades and the park they stood in—the park *we* stood in—to atoms," I said. "That same beam and several more like it tried to atomize us. And your response is: *Be calm and take a deep breath?*"

"Losing control will not repel a beam of that magnitude," Monty said. "We must assess what we know and act accordingly."

"Here is what I *know*: we just barely escaped being charbroiled to dust by a mage we didn't even see," I said. "All because another mage was wearing a medallion and we were standing too close to him."

"It must have been keyed to the medallion and triggered the moment it sensed our energy signatures," Monty said. "This was no ordinary cast. In fact, its execution is quite impressive. As far as long-range attacks go, this one nearly worked. Someone powerful must have assisted in the timing of the attack."

"So glad you're impressed," I said, amazed at how he seemingly missed the obvious threat to our lives. "Why would it be keyed to the medallion?"

"The medallion held a cast of unearthing," he explained. "The fact that my uncle used a fixed circle made it easy for them to shunt us to the park. That, together with the trigger he cast, made us easy to locate, but there must have been a miscalculation on their part because they missed your creature in the initial shunt."

"Maybe the medallion was only keyed to you?"

"Perhaps," he said with nod, keeping an eye on the area around us. "The rest of the trap was to stall us while the blight of undoing, well, undid us."

"It nearly did. Is that what that beam was?" I asked. "A blight of undoing?"

He nodded.

"It's a terribly difficult cast to execute," Monty said, "which is why the medallion was used. Think homing beacon and missile. The blight can be cast from a considerable distance, allowing the caster a certain degree of safety. I didn't think anyone still used it, outside of mage warfare. On the battlefield, that cast is devastating."

"Guess what—on the streets of this city, it's just as devastating," I said. "If that had been midday, she would have wiped out everyone in that park."

"Actually, she did," Monty said. "All of the Verity Blades were incinerated."

"You know what I mean. It would have been families with their kids in that park instead of Verity," I countered. "How would they have explained that?"

"A random explosion in a park in this city? Some rogue terrorist group detonated a device to make a point because they could?" he offered. "The general populace would have accepted it, and Verity would be free to strike again and again, until they succeeded in their mission. It's not so far-fetched."

"I hate it when you're right," I said. "Did Davies know he was standing on ground zero?"

"Unlikely," Monty said, pulling on his sleeves. "He was used as bait and then discarded. The High Tribunal is not known for their compassion. I doubt their Enforcer would show any towards what they consider pawns. They are an *end justifies the means* type of group."

"Even if it means sacrificing their own?"

"Expendables, according to them," he answered. "All of Verity is expendable to the High Tribunal it seems, if it means they achieve their objective."

"Which is removing us from existence, apparently," I said.

"Something is still off. I've never heard of a blight of undoing being so precise. This is a battlefield weapon—think something to unleash destruction in a general direction, not a precise location."

"You're saying it's a sword that's being used as a scalpel?"

"Precisely," he said with a nod. "It's not supposed to be able to be used for precision strikes. It's unwieldy, and the potential for error is too great."

"Seemed pretty precise to me," I said, thinking back to the nightmare of what remained in the park. "It was contained to the park—Davies specifically, and the area around him broadly."

"That is what concerns me. That degree of control is beyond an Enforcer, beyond even the High Tribunal. Someone is working with them, someone powerful enough to convince the Tribunal to accept their assistance."

"How powerful exactly?" I asked, looking over at the Foundry. "Archmage level of power?"

"At least, if not stronger."

"Well, that should narrow it down, don't you think?"

"You'd be surprised at how many powerful mages currently exist on this plane."

"Powerful mages that want us dead?"

"A valid point," he said, giving it some thought. "*That* should narrow it down somewhat."

"You think Gault is working with this Gray Shadow?"

"There is a distinct possibility he is using the Gray

Shadow to act as his weapon, while maintaining an illusion of non-involvement. It's what he did with Tellus and the Arcanists."

"You know we're going to be blamed for the deaths of the Verity Blades."

"It can't be helped at the moment," Monty said with a nod. "Let's not keep Julien waiting any longer. I'm certain he is aware of our presence; at the very least, I'm certain the blight of undoing did not escape his notice."

We crossed the street and approached the Foundry.

TEN

The Foundry was a neutral ground of sorts, in the sense that most of the people who entered its doors were neutralized and vanished from existence.

It wasn't that Julien was evil, exactly—it was more that he was involved with people and beings that valued their privacy beyond what would be considered normal levels.

Most of *them* were evil.

Showing up uninvited to the Foundry was one of the fastest ways to be permanently retired in the city. In fact, the entire block where the Foundry sat was covered in aversion runes. I was sure that people had a tendency to cross the street when they came to 91st Street and 5th Avenue. If you asked them why, they wouldn't be able to give you a reason except that, maybe something about the area felt off.

It was the same reaction people had when getting too close to the Dark Goat; although with the Dark Goat, Cecil had pushed it to 9,000 on a scale of 1 to 10. The runes Julien placed around the Foundry made sure the property was secure and empty at all times.

The fact that Dex had sent us here with his two-phase trigger made me realize a few things.

One, he was way out on the fringe of scary if he could get Julien to cooperate with one of his requests.

Two, Dex was truly and completely out of his mind if he thought this was a good idea after our last visit had left *major renovations* at the Foundry. Renovations that required we make some kind of reparations to Julien. We *had* been on site during major destruction to his home.

Three, despite all of that, I knew Julien wouldn't risk harming us. At least, I really hoped so. It made me realize how wide and far-reaching Dex's influence extended.

Being associated with him was a risk, yes, but it also came with some major street cred where it counted.

Also, Dex was truly and deeply frightening when he really wanted to be—and I wasn't talking about the times he wore a kilt and nothing else. When he wielded Nemain, I had serious doubts about my continued existence, cursed alive or not.

I shuddered the memory away.

Located at 2 E. 91st Street, the Foundry had purchased the property once known as the Cooper Hewitt Museum, and created a meeting space and home for the elite criminal magic-user.

It also boasted state-of-the-art conventional security along with nasty runic defenses designed to erase anyone suicidal enough to attempt an unscheduled visit.

Neither the NYTF nor any other body of authority ever set foot in the Foundry without being specifically summoned by Julien, and he never dealt with external authority.

These same authorities had no jurisdiction within the walls of the Foundry. The Dark Council acknowledged its presence, but chose not to interfere with its activities. Probably had something to do with the fact that a few members of the Dark Council were also members of the Foundry.

Like the Vatican, the Foundry existed as a de facto sovereign state within the city. Similar to the Vatican, it was controlled by an absolute monarch: in this case, an Archmage.

An Archmage named Julien Durant.

Within the Foundry walls, Julien's word was the absolute law. It also helped that he had the firepower to back up those words. As an Archmage, he was a real and present threat no one I knew took lightly.

He had a tendency to keep a low profile. I had long realized that those who wielded the most power did that. They attracted little to no attention to themselves, preferring to dwell in the shadows.

As the caliber of our enemies grew stronger, I learned that what dwelled in the shadows was truly dangerous and lethal.

I wasn't a big fan of what moved in the shadows of this world. When we encountered them, they usually wanted to kill us, exploit us, or engage in some combination of the two.

I looked up at the building as we approached. It was an impressive structure, belonging to the age of mansions of the early 1900s. It had first belonged to Carnegie before being donated to the Smithsonian. Julien's sect, the Fleur de Lis, had purchased it in the late 1970s according to my research.

Just because I didn't like Julien or his sect didn't mean I was going to hold back on collecting information on him. The best way to defeat an enemy, or a potential enemy, especially one as powerful as Julien, was to gather as much information as possible.

Knowledge was power.

I didn't enjoy the idea of having to revisit this place—much less seeing Julien and his ever-pissy assistant, Claude, again—but if Dex said we needed to go to the Foundry, then we were going to the Foundry.

I just hoped it wasn't the last place we would visit...ever.

The last time we were here, we had to beat a hasty retreat. Between a psycho Blood Hunter named Esti losing what little mind she had left, and an even more psycho Arbiter, Ian Macintyre, who had a particular axe to grind with Monty, we might have been present when they *redecorated* parts of the Foundry.

I didn't think that saying it wasn't our fault would fly with Julien. He didn't seem to be the understanding type when it came to his home and the very expensive items it contained.

I knew for a fact, that he didn't appreciate Monty and me creating a new exit from the second floor—through the wall. In fact, the term 'murderous rage' may have crossed my mind a few times in the aftermath of Foundry renovation, when I thought of Julien's reaction.

It was a *renovation* that included blowing an enormous hole in a wall, and disappearing a fireplace I was sure was some sort of irreplaceable and priceless antique.

Yes, the entire fireplace had been obliterated and gone by the time Monty and I jumped out of the hole that used to be a wall. I would imagine Julien would remember something like that and possibly hold a grudge.

But maybe time had mellowed him out?

"You think Julien still remem—?"

"Of course he does," Monty said, cutting me off. "An original Saint-Gaudens fireplace was obliterated. I'm fairly certain Julien will remember its destruction. Wouldn't you?"

"Sometimes it's best not to get attached to material things," I argued. "He should really consider a minimalist lifestyle. Less stuff to worry about."

"I'll make it a point to inform the Archmage that he should detach from his personal belongings—items that he acquired over his long life and which probably hold significant amounts of meaning for him. I'm sure he'll be amenable to that concept. Why didn't I think of that earlier?"

"No need to get snippy," I said. "I was just pointing out that if it was really priceless, he may have wanted to keep it somewhere safe."

"He *did*," Monty said. "It was in the Foundry, behind several layers of protection, until we arrived."

"Well, when you put it that way..." I said, realizing that my only recollection of a Saint-Gaudens of any kind sat in the Metropolitan Museum of Art. "Just to be absolutely clear here—when you say Saint-Gaudens, do you mean the same Saint-Gaudens that has pieces displayed in the Met?"

"The one and the same," Monty said. "Perhaps now you could understand why Julien would be upset at its destruction?"

"But that wasn't *us*," I protested. "That was your psycho-arbiter pal, Ian. He shouldn't place any of the blame on us for that one."

"He expressly instructed us not to destroy anything," Monty said. "He left us alone for a few moments, and his fireplace was blasted into nothingness. What would *you* think?"

"I would think that my two amazing guests, who I just warned not to break my home, had nothing to do with the destruction I had just witnessed."

Monty stared at me.

"In this world, where your brain lives," he said, pointing at my head, "do you ever get visited by reality?"

"Reality is overrated," I said. "I still say we argue our innocence. We just happened to be in the wrong place at the wrong time. The property destruction was collateral damage, completely unintentional. Did you forget that Esti was armed when we were specifically instructed not to bring weapons into the Foundry?"

"I recall."

"So what? We take the fall because they blew a hole in Julien's home?"

"Why were Esti and Ian there in the first place?"

"One wanted to skewer me, and the other wanted to disintegrate you," I said. "I'm not understanding the question."

Monty shook his head.

"*We* were the catalyst for the destruction."

"By that logic, we're responsible for all of the destruction in the city related to us," I said. "Even the destruction we didn't cause."

"*We are*."

"Excuse me?"

"According to the authorities, we are guilty by proximity," Monty said as we stepped close to the gate that led to the front door. "I trust that Julien respects my uncle more than his desire to exact retribution."

"Forget respects, I hope he *fears* Dex more than he wants to strangle us."

"We shall see."

We approached the large black wrought-iron fence. Even from a distance, I could see the rune work along its surface. Angry red symbols threatened a painful and excruciating death for any who trespassed on the property.

A winding, stone path beyond the gate led to the front of the mansion. I saw the runic defenses inscribed on the ground on both sides of the path as we stepped close to the threshold of the gate.

"Those aren't oblivion circles like last time." I pointed at the circles slowly pulsing a dim red in night. "They look more like—"

"Obliteration circles," Monty finished. "It would appear

Julien has taken measures to upgrade the lethality of his defenses."

"Deadly measures," I added. "Aren't those circles supposed to be unstable? You told me they were nearly impossible to control."

"They usually are," Monty said with a short nod as he examined the circles. "It would depend on the level of the caster. I would assume these are Julien's handiwork, and therefore extraordinarily lethal and stable."

"Well, that's good to know," I said. "Note to self: stay on the path."

"That is, provided we get past this gate," Monty said, being careful not to touch the actual gate. "He enhanced the defenses here as well."

"Enhanced is an understatement," I said, pointing at the fence. "Those runes look lethal."

"Because they are," Monty said, keeping his distance. "However, I'm certain Claude will be with us momentarily."

"Ah, Claude," I said. "I'm sure *he'll* be happy to see us."

"I find that highly unlikely."

I heard a string of French curses slowly get closer to the door, from the interior of the property. Several lights came on as the voice became louder.

The large, ornate door opened, and I realized that while it wasn't Australian Buloke, it was covered in more of those deadly runes that were all over the fence.

Claude stepped outside, careful to stay on the path, and remained a good distance from the fence. He glared at us and crossed his arms. He was a small man with piercing eyes, who used his stature to his advantage.

I recalled what I knew about him. None of it was good.

Claude was an accomplished mage and world-class assassin who had been trained personally by Julien. No one underestimated Claude twice—*if* they survived the first encounter.

We still didn't like each other much.

"*Bonsoir*, Claude," I said diplomatically with a wave, trying to get off on the right foot as he scowled in response. My French was rusty, but I still remembered the basics and most of the curses. Actually, I was fluent in curses in several languages. "We're here to see Julien."

"*Je m'en fous*," Claude said with a sneer and pointed to the park. "Go away. Julien is not here, especially not for you and your abomination of a creature. *Bonsoir, connard.*"

I ignored the remark directed at me. Insult me all you want. Insult my hellhound, and we had a problem.

Claude stepped back inside and made to close the door.

Monty and I moved back from the fence. The last thing we needed was to appear to be storming the Foundry. Monty cleared his throat and Claude paused.

"I believe my uncle arranged this meeting," Monty said matter-of-factly as he pulled on one of his sleeves. "What message would you like me to convey to him about your lack of hospitality?"

"Dexter?" Claude said with a hint of surprise. "*Putain de bordel de merde.*"

"You know, Monty, my French gets better every time I visit this place," I said. "I know for a fact that Clyde here wouldn't be using vulgarities directed at us. He's much too sophisticated, being French and all, to use such base language. What do you think?"

"Impossible," Monty said with mock seriousness. "After all, he represents the Foundry and, more importantly, Julien. I'm sure he realizes any behavior he exhibits is a direct reflection on *Archmage* Julien's reputation and standing."

Claude stood with the door ajar for several seconds and

stared at us. If looks could maim, Monty and I would be missing several limbs right about now.

"*Merde*," he said under his breath, and gestured as he stepped close to us, unlocking the gate. He turned around and walked back to the Foundry door. "This way."

We stepped through the iron gate, and my exposed skin burned for half a second. I rubbed my face and hands, realizing the defenses were beyond upgraded. My skin felt sunburned after simply walking past the threshold.

If that was entry with the defenses disabled, I'd hate to see what happened to someone trying to get past the gate with the defenses enabled.

"Stay on the path," Claude warned. "The circles do not know mercy or recognize friendships. I would *hate* for you to step on one of them. You would not survive. It would be a terrible accident. Everyone would weep at your demise."

"See, Monty? I told you he cared."

Claude muttered some more curses under his breath.

We arrived at the front door which Claude held open for us as we entered the Foundry proper.

ELEVEN

Claude led us past the expansive foyer and into a sitting room.

At the far end of the room he placed his hand on a door and, whispering some words under his breath, caused it to *click* with a subtle release of power as it unlocked.

This library was different from the one we had visited the last time we were here. The tomes on the shelves were covered with runes, making the titles indecipherable.

Power bled off the books—looking at them for any extended period past a few seconds hurt my eyes and increased the pressure around the base of my neck. I slid my eyes away from the books to prevent the melting of my brain and kept my gaze soft, not focusing on any particular book.

Every wall was covered with shelves—and the shelves were floor-to-ceiling affairs that looked more at home in the Reading Room of the New York Public Library than a private residence.

Several tables were situated around the room, banker's lamps sitting on each. All of the lamps were currently off. Comfortable chairs were placed around each of the tables.

"You will not destroy our home in this place," Claude said. His accent seemed to be more pronounced when he was upset. "Wait here and touch nothing, if you wish to see the morning."

I heard the door lock as he left the library.

"I get the feeling he doesn't trust us," I said, looking around the library. "Can you read these titles? Because if I stare too long at them, I feel like my eyes are going to bleed and my brain is going to pour out of my ears. Other than that, it really is a cozy place."

"Some of them, yes," Monty said, stepping close to some of the shelves. "This is an Archmage reading room. The mages who would come here would need to be high-level practitioners of their respective disciplines."

"Mages come here to read? Really?"

"I'm certain it's by invite only, but there are some rare and obscure volumes here," he said. "The only other place to find them would be—"

"Professor Ziller's Living Library," Julien finished, his voice carrying a slight accent as he entered the room otherwise without sound. "Some of my associates would rather not trouble the esteemed Professor with such trivialities as reading a specific book."

"I think some of these would be missing even from the Living Library," Monty said, turning to Julien and giving him a short bow which Julien returned. "Thank you for welcoming us into your home again."

I followed the example and gave him a slight bow. My diplomacy skills were getting better by the second. Julien returned our bows with another one of his own before he moved to the center of the library.

A large, marble fireplace dominated one of the far walls. What was it with mages and their fireplaces? Thankfully, this one didn't seem priceless or antique. It had a pair of impressive dragons sculpted into the white marble facing away from each other. They held a fortress in clouds in their claws overhead. It was an ornate work of art that gave off a low-level sensation of vertigo. If I stared at the dragons for too long, they seemed to move.

It wasn't as bad as the books.

My eyes didn't want to bleed out of my skull, but I could sense the subtle power in the fireplace. It wasn't just a fireplace, though; it felt like...more. It was currently dormant, the room being comfortable and not needing additional heating.

We had been in the Foundry ten minutes and nothing had exploded or been blown to bits. Both of us were still intact and no one was actively trying to kill us—as long as you didn't count the High Tribunal, Korin, Dira, most of Verity, the Arcanists, Keeper Gault, and probably Claude. I was certain I had missed a few groups, but overall things were going smoothly.

This had to be some kind of record.

Julien wore a gray Alexander Amosu Vanquish II Bespoke over a white Eton shirt with no tie. He was barefoot as usual; in fact, I had never seen him wear shoes. He reminded me of Gandalf, if in a suit. His long white hair, usually loose, was pulled back into a low ponytail.

"Your uncle is a difficult man to refuse," Julien said. "He and I have an understanding, and I owe him too many favors to take his requests lightly."

"We can make an exception," Claude said from behind Julien. "These two are *un mal de tete*. Allow me to send them home, seigneur."

"They are here as our *guests*," Julien said with an edge to his voice. "However, please activate the defenses of the Foundry. We will be moving to the Chateau shortly."

"Defenses?" I echoed. "Why are we—?"

"The defenses?" Claude asked, cutting me off with a look of disdain he had probably practiced for a few decades. "For these two? *Mon dieu,* what for? They are insignificant. No, my apologies! Ants are insignificant. These two are lower than ants."

"Claude," Julien said, his voice a warning. "Now, please."

"Right away, seigneur," Claude said, properly chastised. "Will they be staying the evening?"

"Prepare the passage to the Chateau," Julien answered. "We will speak here for a moment, before retiring there for the evening."

"Of course," Claude said, giving us an extra dose of stink eye. "I will make sure everything is ready, seigneur."

"See to the defenses first," Julien said. "Then prepare the passage."

Claude bowed and left the library.

"I get the distinct feeling Claude doesn't like us much," I said. "Was it something I said?"

"As you know, Claude is zealous in his protection of me and this place, but he has lost some of his social graces over the years," Julien said. "We have had fewer guests of the Foundry since your last...*visit.*"

"We regret the loss of the Saint-Gaudens," Monty said. "If you allow, I'm sure we can find a way—"

Julien waved Monty's words away with a faint smile.

"Your uncle resolved that issue shortly after your departure," Julien said. "Did you really think I would have let that insult go unanswered? You came into my home and destroyed it, after I specifically requested you refrain from doing so."

I didn't see the point in explaining how it was really the crazed Blood Hunter, Esti, and the psycho-arbiter Ian Macintyre who really caused all of the destruction.

Still, somehow Dex had resolved the issue. What exactly did that mean?

"Dex did what?" I asked. "He resolved the issue?"

"He saved your lives," Julien said. "By replacing the Saint-Gaudens."

"He didn't say a thing," Monty said, looking away. "He never mentioned it to us."

"Why should he?" Julien asked. "He took on the obligation of reparation; you had no part in it except to have your lives spared."

Monty remained silent for a few moments.

"You heightened the defenses of the Foundry," Monty said. "Has our presence here caused you difficulty?"

"The last time you were here, you were being pursued by your sect," Julien replied. "Now you are being pursued by the High Tribunal, Verity, and have managed to get the attention of a Keeper—impressive."

"We're special that way."

Julien shook his head as he turned to the fireplace. While his back was turned, Monty gave me a formidable glare—at least a two on the glare-o-meter—which said: *Do not antagonize an Archmage who could kill us without breaking a sweat.*

I raised a hand in surrender at his look, and made a vow to remain silent, even crossing my heart and throwing away the imaginary key to convince him.

"I judge a person by the enemies they make," Julien said, turning from the fireplace. "Most of your enemies are inconsequential, but a Keeper? Now, I am interested."

"Why did Dex send us to you?" I asked. "I mean, not that we aren't grateful for your hospitality. I'm just curious why he sent us here."

"It is a good question," Julien replied. "Allow me to answer it with one of my own. Where else could you go? Did you have other options?"

"I'm sure the Dark Council—"

"No," Julien said, cutting me off. "The Director is

currently dealing with internal strife in her reorganization of the Dark Council. She cannot help you, even if she wanted to."

I wracked my brain thinking of mages powerful enough to face off against Keepers and their minions—then the thought came to me, and I smiled.

"Fordey Boutique," I said with smug satisfaction. "They could help us *and* face off against the Keeper."

Julien stared at me for a good five seconds, and I stared back. I would never admit that impromptu staring contest shook me, but it did. Looking into his eyes was not the best of ideas.

Julien was old and wore his age like a mantle of authority. It chilled me much in the same way Dex did when he would stare at me sometimes. I felt I could see across time in his eyes.

I looked away first.

"You are a dangerous man, Simon," Julien said, lowering his voice. "It is true, the Ten could assist you, but it is not the end of the world...yet. That would be like using a hammer to kill a fly. The damage would be incalculable."

"My uncle sent us here because it was the safest option," Monty said, giving me a glance and reminding me to stop sharing so much. "You were the best option, not the only option."

"Spoken like a true Montague," Julien said, pronouncing the last part of Monty's name like *goo*, which caused me to snort. It was a reflex and Julien turned to me, his expression mildly amused. "Are you always this infantile?"

"Only when he is awake," Monty answered, preventing me from sharing some of my sage wisdom. "My apologies. He meant no insult."

Julien remained focused on me a few seconds longer.

"You feel fear," he said after scanning me. "This is wise.

You *should* feel fear. The beings you face are indeed powerful, and you are no match for them in your current state. Even with your"—he waved a hand in front of him—"advancements. They will not be enough."

I grew serious, all humor gone.

"Can you help us?"

"Three days you will remain with me at the Chateau," Julien said, pointing to the two of us and shaking his head. "In that time, we will sort out that mess you have between you."

"What mess?" I asked. "Can you be a bit more specific?"

"You share a stormblood and an elder rune," he said incredulously. "You are also *his* Aspis. How either of you are still alive astounds me. Kali, I can understand—she can be somewhat deranged on a good day—so the Aspis designation makes sense. Becoming her Marked One was not prudent."

"She didn't exactly consult with me on the decision," I said, glancing to the sides at the mention of her name. I put some distance between Julien and me, just in case she was listening. "She's not exactly the consulting type."

It didn't surprise me that he knew about Kali. I was already aware that my upgraded status to the Marked of Kali meant I showed up on a few high-powered radars now. Some of them I knew belonged to the heavy hitters club.

You didn't get to be a thousand years old and not have a way of staying informed about what was going on in your city. Julien had vast resources and used them when he needed to.

"Be that as it may," Julien continued, "why you two trusted that madman, York, to perform a stormblood merge is beyond me. That man is an unstable psychotic."

"I don't know," I said. "He seemed like a nice guy. A little frayed around the edges and a few pieces short of a full puzzle, but his intentions were in the right place, I think."

Julien stared at me and then turned to Monty.

"You work with him every day? How?"

"With great patience," Monty said. "But he is right. York wasn't trying to actively harm us."

"Merging a stormblood is usually a death sentence," Julien answered. "He is a mad genius to be able to do this, yes, but it does not change that he *is* mad and you two are madder still to have allowed it to happen."

"Not like we had much choice," I said. "We needed the stormblood."

"And the elder rune?" Julien asked softly. "Did you *need* that as well?"

"That's his department," I said, pointing at Monty. "This goes deeper than I can understand, but I know we are maintaining the balance that Gault wants to destroy."

"You have no idea what you two have gotten into," Julien said. "Do you know why I agreed to your uncle's three days? Aside from that being how long the cast can hide you?"

"I don't know," I said. "Aside from the cast, three days seems like it's enough. I thought that was *your* condition for helping us—that you could only tolerate us for three days before you wanted us gone."

Julien gave me a look and shook his head.

"No, he said you had to learn how to activate the elder rune in three days. I told him that it was impossible—Tristan is not an Archmage, not even close. We would need closer to three centuries, and that would only be the beginning. Then he suggested the Chateau."

"The Chateau?" Monty asked. "Which is?"

"Something you will discover soon," Julien said, his response cryptic in the way of all mages. "We must start the process soon."

"It has to do with the trigger," I said. "Dex said the second phase would hide us completely, and then in three days it wouldn't."

"That is the explanation of the cast, the inner workings, but not the reason *I* agreed, no."

"Verity will be able to locate us in three days' time, despite your defenses," Monty said, his voice somber. "It is the rule of the cast."

"Yes…and no," Julien answered. "It will not be Verity, no."

"Korin," I said, seeing where he was going. "The Gray Shadow will find us."

"Yes, the *sword in their hand*, Korin, will find you," Julien said. "She is good, very good. My reason will become clear soon enough."

"She used a—"

"Blight of undoing," Julien finished. "How close did she come to succeeding?"

"Too close," Monty said. "She vaporized an entire Blade Recovery Team to show us how serious she was."

Julien nodded.

"She used a medallion?" He held out his thumb and forefinger "About this big, made of gray stone with one rune on its face, yes?"

"Yes," Monty said. "How did you—?"

Julien reached into a desk and pulled out a medallion. It was identical to the one Davies had worn. I stepped back, looking up in case another beam of purple death was headed our way.

"This was sent to me several days ago," Julien said. "It would seem she, and whomever she answers to, knows you need assistance."

"Not just any assistance—the assistance of an Archmage," Monty said, looking at the medallion. "You disabled it?"

"I do not wish to have a blight of undoing arrive in my home, although it could be said that, with you here, it has already arrived," Julien said as he whispered some words under his breath. The medallion turned to dust a few seconds later. "She will come. You must be ready when she does. I will help you to meet her."

"How do we get ready in three days?" I asked. "It's impossible."

"We have three days to do the impossible," Monty said, looking at Julien. "Can you do it?"

"*Oui*," he said with a nod. "This is why your uncle sent you here. We will use the Chateau."

"No one else would even try this," Monty said. "Not in this timeframe."

"It would be madness to even attempt it," Julien said with a shake of his head and a wicked smile which reminded me of Dex. "It is fortunate that we are all mad then, no?" I understood why Dex had reached out to Julien—they were both old and crazy. It made sense. "

"You can really do this?" I asked. "In three days?"

"Yes. It will not be easy or painless, but I can do the unthinkable and facilitate a major shift in Tristan, with the assistance of his bond brother. I do hope you both survive."

TWELVE

"This will not be a true shift to Archmage," Julien said. "That would certainly kill you."

He turned to the fireplace and pointed at it while looking at me.

"What?" I asked, examining the fireplace. "It's an excellent fireplace. I especially like the dragons. I like these better than the actual thing. All in all, a most excellent fireplace. Very marbly and sturdy. I'm sure it can hold impressive fires."

"Light it," Julien said, crossing his arms while staring at me. "If you think you can."

"Of course I can," I said, looking around the top of the fireplace for matches. "Where do you keep the matches?"

"I didn't say to use matches," Julien replied. "Light it."

"With what?"

"With your ability," he said. "Once we cross over, that will start our timetable."

"You want me to light the fireplace?" I asked in disbelief. "Did you forget what happened to the last fireplace?"

"I have not," he said dryly. "Light *this* fireplace, Simon Strong, *Aspis* to the Mage Montague, bearer of the stormblood, catalyst to the first elder rune, bondmate to Peaches, the scion of Cerberus, Marked of Kali, and holder of the necrotic seraph Ebonsoul, blade of Izanami. NOW."

I felt a buildup of power crossing the room from Julien as he spoke. He gestured and pointed at me as he said the last word.

Power flooded my body as Julien focused on me with those ageless eyes. Violet energy erupted from my hands, and Julien pointed at the fireplace again. I raised my hand and unleashed a magic missile of epic proportions.

For a few seconds, my brain protested at what I had just done. Clearly I had just destroyed a second fireplace in the Foundry. My magic missile was a blend of energies, bright violet, a gleaming black, and tinged with hints of gold and red.

It shot forward from my hand, almost eagerly, and raced at the fireplace. I had never created anything near this, and the energy around the missile warped the space around it similar to the mirage effect I'd only seen in a desert landscape.

There were several things wrong with that. First, we weren't standing in a desert but rather in the Foundry, and second, I didn't possess enough power to warp space with my magic missile—or at least I didn't think I did.

Julien raised a hand, and froze my missile mid-flight.

It strained against whatever was holding it in place, and my opinion of Julien's power level ratcheted up a few notches.

"You've grown somewhat since we last met, Strong," Julien said, looking at the missile. "Did you know you possessed this much power?"

"No," I said, being honest. "I've never created something like that before in my life. How is it so powerful?"

"You are more than you seem, evidently," he said, turning

to Monty. "Tristan, were you aware of this increase in his power?"

"No," Monty said, shaking his head as he observed the missile. "It is a considerable increase from the last time he used this cast."

"We will tap into that new power, then," Julien said, looking at me. "You no longer need to feed your cast, Simon. I can handle it from here."

He waved a hand, and the power that had erupted from me dissipated almost instantly. I staggered back a step from the sudden disconnect.

"Your turn," Julien continued, focusing on Monty. "Mage Montague, Ordaurum of the Golden Circle, bearer of the rune of seals and the first elder rune, Master of the seraphic Sorrows, please, if you would be so kind, unseal the doorway before you."

Monty, like me, was still in some kind of mild shock at hearing Julien list who we were with such ease. How did he know so much? Was this what it meant to be an Archmage? Did he just sense all those things about us?

I had underestimated Julien and the power of an Archmage. I glanced over and saw how he held my magic missile frozen in the air as he spoke to Monty. He didn't even bother to give it a second glance.

He was either extremely confident in his ability to control our casts, or he was willing to risk exploding the Foundry into a blasted-out crater, because now he was asking Monty to do the same thing—unleash a devastating cast inside his home.

Monty gave me a look and then looked at Julien, uncertain.

"The rune of seals...the power it now contains," Monty said. "The damage it could unleash would be catastrophic. Your home—"

"Will be just fine," Julien finished, his voice holding a calm I didn't feel. "Do it. Do you see the doorway?"

Monty narrowed his eyes at the fireplace for what seemed like a lifetime and then nodded.

"I see it," Monty said, still uncertain. "The defensive runes around this doorway cannot be opened, at least not by me. You are asking me to do the impossible. I can't open that doorway."

"I never said, to *open* the doorway, mage," Julien said with an authority I hadn't heard earlier in his voice. "I told you to *unseal* it."

Monty remained silent for close to a minute as he peered at the fireplace. I felt the shift in him as he nodded.

"It's a stasis tunnel," Monty said, his voice taking on the tone it got when he was investigating some cast or runic symbol. "How?"

"Irrelevant," Julien said, dismissing Monty's words. "You *can* unseal it with the rune."

It wasn't a question but a statement of fact.

Monty nodded as understanding illuminated his eyes.

"I can, yes."

"Then please do so, now."

Monty gestured as a black-and-red aura of power surrounded him.

Julien narrowed his eyes at him, but remained silent. I could tell from his expression that he wasn't thrilled about the black energy wrapping itself around Monty.

Black symbols merged with violet ones, and formed a black lattice with hints of violet power racing along its length. The power from the lattice was enough to make my eyes water. After a few more seconds, the waves of energy forced me to avert my gaze.

Monty, his expression hard, focused even more energy into the lattice with a series of black-and-red orbs, which floated over and sank silently into the suspended cast. I took a few steps back as Peaches whined by my side.

If my magic missile didn't tear the Foundry apart, the combination of my missile and this lattice definitely would. There was no way this place could remain standing if our two casts collided.

I braced for impact as Monty released the lattice, letting it float over to the fireplace. Julien, his face impassive, nodded in approval as the lattice moved slowly to where my magic missile hovered.

Monty looked on, an expression of concern growing on his face as the casts got closer and closer.

"Julien, I don't think it would be prudent to allow those casts to collide," Monty said. "The energy released will level the Foundry—"

"I understand, and thank you for your concern," Julien said. "It's under control."

Julien waved a hand and the lattice slowed down, hovering about two feet away from the energy that was my missile, but still moving closer and giving me a mild heart attack in the process.

I didn't want to imagine what would happened if they touched.

"You managed to halt its approach," Monty said, his voice barely above a whisper, as the lattice slowed down. "Fascinating."

Leave it to Monty to go full Spock when faced with impending death.

"You've been using blood magic," Julien said, his voice and expression neutral as he observed the lattice. "There are considerable dangers to exposing yourself that way, not to mention who and *what* you may attract. The benefits rarely, if ever, match the costs."

"It was necessary to do so."

"Was it?" Julien asked. "Or did *you* feel it was? Are you justifying the act after the fact?"

"It was needed," Monty said with conviction.

"We shall see," Julien said, waving a hand at the lattice. It slowed down even more, then came to a stop, inches away from the missile energy. "You may have to reevaluate what is needed, against what you *want*."

As soon as the lattice stopped moving, Julien ignored it and turned from Monty.

Monty looked the way I felt: controlled awe and disbelief, except he showed more control than I did. I was heavy in the disbelief stage, which I was sure showed on my face, as Julien turned to me.

He stepped forward, ignoring me, and crouched down to gaze at Peaches, locking his eyes with those of my hellhound.

"I have not forgotten you, Mighty Peaches, bondmate to the Marked of Kali, scion of the Gatekeeper to the Underworld. You will be the catalyst for this special cast," Julien said, placing a hand gently on my hellhound's ginormous head. "I need you to speak your most powerful word. Can you do that for me?"

I looked on in barely contained shock.

If Peaches spoke his most powerful word, the Foundry was going to be reduced to a memory, along with everything inside of it—including us.

I couldn't let him do that.

Peaches rumbled back to Julien and stepped into shred-and-disintegrate mode. He stood firm and leaned back on his haunches.

"Julien, no!" I said, raising my voice. "You can't let him unleash his most powerful bark!"

Monty was gesturing fast and I saw the beginning of a shield appear around our feet. Julien looked at us and smiled, oblivious to the destruction he had just requested from my hellhound.

"You don't think his bark is powerful enough?" Julien asked, still looking down at my hellhound. "I hear it can be quite formidable. It will provide an excellent catalyst."

"Are you insane?" I asked. "His most powerful bark can tear down buildings! You want him to unleash that in here?"

"Yes," Julien said, still looking at Peaches. "Mighty Peaches, mightiest of all hellhounds, please release your most powerful word."

Peaches looked in my direction.

<*He is very strong. I think he can stand against it.*>

<*If you break his house, we are all dead.*>

<*His house is stronger than my words. Don't worry, bondmate. I will not break him or his den.*>

<*Not like we will be around to say anything if you do.*>

<*You are my bondmate. Do you trust me?*>

<*With my life.*>

<*And I you. We will not destroy his home and we will not be harmed.*>

I glanced down at Peaches and nodded.

Peaches took a deep breath and released the loudest bark I had ever heard from him. I saw Monty cast, but he was too late. The shield was too slow. I felt the pressure build up in my ears, realizing the sound was going to rupture my eardrums.

The marble floor around Peaches exploded into fragments. The runes along his flanks exploded with pulsing red energy, glowing brightly. It created an image of my hellhound standing in a cloud of powerful energy.

The entire Foundry shook on its foundations as a visible sound wave of red energy raced at Julien.

With a gesture from Julien, the pressure around my ears dropped and the stone fragments that had been the floor around

Peaches suddenly froze mid-explosion. Julien stepped forward, that small smile still on his face, extended an arm and caught it.

My brain saw what had happened, but couldn't process it, nearly exploding as it tried. He had controlled and caught Peaches' bark before it could unleash total devastation on the Foundry, and us.

Julien turned away from us and brought his hands together, merging the three expressions of power into a silver orb that resembled a sun in mid-supernova.

He held the supernova in one hand and released it slowly in the direction of the fireplace. I braced for the Foundry to disappear from existence, along with the rest of us.

The orb floated into the fireplace and flashed with silver light, but no heat or kinetic energy. We all looked away, except for Julien. When I could see again, without a large silver blob blocking my vision, I looked at the fireplace.

Julien was still standing in front of it, except it wasn't a fireplace anymore. The entire side of the library had changed.

The fireplace had grown to five times its original size and was now a doorway. Above it, was the image of a fortress that, to my eyes, moved as if alive. A silver dragon, one on each side, framed the door, forming part of the threshold.

Both the dragons' heads moved, focusing on me. Small clouds of silver dust escaped their mouths and I could just catch a gleam of silver light in their eyes.

"What are those?" I asked, pointing at the dragons. "Where did the fireplace go?"

"Those are the dragons of delay," Julien said, turning behind us as Claude raced into the library. "Everything is fine; we will be taking our leave shortly. Please make sure all appropriate measures are enforced."

Claude gave Monty and me a barely concealed look of disgust before turning to Julien.

"How long, seigneur?"

"Three days if it all goes according to plan," Julien said. "Much shorter if it doesn't. *Au revoir*, Claude."

"*Au revoir*, seigneur," Claude said with a bow. "I shall take my leave, and seal the room until your return."

"Please do," Julien said. "I will open it from the Chateau if needed."

Claude nodded silently as he left the library.

I could feel an energy spike as the door frame glowed white for a few seconds. The door was suddenly covered in orange-and-white runes that flowed around the surface.

From the little I could understand: unless you were an Archmage named Julien, that door wasn't going to be opened by you at any point in the foreseeable future.

"Those are some major failsafes," I said, looking at the door. "Can anyone besides you open it?"

"Of course," Julien said. "If they wish to disintegrate five square blocks of this city along with whoever is attempting entry. Then yes, of course, they can try."

"Try?"

"It won't open unless I open it," Julien said. "The defenses will activate the moment someone presents a credible threat."

"You would sacrifice the entire Foundry?"

"There are items and secrets within these walls that must never fall into, shall we say, questionable hands," Julien said, walking back to the doorway that used to be a fireplace. "If that means they must be destroyed, then yes, I would sacrifice the Foundry."

"What about Claude?"

"Claude is designated as the *Garde de Fonderie*," he said. "He will, and must, protect its secrets to his last breath. Foundry Guardsman is a highly regarded, respected, and coveted position among the most accomplished mages of the Fleur de Lis."

We turned back to the silver dragons which I was convinced had come to life since Julien unleashed that orb of power at them.

"I had heard of the dragons of delay—are the stories about them true?" Monty asked. "They act as timestops?"

"Not entirely," Julien answered. "They delay time according to the design. My last doorway contained caryatids of causality. Are you familiar with them?"

Monty's expression darkened.

"I had no idea," Monty said. "How did my uncle replace *that*?"

"He did it in his own way," Julien said with a small chuckle. "Let us say that the Vanderbilt Mantlepiece currently sitting in the Met is not the original."

"He stole it from the Met?"

"No, not stole, exchanged," Julien said. "And with an impressive replacement."

"Wouldn't the museum notice something like that?" I asked.

"The next time you visit the museum, let me know if you can tell the difference. Now, to our task at hand," Julien continued. "Once we cross the threshold, the delay will begin. We must make the most of our *time*."

"What is the ratio?" Monty asked. "How much of a delay will we experience?"

"We will not sense anything," Julien said. "Time in the Chateau is accelerated. The ratio, as you say, is forty-eight to one. For every hour that passes on this plane, forty-eight will pass at the Chateau."

My brain twisted into knots trying to work out the time difference. I had issues working out Eastern Time to Pacific Time, and that was in the same country. Julien was talking about interplanar time differences. After a few seconds, my brain seized.

"Can you explain that in non-mage?" I asked. "For those of us who don't make a habit of traveling across planes?"

"Three days equals roughly five months," Monty answered. "Four months and three weeks, to be precise."

"We're going to spend five months in there?" I asked, pointing at the doorway. "How is that going to affect our bodies?"

"The same way regular time would," Julien said with a wicked smile. "Consider this a method of *tricherie*. This is part of the reason Dexter sent you to me. Only the Fleur de Lis has a Chateau like this. With the Chateau, we will cheat time."

"Why did that sound like treachery?" I asked. "So when we leave this Chateau, only three days will have passed here?"

"Exactly, and by that time you will have trained enough to access the First Elder Rune."

"Will it help us stop Gault?"

"That depends on the three of you," Julien said. "Gault is powerful, as all Keepers are. They *can*, however be defeated, if you use cunning where you lack power."

"I'm curious. Can you beat a Keeper?"

"Even Archmages have limits," Julien said, touching one of the dragons. "I hope I never have to face one."

My heart sank at his words. If Julien didn't want to face a Keeper, what were the chances of Monty and me facing one and surviving?

"Well, that improves my mood," I said. "What you're saying is that we don't stand a chance."

"No," Julien said, turning to face me. "What I am saying is that you must defeat Gault or die in the process—which for you will be difficult, don't you think? Even a Keeper has weaknesses. You must find and exploit them, but at no moment must you think you are defeated without fighting to the last breath. And, then in some cases, beyond even that."

He turned and focused on the dragons as a rumble filled the room. The silver dragons turned their necks upward as their bodies became covered in energy resembling liquid mercury.

They both let out a low roar, and the door that had been a fireplace moments earlier opened. Julien stepped forward, pushing the door open further and revealing a wide bridge that led to a fortress sitting on an island in the middle of a violet ocean of power.

"Gentlemen," Julien said, motioning to the fortress. "Your three days start now. Welcome to the Chateau."

He stepped through without waiting to see if we would follow. Monty and I moved quickly to keep up, with Peaches by my side.

THIRTEEN

"Where exactly are we?" I asked as we walked onto the small island. "I know it's the Chateau, but where exactly in the planes is this place?"

I looked behind to see the doorway had disappeared, but the two silver dragons remained where the door had been moments earlier, shimmering in the bright sunlight and forming the approach to a wide iron-and-stone bridge.

A bridge that, to my mind, shouldn't have existed. Clouds floated lazily below us as Julien moved forward. It was higher than any bridge I had ever seen or crossed. And yet somehow it felt familiar.

"This way please," he said, stepping onto the pink stone that made the walkway of the bridge. The color of the stone reminded me of the Cloisters and Aria. "If you do not like heights, please do not look over the sides. We are very high. Watch your step."

Far below us was a bottomless chasm. Across the span, the bridge ended on an island in the middle of an ocean. The ocean ended in a waterfall that fell into the chasm below us.

I'd never seen anything like it, and my brain was trying to

figure out how it all worked. Where did the ocean come from? What was below us in the chasm? How had this bridge been created over such a deep chasm? Too many questions and no answers.

"Stop trying to make sense of it all," Monty said under his breath. "Places like this don't adhere to the laws of physics as we understand them."

"I get that on a deep level, but my brain is refusing to read the memo," I said. "This whole place feels like Escher was having a bad day and someone used that for inspiration. It's beyond trippy."

"It takes some getting used to, especially on a grand scale like this."

"Why does this bridge seem so familiar, like I've seen it somewhere before?" I asked. "I know that can't be right. I don't recall ever seeing this particular bridge anywhere, but it still feels familiar."

"You have seen the work that inspired it," Julien said. "This is why it feels familiar."

"I've seen the work that inspired it, where?" I asked. "I've never been here before."

Julien nodded.

"Take the Eiffel Tower, remove the top two sections, and turn it on its head," he said. "Then you will understand."

When I imagined that, I saw what he meant.

"Eiffel built this bridge?"

"*An* Eiffel built this bridge, yes, Gustave's eldest child, Claire. She was a powerful ferromancer of my sect," Julien answered. "I should say *is*. She is still alive and visits often, but she has stopped creating structures like this."

"Probably sprained her brain one time too many, creating things like this," I said mostly to myself as I looked at the ironwork on either side of the bridge. "This whole bridge is impossible."

"Impossible only means it has not crossed from imagination to reality," Julien said. "I would say the things in our imagination are just as real as what we perceive to be reality. Don't you agree?"

"Listen, I'm barely keeping it together walking across a bridge I know shouldn't exist," I said. "I understand the concept, but you need to hold off on the *what is the nature of reality* conversation for another time, like when we aren't suspended miles over a chasm."

We crossed the Eiffel bridge as Julien and Monty spoke about mage topics and the power of the mind over energy. I listened in, but didn't join, being that my mind was too busy waiting for the imaginary bridge to disappear under my feet, dropping us to our deaths in the chasm below. I kept pace with them, remaining a few feet behind, Peaches walking beside me.

The bridge itself was an architectural wonder. The walkway we used still had room on either side of us on the wide iron bridge. The violet ocean was far below us. Its surface looked angry as swells of waves crossed its surface. After a few seconds of sensing the energy around us, I realized that the activity on the surface of the ocean was being caused by the power in the water itself—if it was even water to begin with.

The bridge was one enormous arch, which would have been expected, seeing as how arches are strong elements in architecture. What made me queasy, despite Claire being a powerful ferromancer, was that this bridge was *only* a free floating arch.

There were no supporting structures around or under it.

I cleared my throat.

"And where exactly are we?"

"This location is in-between—it is in the interstices of planes," Julien said, answering my earlier question. "It is no where and no when. Which is why time can be manipulated and controlled here. Do you understand?"

"Absolutely not," I said, even though some of the concepts made sense. "But I'll try to keep an open mind."

"That would be most helpful for our training," Julien said. "You will have to be very open for this to succeed. We do not have much time. We must accomplish in five months what should take much longer than that."

"We'd better hurry up then," I said. "Time is of the essence and all that."

"*Oui*," Julien replied with a nod and picked up the pace, increasing my chances of a heart attack every time I managed to glance over the edge of the bridge. "We should hurry."

Thankfully, while the bridge was impossibly high and looked flimsy, it was actually sturdy, and, most importantly, short, relatively speaking, that is. It felt like we had walked miles, but when I looked back over the span it appeared to be about half a mile long.

Claire knew her ferromancy, because despite the lack of apparent support, the bridge remained intact the entire time it took us to cross it. I breathed out a sigh of relief when we arrived at the other side. We followed a long stone pathway, which was made of the same pink stones of the bridge walkway, and eventually stood before the large door of the Chateau.

"This place is a fortress," I said, looking around at the building as we approached the main entrance. "Not my idea of a Chateau."

The weathered stone was the color of rust, and I could sense the energy flowing in and around the stone that made up the castle. If I tried to focus too hard on one spot, the area would slide away from my vision, as if it constantly shifted under my examination.

I got strong Scola Tower vibes from the location, except

that this island was almost a mile across, unlike the tiny island where Scola Tower sat. This fortress was also more robust. It looked like a real fortress and was still intact. Scola Tower had been a blown-out relic, missing most of its walls.

"That is what *chateau* means in French," Monty said, looking up at the small castle for a few seconds before turning to Julien. "Is there a counterpart to this location on our plane? An anchor point?"

"Yes. Chateau D'if shares temporal passages with this location," Julien said. "Here, it is known as Le Chateau du Temps, but we call it the Chateau to keep it simple."

"Castle of Time?" I asked. "Is that right?"

"Yes," Julien said. "Now, one moment—I must unlock the door in a specific way, or we will be ejected from this plane because of the security measures."

"Really not in the mood to get ejected anywhere," I said, moving back from the large door, making sure Peaches was next to me. "Please unlock it correctly."

"It would be more accurately 'anywhen,'" Julien said, approaching the rune-covered door. "The security measures will remove you to some random point in the past and strand you there, without abilities."

"Whoa, that's serious security," I said. "Couldn't that cause some time anomalies? If you get sent to the past and start messing around with events or meeting people you shouldn't, you could influence the future."

"I never said you would arrive *alive*."

"I see," I said, watching Julien touch several areas of the door in sequence. "The security is beyond serious, and steps into lethal with both feet."

"Yes," Julien said, finishing another sequence before the runes on the door flashed white. "Ah, success. I was afraid I had forgotten the sequence. That would have been terribly unfortunate."

He pushed the massive door, which moved easily beneath his hand, and proceeded to enter the Chateau.

I stood there staring at his back for a good five seconds, before Monty tapped me on the shoulder.

"I'm certain he wasn't being serious," Monty said. "Recalling security sequences is just as important a skill as remembering casts, their gestures, and words of power."

"That wasn't even a little bit funny," I said, walking past the large door. "We have to deal with French Archmage humor for four months?"

"Four months and three weeks," Monty said, reminding me of the added weeks of torture. "When it gets bad, and it will get bad, remember that we're doing this to stop Gault from destroying the balance of magic in our world."

"We're doing this to stop a Keeper," I said as we moved deeper into the castle. "A Keeper that even an Archmage wouldn't want to face. You heard him—even *he* doesn't want to face Gault."

"We don't have the luxury of choice," Monty said, looking off to the distance, his face pensive. "I'm sorry, Simon. If it wasn't for me and my desire to acquire the rune of seals, things would not have escalated this far. You're here because of my intentions."

"Well, if we're going to be all honest and soul-searching, you're right," I said, as he looked at me suddenly. "Most of this *is* your fault, but I'm not a child. When Ramirez gave me that case to look into, I could have walked away. I could've said no thanks."

"There were children involved," Monty said. "I can't see you walking away from helping innocents, especially children. I see how you interact with Cece; it's one of your strengths."

I nodded as I thought about what we were going to do.

"That's it, isn't it?" I said. "We aren't here just to get stronger, are we?"

"No," Monty admitted. "Many more innocents are at risk if we fail."

"I could've walked away early on, but then I wouldn't have a cranky mage bond brother or my hellhound bondmate."

"Don't forget your complicated relationship with an ancient vampire who seems to have feelings for you, and demonstrated them by gifting you a cursed blade."

"Nothing says *I care* more than gifting cursed weaponry," I said. "There's no way I can ever forget Michiko. She'd kill me if I did."

"True. Could it be that's her preferred method of demonstrating affection?"

"Oh, I see—nothing says *you're special to me* than attempted homicide?"

"That and giving you Ebonsoul," he said. "Especially after she knew it was one-half of the set that housed a bloodthirsty goddess. You're actually quite fortunate. She seems to *really* care for you."

"Not enough to have a face-to-face after our last conversation."

"Perhaps you should seek her out," Monty suggested. "She may be waiting for *you* to go speak to her. You do know where she lives."

"We do have to get some things sorted out," I said. "I just haven't had a moment to breathe after Verity decided to get on our asses."

"If she is important to you, steal the moment, and go speak to her," he said. "What's the worst that can happen?"

"Are you really asking me that question?"

"Apologies. There are too many variables that can impact your response to that question. That being said, you should go see her as soon as possible, before she decides to find out how strong Ebonsoul—and you—have become."

"You really think she'd go that far?"

"You think she gave you that blade for show?" Monty asked as we caught up to Julien. "Your vampire may be many things—frivolous is not one of them. If she gave you Ebonsoul, and allowed you to bond with it, there was a purpose to her act. You should ask her what that purpose is."

"Have you met Chi?" I asked. "That sounds like the perfect way to get stabbed, repeatedly."

"Not like it would kill you. At least, not permanently."

I shuddered at the thought, thankful that Ebonsoul—even though it was part of two blades that had been inhabited by Izanami, a bloodthirsty goddess—wasn't sentient like Grey's blade was. At least, it had never tried to speak to me, and I hoped it stayed that way...forever.

"I've made some nightmarish enemies, but I've also made some incredible friends I consider part of my family. All in all, no matter what happens with Gault, I'm glad I stayed on the case and learned more about your world, even if it kills me."

"*Mon dieu*, that is touching," Julien said as he turned to face us. "But we are here to prevent your deaths, not to utter pretty words as you breathe your last."

"Do you think we can take out Gault if we really have to?"

Julien remained silent for a few moments.

"You are here to learn two techniques," Julien said. "One will provide you access to the First Elder Rune to enhance your power, mostly Tristan's. It should prove enough for you to stop Gault's plans."

"That doesn't sound like we are facing Gault directly."

"Because you are not," he said. "Are you familiar with the term 'guerrilla warfare'?"

"Smaller force takes on a larger force in a battle," I said with a nod. "The smaller force attacks in unconventional ways and using similarly unconventional tactics. We called it asymmetrical warfare. It can be very effective."

"That is what you will be using against Gault and his Dark Arcanists," Julien said. "The first technique will be for that."

"Dark Arcanists?" I asked. "What exactly are those? Angry librarians with a temper?"

"No," Julien said, shaking his head. "You have met Tellus. He was one, but you will meet more. These are Arcanists that only serve Gault, and his cause. His influence is extensive."

"Does his influence reach Verity?"

"You ask the questions you know the answers to," Julien said. "His influence extends to Verity and beyond."

"Even to The High Tribunal?" I asked.

"If you were a Keeper and wanted to hold onto power, which groups would you control, making sure that control was indirect and layered in shadows?" Julien asked. "Would it not make sense to control those who police the others?"

"Like Korin?"

"Korin has been the sword of the Tribunal for many years," Julien said. "I would think her to be beyond the corruption of Gault, but she is human, and therefore vulnerable."

"No one is beyond corruption given the right incentive," Monty said. "Everyone has weaknesses that can be exploited."

Julien nodded.

"When you put it that way, it makes perfect sense," I said. "Wait—that means that this Korin could be working indirectly for Gault?"

"That is for you to discover," Julien said. "However, I would behave as if that were the case, and act accordingly."

"The second technique?" Monty asked. "What is *that* for?"

Julien turned and headed past the courtyard and up some stone steps. Monty and I followed with Peaches right behind me.

"Did he hear you?" I asked Monty under my breath. "Maybe he didn't like the question?"

"I heard him," Julien said from the top of the stairs. We reached the second level and he began to walk down a corridor. "Eventually, you will face Gault. You would be fools to think you can do this and not face him one day. I would hope that day would be many, many centuries from today, but life sometimes chooses for us."

"You're saying we're not ready," I said. "I could've told you that, and saved us the trip here. We know when we are outclassed."

"Do you?" Julien asked as he came to a stop in front of a door. "Your first job, the one you mentioned earlier. What was it?"

I was certain Julien knew our first case. He knew *everything* else about us.

"Children were being abducted, and we had a lead on who was doing the abducting," I said. "It wasn't what we expected."

"Who hired you?" Julien asked, looking at me. "Before Ramirez assigned you the case. Who approached you initially?"

"Shiva," I said, being honest. "He was trying to get me to stop Kali. Not that I knew it at the time."

"And you, Tristan—who called you in? Ramirez?"

"As a consultant only," Monty said. "I had no idea the depths of the case, not until Simon became involved."

"And after?"

"After what?" I asked. "The case?"

"No," Julien said, giving me a look that said, *Stop being so dense*. "After you discovered gods were involved, why didn't you drop this case?"

"Did I mention the part about children being abducted?"

"Yes," Julien said. "But you were outclassed—by not one, but two gods. You, a mortal detective, and him, a mage in hiding from his sect. How could you possibly go up against two ancient gods and expect to succeed?"

"We did what we needed to do," I said. "I didn't really think about the whole gods thing, at least not until the warehouse full of kids and the Rakshasas. By then, it was too late to do anything else but see it through."

"If I gave you the choice now, would you take it?"

"What choice?"

"There are passages in this place that would allow you to disappear into the past," Julien said, looking past us and into the corridors. "Many have done it before. Escape life and step into the shadows for the rest of their lives. If you had that option, would you take it?"

"No," Monty and I said at the same time.

"But you *are* outclassed," Julien said. "There is a slim chance you can succeed against a Keeper. You could very well face your death at Gault's hands."

"If that's how it has to go, then that's how it has to go," I said. "We will do everything we can to stop him."

"And you, Mage Montague?" Julien asked. "You have a deeper understanding of war and death than your associate here. What say you?"

"It's true that I may have a deeper understanding, but on this we are in agreement," Monty said. "I have seen evil, and I have seen good people, outmatched and outclassed, rise to face that evil against what seemed to be insurmountable odds. I would rather stand on the side of those who would confront evil in all its forms, than run away and disappear in the recesses of time. Knowing I could have done something to make a difference, but refusing to do so, would make my existence intolerable."

Julien nodded again.

"The second technique is for when you have to make that decision," Julien said. "There will come a time when you stand before Gault, and will have to choose between continuing to live or knowing you will die by removing him from existence with you."

"If you know a technique that can wipe him out of existence," I said, "why not just use it now, and resolve this whole mess?"

"*I* do not possess the First Elder Rune," Julien said. "However, you two do."

"Does this technique have a name?" Monty asked. "Is it related to the Restoring Palm?"

"You are aware of the Interrupting Palm and the Restoring Palm," Julien said. "There is one more."

"Impossible," Monty said, sure of himself. "There are only two palms—Interrupting and Restoring—recorded in the tomes. Both were created and taught by Mage Santiago. Nowhere in his notes was there a mention of a third. I learned directly from him, and he never mentioned a third. You are mistaken."

Julien stared at Monty for a few seconds before continuing.

"It must feel very satisfying to be right all of the time," Julien said. "You are saying that, because Mage Santiago never shared this palm with *you*, it does not exist? And I am called arrogant?"

"That...that is not what I meant," Monty said, trying to backtrack. "I only meant to—"

"You may want to quit while you're behind," I said, keeping my voice low. "Your mage ego is showing."

Monty shot me a dark look, and composed himself.

"My apologies, Julien. To my knowledge there is no third palm," Monty corrected. "However I will defer to your greater experience. I meant no offense."

"None has been taken—I, too, was once young and knew everything," Julien said. "There is, however, a third palm that is not mentioned in any book and has only been taught to a select few. Its very existence is forbidden."

"I was always under the impression there were only ever two palms created," Monty reiterated. "Even those two are considered too dangerous to use."

"The last palm will be the second technique that you will both learn."

"Both of us?" I asked, surprised. "How am I going to learn a palm? Isn't that—?"

"For mages?" Julien finished. "Not this one. This technique only requires three things: knowledge, power, and lifeforce. You have two in abundance, and will acquire the third. It's part of what makes this palm so dangerous in the wrong hands."

"Why don't more people use this technique?" I asked. "I mean, I understand it's forbidden, but it sounds ultra-powerful. Why isn't it used?"

"Because it's a one-use technique," Julien said, pointing to the door. "You will both stay here. I trust the accommodations meet with your approval."

"One-use?" I asked. "What are you saying?"

"When it is executed properly, the person who uses it is gone."

"It's a kamikaze technique?"

"Crude, but correct," Julien said. "Get some rest. Training starts at first light."

"First light?" I said. "It was the middle of the day when we got here."

"Look again," Julien said, pointing to a window.

I looked out a nearby window and saw it was pitch black outside. All around us, the sea glowed violet.

"That is going to take some getting used to."

"You will adapt quickly," Julien said. "The days here are roughly the same as the days on our plane. The change between night and day will feel abrupt at first, but over time, you will hardly notice it. Your evening meals are inside your rooms."

"You never mentioned the name," Monty said as Julien turned to walk away. "What is the third palm called?"

"Survive through the first half of training, and you will have earned the privilege of learning the name, along with the technique of the forbidden palm. Goodnight."

Julien disappeared around a corner and left us to our thoughts.

FOURTEEN

The room was actually two adjoining rooms of equal size.

Even though it was an ancient castle, it had some modern features I was thankful for, like electricity, running water, and glass windows. I could tell the windows were a fairly recent addition, and through the two in my room I had an amazing view of the violet sea.

A little further down the island, I could see smaller structures and buildings that seemed to be unpopulated. The antennas and satellite dishes let me know that, like the castle, they had also been modernized.

The rooms Julien provided weren't luxurious—it's possible he was concerned we would obliterate them—but they were clean and had everything I needed. With a good-sized bed and access to a working bathroom, I was good.

A small table on the far side of the room had one sturdy-looking chair. A large, delicious-smelling meal sat on the table, filling the room with a fantastic aroma of steak and seasoned potatoes.

I worried about Monty, though. He *was* a mage and I had the feeling that he was used to the finer things in life. This was practically slumming it for someone used to wearing Zegna, Armani, and Patek Philippe time pieces.

Although Monty did prefer luxurious things, especially his clothing, he was never totally over-the-top attached to those items. He was fastidious, but at the rate he went through suits, if he had been truly pretentious, he never showed more than a mild annoyance at having his runed suits shredded or destroyed.

My hellhound rumbled as he found a spot in the corner near the bed. He padded away to the corner of the room that had a small rug and a large bowl next to it. The bowl was filled with fresh pastrami. Peaches stepped up to the bowl and gave me a look. I nodded and he proceeded to disappear the meat in record time.

<*Was it good?*>

<*Very good. I can rest now.*>

<*You can't rest without eating a bowl full of meat?*>

<*Meat helps me rest. Are you going to sleep now?*>

<*I'm going to check on Monty, and then I'm going to crash.*>

<*What are you going to crash into? Do you need my help? I'm very good at crashing into things.*>

<*Crash as in "get some sleep," not crash into anything. Go to sleep.*>

<*I will. If you are going to do any other kind of crashing, I will help you. I go where you go.*>

<*I promise not to do any other kind of crashing without you. Goodnight, boy.*>

<*Goodnight, bondmate.*>

He turned around in a few circles on the rug, sniffed the air a few times, let out a huge chuff and plopped down, settling in.

I looked around at the room.

Calling the room Spartan was a stretch. It was about as

bare bones as it could get without us sleeping outside in lean-tos.

I moved over to the door connecting our rooms and peeked into Monty's room.

It was a duplicate of mine, and I winced as Monty tested the bed.

A mild expression of disdain crossed his expression, which was quickly replaced with a look of determination. He nodded to himself and peeked into the bathroom, as if making sure it was serviceable.

With a satisfied nod he stepped back into the main room.

"This will do," he said as he saw me in the doorway. "It is sparse, but it will suffice."

"You going to be okay?" I asked as Peaches began to snore behind me. The chain-sawing effect he unleashed guaranteed I would get little-to-no sleep tonight. "I know it's as no-frills as it gets, but at least it's clean."

"This is not a vacation," Monty said, hanging up his jacket on a wall peg. "We are here to train to access the First Elder Rune. I've slept in worse conditions during the war."

"Seems like Julien is going out of his way to help us," I said, examining the room. "Doesn't that seem odd? Considering we destroyed—well, mostly you and Ian destroyed—his home the last time we paid him a visit? This seems extra generous."

"Agreed. This has been an extraordinary gesture by Julien. I find it hard to believe that all of this was merely because my uncle asked him to help us."

"Dex *is* hard to say no to," I said. "Do you think Julien has an ulterior motive?"

"If you're asking if he has some nefarious plot to do away with us, I doubt it," he said. "He could have eliminated us at the Foundry. There was no need to bring us here for that."

"True, but he was being all cryptic with the third palm," I said. "Did you really not know there was a third palm?"

Monty shook his head as he gave it thought.

"Why wouldn't he share the name of the third palm?" Monty said, frustration clear in his voice. "How could there be a *third* palm? Mage Santiago never mentioned a third palm to me, or to Ines, his own daughter."

"That's probably the answer right there."

"What answer?" Monty asked, exasperated. "What are you going on about?"

"We need to learn *two* techniques," I said, holding up two fingers. "But you're focused on this third palm. It's distracting you. Now you're even questioning Mage Santiago's motives."

"I was merely stating fact," Monty snapped. "He didn't teach Ines, his own daughter, this hidden forbidden palm. That is plain fact, not conjecture."

"You mean the daughter that joined Verity against his wishes, and was hunting us down until recently? *That* daughter?"

"A valid point," he admitted with a nod. "That would have been a disaster of epic proportions, if he had taught her some incredibly powerful technique and she had shared it with Verity."

I shuddered at the thought of Verity possessing a technique powerful enough to confront a Keeper. We would've been erased a few times over if we'd had to face that. Edith was bad enough without her having some forbidden technique to use against us.

"Is it possible that Mage Santiago realized you weren't ready for the third palm yet?" I asked. "Maybe he thought you were too young?"

"Preposterous," Monty said, dismissing my words and proving my point. "I mastered his teachings in record time. I would have been able to learn the third palm with ease, if he had deigned to reveal it to me."

Mage egos, as delicate as they were, could be enormous and sometimes barely fit in the rooms the mages occupied. For such a powerful group of people, they were easily insulted and slighted. Their emotions and feelings easily bruised. It made them predictable if you knew which buttons to push.

It had been my experience that the more powerful the mage, the bigger the buttons, and the easier they were to push. It wasn't always the smartest play. Antagonizing someone who could obliterate you with a gesture is *never* the smart option. The times I had done it, I knew I was risking my life. But in every case it had created the opening we needed—sometimes painfully—to stop the threat we faced.

Monty wasn't as bad as the megalomaniacs we had faced, but he was still a mage. He was more grounded than most, but his ego was still oversized, and it was on display now as he pointed out that Mage Santiago had neglected to teach him the third palm.

I read between the lines, and what I saw didn't surprise me.

"Basically what you're not saying is: Why didn't Mage Santiago teach *you*, the prodigy, the third palm?" I asked, keeping my voice even, since mage egos were brittle and fragile things. "That's what you really want to know, right?"

Monty narrowed his eyes and scowled at me.

"I'm not being petty," he said. "It's objective curiosity. I can maintain my perspective, and still question the action Mage Santiago took, or in this case, didn't take."

"Of course," I said. "It could be Mage Santiago didn't think you were mature enough to learn it...yet. It seems to be a powerful technique, reserved for powerful mages, like *Archmage* Julien. You know, mages who are older and more powerful than *you*?"

"It is a possibility," he said, rubbing his chin. "There are certainly casts beyond my current understanding."

I nodded.

"You yourself admitted there are things in your own family that have been kept from you, for security reasons. Maybe this is something like that?"

"I wonder if my uncle knows of this technique?"

"I wouldn't be surprised," I said. "Dex seems to be full of secrets he hasn't shared. Probably for your own good. Do you have any idea what the third palm could be named? The other two do seem to have practical names, describing what they do."

"I wouldn't even know where to begin," Monty said, throwing up a hand. "Not without knowing what the technique is capable of. It could be anything, literally."

"How about the Ultimate Palm of Apocalyptic Obliteration," I volunteered as I struck a defensive pose with both my palms in front of my body, set in a fighting stance. "What do you think?"

He stared at me in silence for three seconds, clearly unimpressed.

"I think I need to eat and get some sleep," Monty said, turning away from me and approaching the small table which contained a large bowl of salad. "I've no idea what this training is going to be like. I prefer to be rested for whatever awaits us tomorrow."

"Good plan," I said. "If you get lonely and can't sleep, I'll send over the hellhound Snoremeister. He can keep you company."

"Don't you dare," he said shooting me a look as he started in on his salad. "I'd prefer to get some actual sleep tonight. As solid as these walls are, I can still hear the rumbling of your creature."

I stood still and brought a hand to my ear. The chainsaw

snoring was going strong in my room and could be heard clearly.

"I have no idea what you're talking about," I said. "I don't hear a thing. Are you sure you don't want his company? He could keep you safe."

"No, thank you. We are not in any imminent danger," Monty said, focusing on his meal. "Please close the door on your way out. Goodnight."

"Goodnight," I said, closing the door behind me as I headed back to my room. "See you in the morning."

My brain was still on overdrive. That, along with the monster snores coming from the corner, meant sleep wasn't going to be an option. I looked at my hellhound and envied his easy ability to get sleep whenever he wanted.

I stepped out of my room, leaving my hellhound, whose snores followed me into the hallway, and headed downstairs to the central courtyard of the Chateau. The courtyard, which was open to the sky, was made of stone like the rest of the castle.

A stairway with a black railing led to the second and third levels. In the center of the courtyard, on the ground level, sat an old well that was closed off with a metal grill. Several worn, wooden benches were situated around the courtyard. I imagined they were for mages to take a break in between whatever it was they did while here.

I chose one of these to sit on and took stock of the situation.

It was a few minutes before I realized I wasn't alone.

Julien appeared in the center of the courtyard near the well. I didn't sense him at all, until right before he appeared. I was sure that was intentional. He didn't have to let me sense him at all.

"Can't sleep?" he asked, taking in the courtyard. "It's always like this on the first night."

"How many times have you done this training with mages?"

"Many times over the years for my sect," he said, sitting on the edge of the well. "My first time here, I was the student. It was the longest year of my life."

"You spent a year here?"

"Well, a year here, yes, but closer to a week in our plane," he said. "My instructor, Mage Durand, took his name to heart." He turned to the well with a knowing look. "I endured countless hours of training within these very walls, specifically the depth of this well."

"Did you pass?"

"Pass? I don't know if *pass* is the right word," he said. "I survived to the end of the year. That seemed to surprise all of the Elders in the Fleur de Lis, especially Durand."

"Survive? Did many of the students *die* in the training?" I asked with a smile at what I thought was Julien exaggerating. "How bad was it, really?"

"Yes," Julien replied, still gazing at the well. "Many fellow students did die under what was the torture disguised as training. It was brutal and needless. I lost many good friends to the mage training of the Fleur de Lis on this island."

"I'm sorry to hear that," I said and meant it. "It's never good to lose friends, especially not that way."

"We no longer use this as a training facility," he said. "I made sure of that."

"What is this place now, then?"

"A place to deepen one's understanding."

"You come here to deepen your understanding?" I asked, confused. "Wouldn't that be easier back home? Seems like a lot of trouble to go through, just to reach a deeper understanding of anything."

"True," Julien said, turning back to look up at the sky

above us. "Although, sometimes, a change of environment is needed to see plainly. Why are you here, Simon?"

The question took me off guard.

"What do you mean?"

"It is not so difficult a question," Julien said, keeping his gaze on the night sky, which had highlights of violet from the sea around us. "Why are you *here*?"

"To learn how to stop Gault."

"A lie," Julien said, fixing me with his gaze. "*That* is a lie. You may lie to yourself, but do not insult *me* by lying."

His response surprised me—not the words, but the anger behind them. It felt as if I had personally insulted him.

I raised a hand in surrender. "I'm not—"

"Lie," he said, cutting me off. "If you cannot be honest with yourself, I can assure you, you *will* fail this training and cost Mage Montague his life when you stand before Gault. Is that your intention?"

"To get Monty killed?" I asked, disliking Julien more by the second. "Are you insane? Of course not."

"Then answer the question plainly," he said, pointing at me. "Why are *you* here?"

"I'm tired of running," I said, the words spilling out. "Tired of having people after me, trying to kill me."

"That is only part of the truth," he said. "What is the part you don't want to admit to yourself? The part you only whisper in your mind? The part you don't want to say aloud."

"What the *hell* are you talking about?" I asked, feeling the rage build up in me. "First you call me a liar, now you're saying I'm confused?"

"Are you saying there is no fear?"

"Fear? Of course there's fear. I would be an idiot to not feel fear—we're going up against a Keeper. That's—"

"No, stop," he said, cutting me off with a slash of his hand. "This is external fear. You have a deeper fear. A fear which drives you. Can you speak it? This is a new fear, a deep fear that robs you of sleep and peace. Can you say it?"

I stood up and stepped outside.

The violet sea raged in the distance, and I could feel Julien's presence as he joined me outside.

"I'm afraid...I'm afraid Monty is going to go dark."

"*That,* finally, is honesty," he said. "Step into the full truth: say it, and rob it of its power."

"If Monty goes dark, I'm going to have to stop him," I said, keeping my gaze locked on the violence of the sea. "The only way of stopping him if he goes dark...is to end him."

"And? There is more."

"And, if I learn a palm that can take out a Keeper, wouldn't that same palm work against a dark mage?"

"That is *precisely* why you must learn it, *Aspis*," Julien said. "There must be a check and balance—always."

"You suck as a teacher, do you know that?"

"Oh, I don't know," he said. "I managed to get you to admit the truth to yourself. I would say that was a good first lesson. We must build on the truth."

"The truth?" I asked. "Whose truth?"

"That is an excellent question," he said. "You think truth is subjective, and in many cases it is, but there are absolutes even in this world of magic and power. You didn't enjoy your first lesson?"

I stared at him for a few seconds.

"You're kidding, right?"

"It is a bitter lesson, yes," he said, looking at the sea. "It was a lesson I did not learn until it was too late. I do not wish for you to go through what I did."

"Why do *we* have to be the check and balance?" I asked. "Monty and I didn't ask to be the guardians of the balance."

"Your actions speak much louder than your words," he said, raising an eyebrow at me. "You confronted gods, accepted a hellhound, merged a stormblood, and faced many enemies threatening the very existence of our plane. Your protestations do not align with your actions."

"Those were extenuating circumstances," I said with a grumble. "Most of the times we were just trying to stay alive."

"Spoken like a true mage," he said after a short laugh, before growing serious. "Tell me, do you understand the concept of *on*—duty, obligation, a debt of gratitude?"

"Yes, I'm familiar," I said. "Are you saying this is our *on*?"

"When I was a much younger mage, I unleashed a cast while I was out on a mission. This was many centuries before, during the War of Mages."

"The War of Mages? I've never heard of this war."

"It has been forgotten by all except the oldest of us," he said, waving my words away. "During one battle, I unleashed a cast that was beyond my capacity to control. It endangered my sect and those of our allies."

"What was the cast?"

"The Endless Night," he said. "It creates absolute darkness, before attacking the senses and destroying your enemies from within. Those under its influence usually end their lives, before the cast is complete. It is absolutely horrible, and terribly efficient."

"That sounds beyond nasty and like major mage overkill."

"It is, and has been banned in all warfare since that war," he said. "In any case, I had just learned it, and being eager to demonstrate my ability I unleashed it. It took me mere seconds to understand that the cast had escaped my control and I knew I had killed myself, my sect, and our allies."

"How did you survive?"

"I didn't survive. I was *saved*," he said, still looking out into the violet sea. "One mage stepped into the Endless Night in what I thought was attempted suicide, and unleashed a sun of power to dispel it. I had never seen so much energy wielded with such ease. It was beyond my imagination at the time."

"What happened to the mage?"

"He was irrevocably changed and transformed," he continued. "You see, I thought he had dispelled the cast, but he saw that was impossible. What he did was even more impossible to my mind at the time. It is only with the wisdom of time that I could understand his choice—and the terrible price he paid."

"What did he do?"

"The Endless Night is a dark cast. It unleashes a darkness which preys on the intended target. It is a devastating and monstrous thing, leaving behind broken objects that used to be mages, but are little more than mindless animals destined to die a gruesome death shortly after being exposed to the cast."

"Is that how the mage died?"

Julien turned to face me.

"I never said he *died*," he answered. "The mage survived, but in order to withstand the Endless Night he made a pact to channel the darkness. He embraced the darkness into himself, making it a part of him."

"He became dark?"

"No. In that moment, he became the bringer of ultimate darkness. He became the Harbinger of Death."

"You're talking about Dex."

"Yes," Julien said. "Now that you understand a small portion of my *on*, I hope that helps you understand *yours*. You have a duty to Mage Montague. More importantly, you have a duty to *all* who depend on you. One does not negate the other. In fact, they support each other."

"I don't entirely understand," I said. "What exactly is my *on* here?"

"I cannot determine that for you," Julien said. "I can only

share some of what I have lived through, and hopefully illuminate the path for you. Do you still fear learning the third palm?"

"Yes. I think it's probably too dangerous, which is why it's been forbidden. At least *I* think it's too dangerous for me... and Monty."

"It is good you feel this way. It *is* dangerous."

"But you still think I should know it."

"Check and balance," he said. "The two must always be present."

"Is that what's happening with the Keepers? The check and balance is broken?"

"It is good to see that you occasionally pay attention," he said with a look of approval as he turned to walk back inside. "There is still hope for you yet."

He disappeared a second later.

I returned to my room and caught what sleep I could.

FIFTEEN

The sun crashed into my room, illuminating the area where my bed sat with an angry determination to burn my sleep into dust. Joining the merciless sun was the sound of an enormous bell that was designed to prevent any thought of sleep from re-entering my mind.

I slid out of bed feeling like a crash of rhinos had stampeded over me in my sleep. Soreness and dull joint pain each screamed at me for attention, causing me to move slowly into the bathroom and splash my face with ice-cold water to regain something approximating functioning consciousness.

What I really needed was a strong cup of Deathwish.

This wasn't acute pain; it was the dull pain of a week's worth of soreness, except it had been compressed into one night. My curse didn't kick in because it must have figured my life wasn't in danger, or it just felt I needed to deal with the pain on my own.

Knowing Kali, it was probably the latter.

Either way, my everything hurt, and even keeping my thoughts straight was a challenge through the overwhelming stiffness and achiness that seized my body. I suddenly felt about three hundred years old, and moved like it too.

"What in the actual hell?" I said with a groan as I got dressed. "Did we have a fight last night and I wasn't aware of it?"

"It's the response of your body to the different flows of time," Julien said from the doorway. "You will get used to it in a few days. Until you do, every day with time lag will be… uncomfortable. We will begin training in the rear courtyard once you and Mage Montague are ready. This will be your training gear."

He held a set of silver-gray training robes in his hand, and placed them on the bed. They gave off a faint energy signature as the material shimmered in the light. I noticed the subtle repeating pattern of the Fleur de Lis symbol all over the robe—the energy signature emanated from them.

"What's wrong with this?" I asked, motioning to my clothing. "These were runed for me."

He sniffed in my direction and gave me a disdainful look that let me know my clothing was barely acceptable in decent company, much less in his rarefied Archmage presence.

"As usual, Piero does excellent work," he said, glancing at my clothing again. "However, what you are wearing is impractical for the combat training phase."

"This clothing was runed to keep me safe," I protested. "Are you telling Monty he can't wear his Zegnas?"

"Yes, I am," Julien said. "He has been provided with a similar set of training robes, just like yours."

"But these clothes were runed to keep me safe," I said again, stubbornly.

He stared at me, and then shifted his gaze to the robes on the bed for a few seconds, before looking at me again.

"Wrong," he said. "The clothes, like your gun or your blade, are merely tools."

"Tools that keep me safe."

He sighed.

"No, Strong," he continued. "Are you telling me you are only the sum of the weaponry you carry?"

"No."

"Would you give up and surrender if you were stripped of everything by an enemy?"

"No way."

"Then we can agree that this runed clothing you wear,"—he waved a hand in my general direction—"much like the curse of Kali upon you, provides you with a false sense of security, precipitating behaviors and comments that could easily result in your death, were the circumstances different."

I paused before answering, because prior to his mentioning it, I hadn't really considered that I acted the way I did because death was off the table as an outcome—well, an *easy* death was off the table. I could still die, but it would take work to put me down permanently, if it could even be done.

Not that I was eager to test out *that* theory.

"When you put it that way, I'd have to agree," I admitted. "I do have certain advantages when it comes to fighting the monsters and beings we face on a regular basis."

"You do," he said with a nod. "An advantage Mage Montague doesn't share. Have you considered the danger you put him and your hellhound in?"

"My hellhound is virtually indestructible," I said with a smile. "I've seen that with my own eyes."

"Only because you've faced enemies unprepared to deal with what he is."

"What he *is*, is impossible to stop," I said, some pride entering my voice. "He's a hellhound, after all."

"Impossible to stop?" Julien said with a small headshake. "I will show you how mistaken you are."

"You are *not* going to hurt my hellhound," I said harshly.

"That would take this from training to actual battle in a heartbeat."

Julien looked off to the side and nodded as if in deep thought.

"No, I'm merely going to neutralize any threat he may present," Julien said. "From there, I'll let you extrapolate how easy it would be to dispatch your *fearsome* bondmate. Don't you consider any of this when you confront beings with mind-numbing power?"

"Not really, no."

"Why not?" he asked. "Where does this sense of bravado stem from?"

"It's not bravado," I said, grasping at an explanation. "Monty is part of this world. He was born into all of this. I wasn't, so excuse me if my first reaction is to inform the current megalomaniac we're facing that their plans suck ass, and we aren't going to stand by while they kill innocents and destroy the world just because they want more power. Not going to happen."

"Good," he said with a small smile. "That conviction will prove important later on."

"So can I wear my runed clothing?"

"No. It's a crutch, and a debilitating one," he said. "And one you must cast off. You have to be able to fight without that safety net. I can't disable your curse because it would needlessly jeopardize your life, but I *can* remove your runed clothing, which is only one layer of protection. I do expect you to use your weapons, however."

"This *crutch*, as you call it, has kept me alive more times than I can remember," I said, looking down at my clothes. "Are you sure this isn't a fashion thing? I know how you mages get about clothing."

"This is precisely why I provided you with training gear," he said, heading to the door. "No overly runed clothing. This training gear will keep you alive but offer only *minimal* protection. You will learn to experience and mitigate the pain of training."

I could almost hear the smile in his voice.

I stopped being surprised by the things he knew about us. Apparently, it was common knowledge that Piero provided high-end runed clothing to mages—common knowledge to everyone but me, of course.

"This training sounds like it's designed to be as painful as possible."

"Pain seems to be an excellent catalyst for you and Tristan."

"What are you talking about?"

"How often do either of you end up in Haven after your battles?"

"Do you see who and what we're fighting?"

"Do you?"

"I don't understand."

"That much is evident."

"Can we pause the mage cryptic magespeak? Explain."

"It's another aspect to your fighting," he said, with a small sigh. "You three constantly rush headlong into confrontations, learning about your opponents as you fight them. It's akin to learning carpentry by hammering your fingers to bloody pulps: painful, slow, counterproductive...and with Gault, deadly."

"Sometimes we don't have the luxury of time to study our enemies," I said. "They don't exactly provide dossiers on themselves before trying to eliminate us."

"If you know the enemy and yourself—"

"You need not fear the result of a hundred battles," I finished. "I know my Sun Tzu."

"You cannot fight Gault blind," Julien said. "You and

Tristan need to be proactive about those who would prefer to see you both gone, now more than ever."

"Isn't that what we're doing here?"

"No," he said. "You're here to unlock access to power. You must study Gault and discover his weakness."

"What if he doesn't have any?"

"*Everyone* has a weakness, and you must discover his," he said. "To start, he has revealed a major flaw: he blindly desires more power. *That* can be used and exploited."

"Is there anything about us you don't know?"

"I don't know how well you will react to the training," he said, stopping at the door. "That still remains to be seen."

Flashbacks to Master Yat appeared in my mind. I wondered if all mages were closet sadists, just waiting for the moment they had students they could torture to share the pain they had received as they were learning.

I was about to say something regarding the torturous mage methods of training, but then remembered Julien's description of his own training and the friends he lost during that training.

I left the thought unsaid.

I did possess *some* tact—that, and the bell from hell was trying to melt my brain with the constant ringing. It sounded like Big Ben on steroids, drowning out every thought in my head.

"Can someone turn off that crazy bell?" I asked. "My head is pounding as it is."

Julien looked around the room as if searching for the bell.

"What bell?" he asked innocently. "I hear no bell. Are you hearing bells?"

He left the room with a small laugh.

I cursed to myself because he was enjoying this entirely too much, while I was suffering through this torture. I only hoped Monty felt as bad as I did.

Misery and agony love company.

I changed into the silver-gray training robes, making sure to adjust my shoulder holster, securing Grim Whisper for easy drawing.

I arrived at the rear courtyard a few seconds before Monty. He was dressed in the same training robes. He looked about as good as I felt. We both scowled in Julien's direction as he smiled back.

I wanted to punch him in the face...several times.

Peaches rumbled by my side. He seemed unbothered by the time lag and yawned wide, exposing his menacing fangs. I rubbed his extra-large head and he rumbled his pleasure.

At least one of us was feeling good. Julien the Sadist didn't count.

I looked around at the rear courtyard and saw it was set up like the circle in Dex's school, where Cece recently challenged Monty for her ascension.

The courtyard was a series of five concentric circles inside a large square. Runes were inscribed into the stone perimeter of the square. Each circle was made of symbols I couldn't understand, but could definitely feel.

The energy of the courtyard was a steady *thrum* in the base of my neck, as the power pulsed through each of the circles, coming up against the edge of the square and doubling back into the circles in a repeating cycle. The square acted as a limiter and kept all of the power contained to the circles.

At each of the corners of the large square stood tall rune-covered columns of stone. They radiated energy with regular pulses that matched the waves of energy flowing from the circles.

"What are those?" I asked Monty as he stepped next to me. "Dex didn't have those columns around his circle."

"Amplifiers," Monty said, focusing on the columns. "Anything cast in this arena will hit harder."

"That's good for us, right?" I asked. "My magic missile will hit harder."

"It's also good for Julien," he said. "The amplifier increases the power of *all* casts."

"Oh," I said. "Not so good, then."

"It's still good. Just make sure not to get hit by anything Julien throws at us," Monty said. "If we manage to do that, we should be able to neutralize him in short order."

"You do remember he's an Archmage?"

"We have a stormblood and a First Elder Rune," Monty replied. "I'd say we can present a serious threat within this amplified arena."

I nodded, but the pit of my stomach clenched at the thought of facing an Archmage in an arena designed to make casts even stronger. The entire courtyard was a power multiplier of staggering proportions.

Julien stood at the other end of the courtyard, opposite Monty and me. He had changed into a robe similar to ours, except his robes had a silver-and-blue Fleur de Lis symbol over the left side of his chest.

Other than that, our robes were identical.

"Today, I will see how you behave as a combat unit," Julien said from his side of the courtyard. "I would like you to attack me freely, without concern for my well-being. Simon, please inform your bondmate he is to attack without holding back."

"Are you sure?" I asked. "He's a hellhound."

"Thank you for clarifying that for me," he said with a smile. "For a moment, I was unsure what he was. Your information has proven to be enlightening."

"No need to be a smartass about it," I muttered under my breath.

"I could say the same thing about you," Julien replied, still smiling.

"You heard that?"

"This arena has excellent acoustics. Your hellhound, please?"

I held up a finger.

"One second," I said. "Let me relay the message that you want to be chomped on repeatedly."

"Certainly," Julien said. "Please let him know there will be extra meat for him if he manages to impede my ability to attack."

<Did you hear him, boy?>

<The silver-man said extra meat. I didn't understand anything after that.>

<Silver-man? Julien?>

<He is the silver-man because he has silver all around him. If I can stop him, he will give me extra meat?>

<Yes. He wants you to really attack him. If you can stop him, you get extra meat. Can you do it?>

<He is very strong. Stronger than you or the angry man, but for extra meat? I will stop him.>

<Good. Don't hurt him, just give him a gentle mangling.>

<No ripping off arms?>

<No ripping off anything. Just stop him from using his power. Got it?>

<I understand. I will chew on him gently.>

<There you go. Get ready.>

"We're ready," I called out. "I hope you have plenty of extra meat. He's going to come at you hot."

"Are you certain you can do this?" Julien asked. "No hesitation. There will be no quarter given."

"And none asked," Monty said. "We are ready."

"I would expect nothing less," Julien said. "Do we have an understanding?"

"Are there any other parameters?" Monty asked. "Do you want to set rules of engagement?"

"Why?" Julien asked. "Do you think Gault will adhere to any supposed rules of engagement?"

"Not likely," I said. "Unless those rules are to obliterate us."

"Quite right," Julien said with a nod. "There is only one rule when facing Gault. Do you know what it is?"

"That there are no rules?" I volunteered. "We use everything we can."

"That goes without saying, Strong," Julien replied. "Try again."

"Survive," Monty said, his voice grim. "We have to be the ones to walk away."

"Yes, exactly," Julien answered with a slow nod. "That is the only rule. Do you think you can shift your thinking to embrace this mindset? There are no gentleman's rules here: there will be no codes of conduct. It's live or die...period. Can you attack me with this mindset?"

"What happens if we can't?" I asked. "What if we hold back?"

"Gault won't be holding back. Neither will Korin, nor any other enemy you face from this point forward," Julien said, his expression hard. "You've grown too strong to be taken lightly. Any intelligent opponent—and Gault is exceptionally intelligent—will do their best to eliminate you immediately and decisively, leaving nothing to chance."

"I guess we'd better not hold back then," I said, cracking my neck. "Do you have a medical facility on this island?"

"Why do you ask?"

"There's a good chance you're going to need it, if you're asking us to go all out," I said. "Remember *you* asked for this."

"I'm glad to see your level of confidence this high," Julien said. "Do you agree with this assessment, Mage Montague?"

"I'd rather reserve my thoughts on that for later, after this training session. However, you *have* been warned," Monty said. "We can't be held liable for any damage you or the arena suffer as a result of our interactions."

"Duly noted," Julien said. "Now that there are no barriers to your full commitment, will you attack me without reservation?"

<*Okay, boy. You can rip off his arms.*>

<*Really? Will the silver-man get angry? What if he doesn't give me extra meat?*>

<*It's what he wants. Maybe just rip off one arm, leave the other one so he can give you the meat.*>

Peaches unleashed a low rumble and stepped into shred-and-crush mode.

"I'm sure we can manage," I said, glancing sidelong at Monty. "How about you, Monty?"

"It won't be a difficulty," Monty said, rubbing his temple. "Can someone disable that infernal bell?"

"What bell?" Julien said with that smug smile. "Mage Montague, are you familiar with the petition of Ascendance?"

"Yes, I am," Monty said with a low growl as he glanced at the arena. "This courtyard is designed to resemble a much stronger version of an Ascendance arena."

"Very good. Consider this your first step toward ascension," Julien said, still smiling and deliberately raising his voice, driving the spike of pain further into my brain. The desire to pound my fist into his smile increased exponentially with the volume of his voice. "Today, we will test your combat cohesion. Use everything at your disposal: feel free to access the First Elder Rune, if you can."

"Can you lower your voice?" Monty said. "I have a splitting migraine. This time lag is quite unexpected."

"Unexpected, yes," Julien said, raising his voice even more

with a nod. "It is good to be prepared for the unexpected, don't you agree?"

"I do," Monty said, wincing. "Except, I have never—"

Julien unleashed a swarm of crackling black orbs in our direction.

"What the—?" I said as I backpedaled. "Where did those come from?"

There were no gestures, no finger-wiggles, no warnings of any kind. One moment there was a large open space between us, and the next the space had erupted with angry orbs headed our way.

Monty cursed under his breath and threw up a shield as I drew Grim Whisper, shooting the orbs which decided to flank Monty's shield and head straight for us.

<*Get him, boy.*>

Peaches blinked out of sight.

"Dawnward," Monty called out as he pivoted around the incoming swarm, throwing up several more golden shields around us, and intercepting the remainder of the swarm "We can use it as a fallback position if needed."

I nodded and focused energy through my body.

I formed a large violet dome of energy in front of me as I saw Peaches blink back in, behind Julien. My hellhound leapt forward with a blazing fast pounce, jaws gaping, which Julien sidestepped, letting Peaches sail past him.

Monty went on the offensive, forming several golden orbs around him as I gathered energy within for my magic missile. He unleashed the orbs with one hand as he created a violet lattice with the other.

"*Ignis vi—whoof,*" I managed as a fist of energy punched me in the solar plexus, forcing the air out of my lungs, causing my diaphragm to spasm, and interrupting my magic missile. I fell to one knee, trying to catch my breath as Monty nudged me into the dawnward. "I need…need a… moment."

"At a loss for words, Strong?" Julien called out in a singsong voice. "Pity. I was looking forward to that magic missile of yours."

My breath came in ragged gasps.

"I'm...I'm...really...hating...him...right...now."

"He hit you with a disruptor, which is why you're having trouble speaking more than a word in sequence."

"Disruptor...sucks."

Whatever hit me was having a lasting effect. It was nearly impossible to speak and get air into my lungs.

Peaches blinked back in, this time above Julien. My hellhound angled his body, and I knew Julien was done. Very few things can withstand a full-on pounce from a hellhound moving at speed.

Julien whispered a word and extended a hand above his head. Peaches crashed into him harmlessly, bouncing off, and floating away weightlessly as Julien tapped him lightly, sending him flying across the courtyard.

My eyes and brain were having trouble processing what just happened. He had removed my hellhound's mass, making the attack about as dangerous as getting attacked by a feather.

We were ten seconds into this fight, and two of us were already out of commission. My curse flared with heat, and I got to my feet.

We weren't going to lose this easily.

Monty put his hands together and whispered some words that caused the hairs on the back of my neck to stand on end.

Three large, black orbs of energy materialized around us.

Julien turned in our direction and raised an eyebrow at Monty. If he was concerned, he gave no indication of it as he gestured, forming a wall of silver energy in front of him.

"What is...that, Monty?" I managed between gasps as the orbs grew to the size of basketballs, picking up speed as they rotated around us. "That...that feels really off and dark."

"He said use *everything* at our disposal," Monty managed through clenched teeth, as sweat formed on his brow. I could see the exertion of creating those orbs on his face. "We are not going to lose to him. Not until I have exhausted every cast in my arsenal."

Peaches had managed to recover and blinked out again.

Monty slashed a hand down. The black orbs froze in place, leaving our orbit, and then raced at Julien.

SIXTEEN

Julien stepped back and remained behind his silver barrier as the black orbs of pain raced at him. Peaches launched another attack. This time I could see my hellhound had increased his mass as his paws dug into the arena, gouging the stone as he ran at Julien.

Peaches leapt at Julien when he was about three feet away.

Julien, without even looking at Peaches, opened a hellhound-sized silver lattice portal. Peaches was locked into his trajectory and ended up sailing right in. The silver lattice wrapped itself around Peaches, trapping him as he disappeared.

"*Ignis vit*—ow!" I yelled, as a portal opened behind me and a hellhound missile crashed into my back, knocking the air out of my lungs, and launching me across the arena floor.

Peaches rolled with me for a few seconds, our limbs getting tangled up in each other. We ended up several feet away from the edge of the dawnward.

It took a few seconds for us to get untangled. I looked up and saw Monty's orbs crash into the silver barrier in rapid sequence.

The first orb hit and cracked the barrier, the second orb managed to create a large hole in the silver wall, and the third made it through and slammed into Julien with an explosion of black energy.

For a few moments, I lost sight of him.

That was a mistake.

When the energy cleared, he was nowhere to be seen, but I sensed him close.

"Where is he, Monty?"

"The energy of the arena has camouflaged his location," Monty said, before sliding to my side and shoving me and Peaches into the dawnward. "There!"

I looked up into Julien's smiling face. He was about twenty feet above us and holding a black orb of his own.

"Mage Montague, I believe this belongs to you," Julien said, looking down at us. "Allow me."

Julien threw the orb at us with an overhand swing of his arm.

Monty slid into the dawnward next to me and began gesturing. A golden lattice of energy reinforced the dawnward as the orb fell on us.

For a second, the reinforced dawnward held—until it didn't.

The black orb of energy descended into us and exploded.

It was the last thing I remembered before the arena vanished.

***

I awoke in my room and looked out of the window. Night had fallen on the island. I had no idea of how long I had been out. I looked around the room and noticed Peaches sprawled out on his rug. He was sleeping soundly, but looked unhurt.

If I had been sore this morning, I had left sore and

entered the familiar land of agony now.

"Ow," I said as movement caught my eye from the other side of the room. "That wasn't fun."

"We severely miscalculated," Monty said from the table. "He outmaneuvered us at every turn."

"What was the first clue?" I said with a grimace. "Neutralizing my magic missile, or the way he literally manhandled my hellhound?"

"I sent obliteration orbs at him," Monty said. "He treated them as if they were nothing."

"Did he hit us with an obliteration orb?"

"No. Had he done so in that amplified arena, we would not be having this conversation," Monty said. "He merely recycled the energy and gave it back to us as an orb of destruction."

"Oh, only an orb of destruction. Well, that was nice of him."

"I reinforced the dawnward, expecting it to withstand the onslaught of that orb."

"I thought for a second that the dawnward would hold."

"As did I," Monty said with a small nod. "It seems we were both mistaken."

"How did he neutralize us so easily?"

"You're predictable," Julien said from the doorway. "How are you feeling, Simon?"

"Like my hellhound chewed me up and spit me out."

"I would imagine," he said. "May I come in?"

"Sure," I said, motioning for him to enter. "It's your castle, after all."

"Not mine," he said with a gesture, materializing another chair. "This location belongs to the Fleur de Lis. I merely borrow it from time to time."

He sat in the chair, looked at us, and remained silent for a few moments, gathering his thoughts before speaking.

"If you confront Gault the way you faced me today, you *will* die."

He let the words hang in the air between us for a few seconds more.

"How are we supposed to go up against an Archmage?" I said. "You completely outclass us."

"Do you think a Keeper will be any easier?"

"No," Monty said. "We underestimated you, and had you been Gault, it would have cost us our lives."

"Yes," Julien said. "I noticed you didn't access the First Elder Rune. Was it because you couldn't, or because you chose not to?"

"I'm not familiar with its inner workings, not yet," Monty said. "It's a merged cast, and Simon and I haven't tried to access it in an active battle environment."

"I truly hope you are not waiting to face Gault before you give it try?"

"Of course not," Monty answered. "It's just that—"

"You don't know *how* to access it."

Monty nodded.

"What about your other shared cast?" Julien continued, glancing at me. "The stormblood? Why didn't I see that used today?"

"We've only used it once," I said. "And it wasn't pretty."

"So you *have* used it successfully?" Julien said. "Why didn't you use it today?"

"I wouldn't exactly say it was a successful cast," I said. "It got away from us, from me, and nearly melted New Jersey. Josephine and Dex stepped in to prevent that from happening."

"I see," he said. "In both cases, you have the potential to wield vast amounts of power, but lack the proficiency to do so."

"Seems like it," I said. "The stormblood was a desperation

play. It was either use it or get fried by Edith. I know I'm the catalyst for the elder rune, but I don't even know what that means."

"Understood," Julien said with a nod, and stood. The chair disappeared a second later. "It would seem I applied the wrong type of pressure in our training. Did either of you feel your lives were in danger today?"

"Not really," I said. "No."

"No," Monty said. "You neutralized us, but didn't retaliate until the final attack, which ended the training."

"I actually thought you would open with a stormblood and follow that up with the First Elder Rune," he said. "I overestimated you both, but the fault is mine. You didn't feel the need to use your weapons either—I didn't see Ebonsoul or the Sorrows. Am I wrong to assume you thought these weapons were off-limits?"

"I... Well, I thought this was only training for the elder rune and accessing power," I said embarrassed. "I didn't even consider using Ebonsoul."

Why didn't I use Ebonsoul? Or at least attempt to get close enough to use it? I packed Grim Whisper, but Ebonsoul would have been more effective.

"I had not considered the Sorrows," Monty said. "Apologies."

"I understand," Julien said with a nod. "I neglected to attack properly. I will rectify this tomorrow."

"Rectify it how?" I asked, curious and wary. "What do you mean, you neglected to attack properly?"

"Tomorrow," he said with a nod. "I apologize for misreading the situation. I will not make the same error again. My sole purpose—our sole purpose—is to unlock the power that lies dormant within each of you. That is why Dex sent you to me. It is why we are here."

"Understood," Monty said. "We will review today's

training."

"Please do so," Julien said and gestured. "Your meals will arrive shortly. Try to get some rest. We start at first light tomorrow. Goodnight."

"Goodnight," Monty and I both said.

Julien left the room.

"What does he mean, he didn't attack properly?" I asked.

"I don't know, but I have a feeling tomorrow's training will be more difficult than today," Monty said. "What can we learn from today?"

"He didn't want me to use my magic missile," I said, going over the training in my mind. "Both times he stopped me from activating it."

"Correct," Monty said with a nod. "He also considered your creature to be a viable threat, which he dealt with directly."

"Your orbs broke through his barrier, eventually," I said. "Can you focus the power of all three orbs into one orb, and throw that at him?"

"I can certainly try," Monty said. "We have to attempt the stormblood tomorrow at some point. Perhaps when he least expects it?"

"I would love to treat him to a lightning flambé, but the last time we activated it, we had no way to control it," I said. "What if we do it and it barbecues us? That would suck."

"Indeed it would," he said, "but our conventional methods are not working. If he was testing our unit cohesion today, we fell apart like a badly made suit. We can't do that tomorrow."

"No, we can't," I said, shaking my head. "He'll take us apart again."

"Do you recall how you triggered the stormblood against Edith?"

I thought back to that moment at the Cloisters.

Edith had unleashed a wave of kinetic energy, Quan had

formed a white circle of energy, and I felt the stormblood inside me. *Frequency, Structure, and Execution*—the blood lessons.

"To be fair, I started it, but you took what I started and ran with it," I said. "We don't have Quan here to create a circle of protection. Do you think you can make one?"

"I don't think Julien will allow me the opportunity to do so. We will need to create a distraction," Monty said. "If we cast a stormblood inside that arena, it will be stronger than what we did at the Cloisters."

"That doesn't sound like such a good idea," I said. "If it wasn't for Josephine, Jersey and most of the area around the Cloisters would've been a blasted-out wasteland."

"I'm aware," Monty said. "It's either that, or we access the power of the First Elder Rune."

"I hope you're not looking at me for that one," I said, shaking my head. "Keeper Evergreen didn't leave a manual or a note somewhere on how that's supposed to work."

"You are the one who's supposed to activate the rune," Monty said. "You bear the burden of causality."

"Just like you bear the burden of holding the magic."

"Yes, I'm the repository," he said with a nod. "At least we're clear on our roles."

"Wonderful. We understand what the words mean," I said. "How do I activate the rune when someone is trying to delete me? How do I unleash the cause that creates the rune to start?"

"I don't know," Monty said quietly. "I think we focus on the stormblood first. If that doesn't work, then we resort to using the elder rune."

"The elder rune we don't know how to activate?"

"Yes, that one."

"Perfect. If we keep this up, Gault is going to shred us," I said. "Evergreen said Dex would have answers."

"I would imagine if we asked my uncle Dex, he would point to our current situation as his way of giving us the answers we need."

"Of course he would," I said. "Why would it be straightforward instructions? No, there has to be some life-altering lesson with the threat of an agonizing death somewhere in the background."

"That sounds accurate," Monty said as a bowl of pastrami materialized in the corner next to my sleeping hellhound. Peaches started awake and began to inhale the meat. "Do you have any other insights?"

"Insights? No," I said as my bowl of food appeared on the table, and my stomach growled suddenly. "Aside from the fact that I'm starving, the one thing that stays with me is that we have to fight together. We were attacking, but it was disjointed. It gave him time to react and counter us."

"Easily, I might add," Monty said. "We have to disrupt his balance."

"That's what I meant: if we can keep him on his heels, we can take him down," I said. "I think the best chance of that is the stormblood—at least until we figure out how to access the elder rune."

"I will meditate on it tonight after my meal," Monty said, heading for the door. "Give it some thought and let's come up with a plan of attack in the morning."

I nodded.

"See you in the morning," I said, approaching the table and my meal.

"Get some rest, Simon," Monty said. "I know Julien is supposed to help us, but that doesn't mean I trust him entirely."

"Understood. You do the same. We need to bring our A-game tomorrow."

He left the room with a nod.

SEVENTEEN

I was up before the sun the next day.

Frequency, Structure, and Execution.

That was the key. I needed to somehow tap into the blood lessons.

The first thing I did was put on my shoulder holster and make sure Grim Whisper was secure. I focused and searched for Ebonsoul, feeling its presence inside.

I would use them after we got the stormblood going. If we opened with weapons, I figured Julien had counters prepared to deal with them. If he was busy dealing with a stormblood, I could probably hit him with a few rounds, or at the very least distract him and let Monty and the stormblood take him down.

If he got close, like he did yesterday, I could always materialize Ebonsoul, cut him, and siphon the energy of an Archmage. If I did that, I was positive I could access the trigger for the First Elder Rune, let Monty take control of it, and unleash the pain on Julien.

If we could manage what I did at the Cloisters, together,

Monty and I could stop Julien, or at least make him think twice about attacking us.

I headed down to the arena with Peaches at my side as the sky began to lighten. Thankfully there was no bell this morning, and my body was less sore. I almost felt human, and after the pummeling we took yesterday, I was surprised the effects hadn't lasted longer.

Monty was waiting for me.

He had finished creating a large circle of pulsing white energy. It was wide enough to provide us ample cover, and give us enough room to maneuver when Julien attacked.

With a gesture, the circle faded from view.

I nodded in approval.

At least we had a circle of protection. Now all we needed to do was activate the stormblood.

"That should provide us enough cover to activate the stormblood," Monty said. "Provided we can…"

He gestured again, and I felt the current of power run through the arena—it flowed out to the four columns, then reversed direction to pool into the center of the arena.

"What was that?" I asked. "It felt, I don't know, familiar?"

"It was the elder rune of sealing," Monty said. "When Julien steps into the arena that will trigger the activation and hopefully diminish some of the amplification in this place."

"Doesn't that place us at a disadvantage too?"

"Not if we remain in the circle I just created."

"It's not a circle of protection?"

"Yes, it is, as well as having a component of stasis," Monty revealed, keeping his voice low and glancing to the sides. "It will preserve the amplification of the arena inside the circle. The rune of sealing will diminish the amplification outside the circle."

"We're evening the playing field."

"We are facing an Archmage."

"Are you sure this is allowed? It seems like cheating."

"There is only one rule, remember?"

"Survive," I said, with a nod. "I remember."

Peaches rumbled by my side.

<*The silver-man is coming.*>

<*Thanks for the heads-up, boy. As soon as we start, you take him down.*>

<*As soon as he steps in, I will attack. He is very clever.*>

<*We are going to be extra clever today.*>

<*Good. That means I can get extra meat.*>

"He's on his way," I continued. "Is he going to sense the circle?"

"Not in the midst of the flowing energy of the arena and the amplification columns. I also masked the circle to mimic the energy present in the arena."

Julien approached the arena and stood outside of it for a few seconds. A cold fear gripped my chest.

Did he sense the trap Monty had placed for him? If he did, this training session is over before it even starts.

Julien patted the front of his robe as if looking for something, before reaching into an inside pocket and drawing out a small piece of silver.

"My apologies, and good morning," Julien said. "I just needed this."

He held up the small piece of silver, which was about the size of a credit card and just as thin. From across the arena, I couldn't make out what it was, but I could sense the energy flowing from Julien.

"Good morning," I said, keeping my voice even. "Same plan as yesterday?"

"Somewhat," Julien said as he stepped into the arena. The rune of sealing fell into place. Julien looked at us, but if he felt a diminishing of the power of the arena, he didn't let it show on his face. "Today, I will approach this situation a little differently, and with one caveat."

"A caveat?" Monty asked warily. "Which is?"

"I want you both to understand that what I do is solely to help you achieve the objective," Julien said. "I want to apologize beforehand for the necessity of my future actions."

"What is he talking about?" I asked Monty and then turned to Julien. "Can you clarify? Use small words for those of us who don't speak mage."

Julien shook his head, and his expression was almost sad. That, more than anything else, set off alarms in my head.

"I find, that in situations like this, actions speak louder than words," Julien said, as he released the card. It floated in the air next to him with an air of menace. "Once again, my apologies, but we must do it this way if we are to make any progress."

"Monty," I said, taking a few steps back. "What is that card?"

"I don't know," Monty said, gesturing and creating shields. "I would say it's safe to assume getting hit by it would be a bad idea."

"Kill," Julien said, releasing the card. It floated near Julien and rotated slowly, as it turned silver-red for a few seconds, then reverted back to a gleaming silver. It hovered next to Julien as if waiting for something more. Julien turned to the card and then looked at me. "Target: hellhound."

Rage and fear clenched my stomach.

"Peaches! Run!" I yelled as the silver card of death raced at my hellhound. "Go!"

Peaches must have heard the fear in my voice because he blinked out immediately at the sound of his name. I drew Grim Whisper and fired several rounds in Julien's direction. He had thrown up a shield, which deflected my rounds. Peaches was still gone, and each second I didn't see him was a lifetime of agony.

He blinked in again next to me, panting heavily. I could see small cuts and slices along his flanks as he fell at my feet, exhausted. What was that card made of that it could cut through hellhound skin?

<It chased me. It found me, even in-between. It...it hurts.>
<Stay close. I got this.>

I focused my will and cast the dawnward, covering us with a violet dome of energy. The silver card of death materialized a few seconds later and raced at us.

<Don't worry, boy. My dawnward should stop it.>

Even as I said the words, a part of me knew it was a lie.

"Monty?" I said in a panic, turning to him as he cast a lattice over Peaches in an effort to protect him from the weapon. "Help!"

"This should stop it."

The card sliced through both the dawnward and the lattice covering Peaches. It cut right into my hellhound and punched through his side, leaving a gaping hole.

The card disintegrated a second later, its fatal mission complete.

My hellhound, my bondmate, yelped as he lay on his side at my feet.

<I'm sorry, my bondmate. I was not fast enough.>

The world froze as he began to bleed out.

"No," I said, barely above a whisper as I fell to my knees and held my hellhound's massive head. His tongue lolled to one side, as tears streaked down my face. "No..."

I looked up at Julien. His expression was hard as he stared back.

"I told you I would show you how mistaken you were."

"And I told you that if you hurt my hellhound, this would go from training to death in a heartbeat, you motherfucker!"

Rage burst in my chest as I got to my feet.

My skin exploded with golden energy. I reached in and

found the feral, ancient, and unknowable raw power of the stormblood. Lightning arcs formed around my body, striking the ground and gouging up chunks of stone, and still I went deeper, searching for more within.

The First Elder Rune called to me, and I wrapped my mind around its power, combining it with the essence of the stormblood. Keeper Evergreen's words echoed in my mind.

Simon Strong, you are the Aspis, the shield warrior, and the catalyst. You will bear the burden of causality. The activation of the rune will rest with you.

I called to that power, summoning it to me, and joining it with the stormblood. Monty's eyes were glowing golden as he stood next to me. Golden energy flowed from his body, as arcs of electricity shot out from mine.

I formed Ebonsoul as Monty summoned one of the Sorrows. His blade wailed, but this time it was different. This wasn't a wailing child. This was the keening of anguish and death.

All around us the stormblood raged.

"End him," I whispered. "He dies now."

Monty remained silent, pointing his blade as a bolt of golden light surrounded by arcs of lightning shot forward, exploding into Julien.

We raced forward to meet Julien, who had summoned a black blade of his own and deflected Monty's bolt into one of the stone columns, shattering it to dust.

"Come and show me your power," Julien raged, stepping into a defensive stance as his voice reverberated throughout the arena. "Come end me!"

EIGHTEEN

Blind rage took hold of me.

I took a step forward and found myself clashing blades with Julien. A distant part of my brain had noticed that I had just crossed an arena of several hundred feet in less than a half-second.

It didn't matter.

Nothing mattered except destroying Julien in this moment.

Monty was by my side and had cast several golden orbs of death, unleashing them at the Archmage.

Julien slashed at the golden orbs, deflecting them out of the arena. They hit the walls around the rear courtyard, exploding sections into dust.

I slid forward and slashed horizontally as Ebonsoul moaned in my mind. Black energy wafted up from the blade and a trail of dark violet energy cut through the air I slashed.

Ebonsoul has never moaned in the past.

Irrelevant.

My target was still breathing, and I wanted—no, *needed*—to fix that, permanently.

All around us, bolts of lightning slammed into the arena, cratering the concentric circles that contained the power of the space.

Julien was a whirlwind of movement.

He slid around the arcs of energy, dodging them with no margin for error. His face was a mask of focus and concentration as he met my every attack with a parry or a deflection.

It was a fearsome thing to experience an Archmage unleash his full power, but there was something even more fearsome: me realizing my hellhound was gone.

I screamed in anguish as those words of death formed in my mind. The sound of my pain reverberated through the arena and for a moment, it felt as if reality heard me and answered.

For the first time, I saw concern flit across Julien's face.

I smiled. It was a feral, hungry thing.

Ignis vitae.

I will burn him to nothing where he stands.

No, that is too good for him. Those are not the words; that is not the command. Let me help you exact the revenge you deserve.

Yes. Help me.

It didn't matter who or what was speaking to me. All I knew was that I needed revenge. Every fiber of my being called out for death. Ebonsoul jumped in my hand, as black energy exploded from the blade.

A violet-gold shield formed around me and Monty, as dark energy covered my hand.

Monty stepped forward and attacked with the Sorrows, the keening from his blade becoming louder and deeper. The sounds escaping from my throat and chest joined the Sorrows as we pressed Julien.

Monty sliced through Julien's defenses and drew blood from one arm. Anger transfixed Julien's expression at being wounded, but his anger was a small, insignificant thing. It would burn away in the face of my rage.

There was no fear. Not anymore.

Only retribution.

Julien slammed his blade into the ground, point first. A shockwave of energy exploded across the arena. Monty had anticipated the attack and gestured, creating a circle of golden light as he slammed the Sorrows into the center of his circle.

I suddenly felt impossibly heavy as Julien's blast crashed into us.

We did not move.

I was immovable, unrelenting, unstoppable.

Julien stared hard at me and then smiled.

That's when I knew.

In that moment, he had decided we had gone too far.

He was going to kill us.

I shook my head and smiled back.

It was possible this was where my story would end, but the world was going to be short one Archmage by the time I was done.

I ran forward, cutting through the winds of the shockwave as if they didn't exist. Julien's eyes widened and he poured more energy into the attack.

The arena floor was ripped up as a massive blast of energy cut across the ground, leaving a trench in its wake as it headed straight for me.

I drove a palm into the ground, stopping the energy blast. I continued moving forward. Julien moved back as I closed in. He raised a hand and screamed words I couldn't understand.

It didn't matter.

Nothing mattered except holding his lifeless body in my fists.

A swarm of silver orbs the size of small marbles materialized and assaulted me. Monty was immediately by my side, deflecting them, his expression a mask of anger and focus. I had never seen him move so fast in my life.

Thunder rumbled across the darkened skies as lightning strikes hit the courtyard all around us. Monty gestured again as the golden aura around him intensified.

The First Elder Rune.

The arcs of lightning crashed through and into us, but I knew that the power wouldn't harm us.

It obeyed us.

We commanded this power.

It belonged to us and we belonged to it.

Golden electrical arcs raced around Monty as violet darkness enveloped me.

"I warned you," I said, my voice echoing in the arena. "Now, you die."

Julien shook his head and laughed as he threw up a silver shield.

"You wouldn't dare. Your fear controls you!" he screamed above the sound of the courtyard being destroyed. "You can't do it! You couldn't even protect your hellhound, your precious bondmate. You are a pathetic failure!"

Something broke in me.

"Death," Monty said quietly. "Do it, now."

"Death," I said, extending my hand. "Death."

Here are the words needed.

What are the words?

Mors ignis. Death in fire; yes, that is fitting.

Thank you.

"*Mors ignis,*" I whispered as darkflame erupted from the ground all around me. "*Mors ignis!*"

The arena—or what was left of it—became an inferno of darkflame.

This time Julien did step back with fear across his face. Every shield he created melted instantly. He gestured and formed a swarm of glowing silver orbs. They covered his side of the arena. Each of the orbs was close to two feet in diameter and shimmered with deadly black energy across their surfaces.

I stood still and looked down, letting the power of the darkflame envelop and empower me.

Frequency, Structure, Execution.

Frequency.

I sensed the storm of lightning and power inside of me, fueled by rage. The energy around the arena swirled around me. The stormblood felt primal as arcs of electricity danced between Monty and me.

Structure.

The ancient power of the First Elder Rune pulled away the veil and revealed the very fabric of all things.

In an instant, I saw—truly saw—the connection between everything. Time slowed and I sensed without using my eyes—everything from the smallest pebble floating in the air, to the violence of the raging sea surrounding the Chateau.

There was no distinction, and there was every distinction.

It was all one.

Execution.

Energy couldn't be destroyed, but it could be transformed.

It could be cancelled out.

I made a fist with my hand and the darkflame around me leapt at my gesture. I rotated my hands as I had seen Monty do so many times in the past, and the darkflame in front of me solidified into an orb.

It hovered in my hand. Monty stepped close to my side, just behind me.

He gestured, summoning another dozen darkflame orbs

around us. They all hovered around us, moving in large orbits around where we stood.

All around us, I felt their power, the power to destroy. The darkflame orb in front me was different.

It hungered.

It wanted to devour, to consume everything around it.

It was perfect.

At this point, Julien dropped all pretense of being fearless.

He was rapidly creating new barriers of silver energy to protect the ones that continuously collapsed around him.

All the while, he kept his gaze on Monty and me.

I glanced to the side and saw Monty focused on Julien.

The sounds of destruction roared around us, but in the space where we stood, silence had descended.

"After you, Simon," Monty said. "He deserves no less than total annihilation for what he did. You have the privilege of first strike."

"Thank you," I said and turned to Julien. "You should have never touched my hellhound."

"I did what was necessary," Julien said. "You can't match my power. Not even in this place. This entire exercise has been a colossal waste of time. Goodbye, Mage Montague and Simon Strong. It has been my greatest displeasure making your acquaintance."

Julien slashed his hand forward, unleashing the swarm of enormous orbs behind him.

Several things happened at once.

Monty whispered something under his breath, causing the darkflame orbs around us to increase in size. With a gesture, he released them at Julien's incoming swarm of silver orbs.

The two sets of orbs crashed into each other, exploding violently around us. Arcs from the stormblood still raced along the edges of the arena, making short work of the stone around the perimeter and destroying everything.

Ebonsoul vibrated in my hand again.

He deserves more than death. He must be undone.

I placed a hand on the orb in front of me and whispered, "Target: Julien. Undo."

Yes. Well done.

The orb rose up a few inches from my palm, vibrated in place, and disappeared from sight. I looked forward with my innersight and saw the strands of matter erupt into darkflame as it moved toward Julien.

Reality itself warped around the orb as it homed in on its target. It didn't matter if Julien was an Archmage—this orb would strike at the very core of his existence.

He would be undone.

There was no power on this island that could stop the undoing once it began. Nothing.

The thought hit me again as Monty gripped my shoulder. He was no longer glowing, and the power of the First Elder Rune was slowly fading from around us. The rage left me, as cold reality settled in.

There is no power on this island that could stop the undoing once it began—nothing.

"We may have a problem," I said, watching the orb of darkflame close on Julien. "I think I just killed us."

"Simon?" Monty asked, suddenly concerned. "What did you do?"

I pointed forward at the orb headed to unmake Julien.

"I told it to undo."

Monty narrowed his eyes and gazed in the direction I pointed.

"Bloody hell," Monty said, furiously moving his hands. "That may have been a bad idea."

"A bad idea?" I said, whirling on Monty. "Did you see what he did to Peaches?"

Monty stopped gesturing, grabbed me by the shoulders, and turned me around.

"Look," he yelled. "Look!"

I saw my hellhound lying on his side, lifeless.

"Way to twist the knife, Monty," I said, trying to shrug him off and staring at my hellhound. "I know he's gone."

Monty shook me hard.

"What the hell, Monty?" I asked, startled at the treatment. "What are you doing?"

"Your bond! Feel for your bond!"

I focused and felt the bond to my hellhound as strong as it had ever been.

"I feel him, but...but he's gone." I pointed at Peaches. "I see him right there."

"Look—*really* look."

I stared at Peaches' body again using my innersight. The darkflame around me burned away the illusion. It wasn't my hellhound on the ground, but some kind of silver, hellhound-shaped construct made of rapidly fading energy.

"I don't understand," I said, looking at Monty. "I held him in my arms. He bled out. He spoke to me."

Monty turned to Julien.

"What did you *do*?"

"Whatever I thought necessary," Julien said, fear tingeing his voice. "In retrospect, I admit I may have gone too far."

"Gone too far?" I yelled, raising my voice. "Where is my hellhound?"

"In the Chateau, behind several levels of energy dampeners, which is why you couldn't feel your bond immediately," Julien said, the words spilling out. "I only meant to use a traumatic event as a trigger to help you access your potential power."

"By making me think you killed my hellhound?"

Julien gazed at his incoming death in the shape of the darkflame orb and gave me a sad smile.

"I'd say you managed to return the favor," Julien said. "You certainly managed to tap into power. Power even I didn't anticipate."

"You are a total ass," I said to him, before turning to Monty. "How bad is it?"

"Any moment now, that orb is going to resurface in this plane and do one thing—"

"Undo," I finished. "I did target Julien." I gave Julien a sidelong glance with plenty of stinkeye. "Won't it try to undo just him?"

"It will *start* with him," Monty said. "But it won't stop. It will undo until—"

"Until there's nothing left to undo. Then what?"

Monty nodded as he played out the consequences in his mage brain.

"Think carefully, Simon. Did you give it a general command to undo, or the specific command to undo Julien?"

"I designated Julien as the target and then gave it the command to undo," I said. "Did I do it wrong?"

"Not exactly; not if you wanted to undo everything in this plane and then the plane itself," he said. "What were your *exact* words?"

I told him.

"That's not exactly how it works," he said, shaking his head. "Not that you would know this. You never received formal training."

"I did what he did with that silver card."

"That silver card must have been an empathetic construct, designed to present you with the worst thing you can imagine in any given context," Monty said, slipping into professor mode. "Did he prime you? Did you discuss your creature with Julien since we arrived here?"

"Yes, I warned him not to hurt Peaches."

"The worst thing you can imagine," he said. "Your orb will do what you instructed it to do."

"Undo."

Monty nodded.

"Starting with Julien, then us," Monty said, his voice grim. "Then the plane, until everything is consumed."

"It won't stop?"

"Once everything is gone, it will undo itself. The explosion of energy should be quite spectacular, not that we will be here to witness it. The solution is quite elegant if you think on it."

I stared at him in disbelief.

"You think this is spectacular?" I yelled. "Are you insane?"

"I think, barring one of us producing an orb stronger than the one headed at Julien, that this is inevitable. We have created what I thought impossible: a world-ending entropic dissolution. It is a horrific and elegant method of destruction."

"Elegant? It's going to undo this entire plane," I said. "Us included. How is that elegant?"

"I just said that," Monty said. "Unless we have a way to remove it. This is the end."

"Mage Montague is right. That is the solution," Julien said. "We need to remove it from this plane."

"Excellent idea. This is the part where one of you two provide the incredibly magetastic answer to this," I said. "How are you going to shift an orb of entropy away, without using any energy or power that it can and will undo?"

"Entropy cannot be destroyed," Julien said. "In fact—"

"How about having the class on runic quantum mechanics when we are not facing extinction?" I asked. "Do we have an exit strategy?"

"All of the portals out of this plane have been destroyed."

"What about the bridge?" I asked. "We can get out the same way—"

"No, the stormblood took care of that," Julien said, looking out of the arena. "Even part of the bridge is gone."

Julien pointed, and I saw the span of the bridge was missing most of the middle, as the elder-rune-powered stormblood continued chewing through the iron-and-stone structure, erasing it from existence.

"There's no way we can jump across that."

"We are trapped here," Monty said. "The stormblood, along with the First Elder Rune, have unleashed too much ambient energy. I can't create a teleportation circle even if I wanted to—and I most certainly want to, but can't because the flux of energy is too violent. We can't create a portal out of this plane."

"How much time to we have before the orb reenters this plane?"

"I would imagine minutes on the outside, most likely much less."

"Much less," I said as I sensed the energy of the darkflame orb and pointed across the ruined arena. "It's back."

The darkflame orb reappeared on the other side of the rubble that used to be the arena. It hovered in the air for a few seconds and then raced at Julien.

"I'm not going out like this."

"I will try and slow it down," Monty said as he gestured. "But it's futile. It will devour the energy. Eventually, we will fail."

I cast a dawnward as Monty created several golden lattices. Even Julien created several thick silver walls of energy.

It should've been enough but we all knew it wasn't going to stop the orb.

"That will only slow it down," Julien said, looking down at

his hands. "I never thought my end would arrive this way. For what it is worth, I'm sorry."

"We still have options," I said. "We aren't going to quit."

Julien looked at me as if I had sprouted another head on my shoulder.

"What options? Julien asked. "Only that darkflame is keeping you going. Once that energy is absorbed, the backlash of that cast will hit you hard. If you manage to survive that, the odds of surviving the orb are nil. Absolute zero."

"Never, ever, tell me the odds," I said, stepping forward and out of the protective defenses. "We still have one shot."

"Simon, no!" Monty yelled as I left the dawnward. "That's suicide."

"What is he doing?" Julien asked. "Has he lost his mind? Going out there is madness."

I'm something more than a mage.

I pressed my mark.

For the first time ever, I really hoped Karma was paying attention. The endless knot on the back of my hand exploded with golden-white light, nearly blinding me with its intensity. It was quickly replaced with black-red energy.

That's new.

Time slowed.

All around me, the destruction froze. Chunks of stone floated mid-air. Bolts of lightning from the stormblood shimmered with the energy of annihilation everywhere in the arena.

The darkflame covering the ground and parts of my body flickered with deep violet and gold energy, but remained still.

My world suddenly ground to a halt; the heady smell of lotus blossoms and earth after a hard rain filled my lungs. This was followed by the sharp smell of cut oranges and an aroma hinting of cinnamon permeating the air.

I braced myself for Karma and the eventual slap of correction.

Something changed.

The smell suddenly shifted to a pungent metallic odor. I heard the cawing of crows in the air around me as the temperature increased. Sweat formed on my brow and a numbing cold gripped me by the throat.

Karma was not coming this time.

NINETEEN

An enormous crow flew into my line of sight, landing on the ground in front of me. It burst into a cloud of black feathers which then froze in place before slowly reforming into an older woman.

More precisely, an older woman who looked like she could pound me into dust without even breaking a sweat in the process. Her energy signature radiated power, anguish, and above everything else...death.

Oh, shit.

This is not Karma.

She was dressed in a blood-red gown of flowing feathers, which matched the blood-red, almost black of her hair. In one hand she held a long, black, rune-covered metal spear with an even blacker tip, which itself was covered in what looked like fresh blood.

On her other arm rested a menacing spike-covered pauldron of black steel with a large, blood-red crow carved into its surface. Despite the difference in appearance, I knew who I was looking at.

Badb Catha—one of the three personifications of the Morrigan.

In fact, this was the scariest of the three, which was saying something, considering how frightening the Morrigan I associated with Dex was.

"You called me," she said, her voice sounding surprisingly young despite her appearance. "I have come."

"I...I...think...I might have misdialed?" I said, struggling to get the words out. "You are *not* who I was trying to call."

"And yet, I am here."

I stared at her in silence for a few seconds.

It couldn't really be her. Why would she be here? How was this even possible? Could my mark really call out to any other being besides Karma?

My innersight was still affected by the darkflame of power that swirled inside me. I glanced at her using it, and she whacked me upside the head with the flat of her spear, turning my head to the side so fast I nearly suffered side whiplash. She was faster than I could have ever imagined. I didn't even see her move to strike me.

"You seek madness?" she continued calmly. "Close your deepsight and face me plainly."

"My apologies, goddess," I said, bowing my head and keeping my gaze averted, not risking another glance with my innersight. "I meant no insult."

I was still wondering what happened to Karma when she tapped me on the head again. This time the intention was to get my attention, not smack wisdom into my skull.

"You were expecting another?"

"Well, no offense meant," I said as I managed to close my innersight. Dealing with the Chosen of the Slain in her warrior-goddess mode was scary enough. "Usually, when I press my mark, it's Karma who manages to appear."

"Do you know who I am?" she asked. "Do you know my name?"

I nodded, my tongue betraying me and choosing that moment to inform me that forming words was out of the question for the next few days—maybe weeks or months, if I was lucky.

"I would like to hear you say my name," she said with a small smile that made me want to run away screaming, as fear, horror, the thought of gouging out my eyes, and biting through my own tongue tickled in the back of my mind. "Say it."

It wasn't a request but closer to a compulsion. The waves of power washing over me crushed me in their grasp. Even if I wanted to move, my body was refusing to listen to me.

"Badb...Badb Catha," I managed after a few moments of wrestling my mind to the ground and forcing myself to speak. "My apologies if I mispronounced it."

"Close enough," she said with a nod before surveying the situation. "Do you know why I'm here?"

"No," I said honestly. "I was actually hoping Karma would show up."

"You didn't call Karma. You called me."

"I think I would remember calling you," I said, making sure not to tread over the line that would end my life repeatedly. "I'm sure I would remember if I called you. I distinctly did *not* call a goddess of death. I really think I would have remembered *that* call."

She smiled again and my insides contracted with fear.

"You're expecting Karma, but let me present you with an alternative idea."

What was I going to say? No thanks, I'm good. You can go back to wherever it was you were before you decided to pay me a visit. Come back and visit me never?

I may be borderline insane and reckless, but I didn't want

to die today. So in the spirit of self-preservation, I gave her the only answer I thought she would accept.

I remained silent and nodded.

"She did say you were daring and had promise," she said. "Let me show you how you called me."

I managed to take a step back—I want to say I stepped back boldly—but the step was closer to a stumble, and the only thing motivating me in this moment was a huge dose of pure, primal fear. If I could run, I would've broken every land speed record to get away from her.

"If you say I called you," I said, raising a hand in surrender, "I'm not going to argue the point. I called you."

"I insist," she said and grabbed my arm by the bicep and squeezed gently. I felt like my arm would snap at any second. "Do you understand?"

"Only that my bones aren't designed for this kind of pressure without snapping."

"Apologies," she said with a nod. "Here, let me adjust your sight."

She raised a hand and tapped me on the forehead. The tap was about as soft as getting smacked on the forehead with a large sledgehammer.

There was a sensation of movement as she tapped me out of myself. The arena and everything around me faded to black for a few seconds before coming into focus again.

There was a moment of vertigo as I adjusted to viewing the scene around me from outside of my body.

I saw myself in the center of the arena after thinking Peaches had been killed. I saw the moment I summoned the energy of the stormblood. I felt when I joined that energy with the visceral power of the First Elder Rune.

I saw Monty covered in golden energy, and the contrast of the darkness enveloping me.

"Here," she continued, her voice low and next to my ear. "This is the moment you called me."

I saw the moment I screamed, my screams joining the keening of Monty's blade, the Sorrows. I felt the anguish, retribution, and hunger for death in my screams.

I felt them connect with something deeper, something primal and ancient, something *other*. In that moment, I felt the hunger in me for vengeance, and I wanted—*needed*— to have the hunger met.

"I didn't...didn't mean to call *you*," I stammered. "That was never my intention."

The image of me screaming disappeared and was replaced with the darkflame orb homing in on Julien.

"I know," she said with an almost gentle smile. "But then you formed and unleashed—that."

She pointed at the orb.

I focused on the orb.

"I know," I said. "It's going to undo everything."

"Yes," she said. "It's an entropic dissolution unlike any I have ever seen in my long life—a world ender. You have somehow managed to merge the power of a stormblood with the creative properties of the First Elder Rune."

"Not on purpose," I said. "All I wanted to do—"

"Was kill the Archmage," she finished. "Yes?"

"Yes," I admitted. "I thought he killed my hellhound."

She nodded, but kept her gaze on the orb.

"A life for a life," she said. "That is just."

"Except my hellhound isn't dead," I said. "And this orb is going to destroy everything."

"It certainly seems like it."

"I didn't think I could call on that much power," I said. "I'm not a—"

"I know," she said. "Rage, loss, despair, and vengeance are excellent conduits to power. They don't last long, but they burn bright and deep, fueling some of the most powerful casts. You didn't do this alone."

"Excuse me?" I asked. "I don't understand."

"I think you do," she answered. "Who gave you the command? *Mors ignis*? That is a cast beyond you. Mage Montague and even the Archmage would hesitate to unleash a cast of that caliber. The cost is steep."

There was no point in lying.

"Ebonsoul, my blade, spoke to me," I said after a pause. "Don't ask me how. I didn't mean to turn it on."

"You speak true, but it was not your blade, but rather the entity that inhabits it," she said, making me feel like I dodged a fatal spear thrust by telling the truth. "You did not awaken your blade alone."

"That sounds like all kinds of bad," I said, giving it some thought. "Do you know who or what helped?"

"I do."

She stared at me for a few seconds, and then went back to looking at the impending scene of death and devastation.

"Can you tell me who helped me awaken Ebonsoul?"

"I can, but I will not. It is not time...yet."

I knew better than to argue the point.

When a goddess says it's not time yet, especially one holding a spear that could turn you into an instant shish kebab, you adapt in a hurry and drop the subject. I focused instead on saving Monty and Peaches, even Julien despite his scummy move of pretending to kill my hellhound. He didn't deserve to go out like that. No one did.

"Is that darkflame orb stronger than the Archmage?"

"It is a powerful, if not slightly inelegant, cast. I suspect Mage Montague had something to do with its creation as well, though he may not know it. The Archmage will not be able to stand against that power. Those defenses will fall, and then so will he."

I nodded, my mouth suddenly dry.

"Can you stop it?"

"This is where I present the alternative, and you...make a choice."

I really didn't like the sound of that.

"There is a cost," I said, nodding. "There's always a cost."

"This is more. You acted as an agent of causality when you formed that orb," she explained. "The Archmage stepped on a path and made a series of choices."

"I don't...I don't understand."

She held up a finger.

"He accepted my love's offer to release your potential."

For a moment my brain seized, then it leapt forward when I realized she was referring to Dex.

I nodded in understanding.

A second finger went up.

"He chose to strike your hellhound, to make it appear deceased," she said. "A clever ruse, indiscernible from the reality, and designed to trigger the release of your power."

"It worked. It was a stupid method, but it worked."

"He failed to consider the ramifications of that action, thinking he could control whatever you could unleash," she said. "Arrogance and regret usually travel together."

"He shouldn't have done that," I said, my voice grim. "That was a mistake."

She shook her head.

"It was a choice, one he made of his own volition. It was a calculated gambit," she said, glancing over at where Julien stood frozen in time. "He underestimated how much rage and power you and Mage Montague could possess. A major oversight for an Archmage, don't you think?"

"I don't know," I said, not understanding where she was going with this. "Earlier, I warned him not to hurt Peaches, and he made it seem like he killed him. What did he *think* would happen? That I would let that go?"

"It was clear he miscalculated," she said. "Now, I will explain why I am here, and not Karma."

"Is she coming?"

Badb Catha gave me a hard look.

"Today, you will have to make a difficult choice, *Splinter*," she said, motioning to the scene in front of us with an arm. "If that orb continues on its course—and it will—it will undo the Archmage and this entire plane, along with everyone within."

"That would be bad."

"No, not bad or good. It would be the consequence of the Archmage's actions by provoking one who bears the burden of causality," she said. "There is always a cause and effect. Do you understand this concept?"

"What are you saying?" I asked, barely able to form the words. "I have to decide if Julien lives or dies?"

"As you said, everything has a cost," she said. "You have to decide if you *all* live or die."

She let the words hang in the air for a few seconds.

"I'm not letting Monty and Peaches die."

"This is not in parcels," she said, glancing at Monty. "If one survives, you all must. All your fates are intertwined in this outcome."

"What is the cost?"

She turned to face me.

"You were concerned for the youngling, the one my love calls Peanut," she said. "Do you remember your conversation with him? About her future?"

"You heard that?"

"My hearing is exceptional," she said. "*That* is the cost."

"Peanut is the cost?"

She shifted the spear in her hand as I winced, bracing myself for another whack. She sighed and shook her head.

"You will take her place when the time comes, Marked of Kali," she said. "When I call upon you, you will serve."

An expression of shock crossed my face, and anger rose in my chest.

This was another ploy, another game played by another god—goddess, in this case. The rage slowly bubbled to the surface, but I kept it in check. Any fear I felt earlier, evaporated.

All I felt now was a deep fury.

"I don't think Kali will be a fan of my serving you," I said cautiously, taking my life into my own hands with each word. I may have been angry, but I wasn't going to do something stupid like piss her off for no reason. I would wait until I had a good reason—and then I would piss her off. "No offense, but she's pretty territorial with the people she curses."

"Do you speak for the goddess?"

I knew a trap when I smelled one. If I dared to say yes, the odds of Kali paying me a visit sooner rather than later shot up astronomically.

That sounded like a conversation I wanted to avoid.

"Absolutely not," I said. "It's an educated guess based on her past actions."

"I understand," she said with a solemn nod. "You have no desire to anger your goddess. That is wise."

"That is called staying alive, and no, I don't want to piss off Kali," I said. "Have you met her? Getting on her bad side is a good way to cut your life short. No, thanks."

"Then it is a good thing I conferred with your goddess before this moment."

"You... What?" I said as my stunned brain reeled. She had spoken to Kali? "When?"

She tapped her spear on the ground, and an enormous golden endless knot formed on the ground beneath us both.

"Do you recognize her mark?"

I saw that the mark on the back of my hand glowed with the same golden energy. Somehow this felt deeper, as if the symbol on the ground lent weight to the words being spoken right now.

I raised my hand in response, letting her see my mark.

"It's familiar."

"This, then, is your choice," she said, staring into my eyes. "Agree to serve me for a limited time of one cycle, when the time comes. If you agree, I will spare Mage Montague, Archmage Julien, the Scion of Cerberus, and the plane they currently inhabit. Refuse me, and I shall allow you to fend for yourselves. It will not end well. What say you?"

I'd had had a feeling something like this was coming—I just hadn't expected it from her. Hades, maybe, but not Badb Catha.

"I have terms."

She smiled.

It was a wicked thing, but filled with a grudging respect.

"State your terms, Kali-marked."

"Everyone, human and hellhound, leaves the plane alive with no lasting effects or reduction in power."

She nodded.

"On your word," I said. "Swear it."

"On my word," she replied. "Everyone, human and hellhound alike, shall leave this plane as they entered—whole and undamaged."

"I'm not done," I said, raising a finger. "Peanut is allowed to choose, free of your influence. If she wants to grow up to be something else besides your assassin, she is free to do so without any influence from *any* of your three aspects."

"Done," she said, her voice holding an ancient menace. "Is there anything *else*?"

"Fifty years of service, with autonomy and veto power in my assignments," I said. "I may be agreeing to this to save those I care about, but I'm not your slave or assassin, and I have no intention of becoming either. We work together. I don't work *for* you. I work *with* you."

She stared at me for a full five seconds with an expression of mild shock.

"Do you understand whom you are addressing?" she said. "I could kill you a thousand times over with a mere thought."

"You could," I said, looking down at Kali's symbol, "but I'm pretty sure *that* would piss off *my* goddess."

"She warned me of your insolence."

"Who? Kali?"

"Who else?"

"You should've listened to her," I said and risked it all. "There's just two more things—"

"*Two more things?*" she echoed as the energy around us increased to massive proportions, threatening to drive me to my knees. "You expect me to agree to *two more* things?"

"Last items, I promise," I said, raising up a hand in surrender. "*I* determine when I start my service. I know how you gods are. You swoop in whenever you want, expecting complete subservience. That's not going to happen. I have a life and a family to care for. Stepping away to work with you puts them in danger. I need to make sure they're safe before I take a fifty-year leave of absence."

"And the *other* condition?"

"Peaches and me are a package deal," I said. "He goes where I go, or this whole deal is off."

"What of Mage Montague?" she asked. "Do you speak for him as well?"

"No," I said, glancing at Monty. "There's no way I can

speak for him in this situation. If he wants to join me, he should be free to do so of his own free will without any outside influence."

"It would almost be easier to blast you to atoms," she said under her breath. "Have you no fear? No respect for power? You are facing a goddess."

"I know what you are," I said, keeping my voice even. "I don't know *who* you are. Most of the gods I've interacted with have lacked a sense of honor and integrity. Plus, it would be beyond foolish of me to take you at your word, no matter how much power you have."

"I have enough power to render you mad with minimal effort. You would be wise to heed that and respect it."

"I respect power," I said, my voice grim. "It's those who wield it that have to *earn* my respect. I don't fear the presence of power. Those who abuse it need to be confronted and stopped."

"By you?" she asked, staring at me. "You think *you* can?"

"Just because you—or any god or goddess—has power, doesn't give you the right to bully those who are less powerful," I said. "I learned that from a wise young girl. Those are my conditions. What say you?"

I saw her mentally count to ten, take a deep breath, let out a long sigh, and then do it again.

If she proposed these terms, she wanted me for something unique.

If she agreed to my conditions, it meant I had leverage to use in the future.

It also meant I had to be careful about how she could manipulate me into working with her. I had tried to cover all the loopholes in the pact, but she was an ancient and clever goddess who had somehow planned for this with Kali at some point.

Talk about playing the long game.

I would need to have a long conversation with TK about working with the Morrigan, if I survived all of this.

Badb Catha stared at me in silence for a few moments more and then slowly nodded.

"Very well," she said, shocking me. "I have heard your conditions and agree to them."

"All of them?" I asked, still shocked. "What if I want to make amendments? Revise some of the terms? Is that allowed? Can I make changes later on?"

"It would be difficult to do so when you're a pile of dust."

"Just checking."

"Let us seal this pact," she said, extending a hand. "The power of the stormblood and the First Elder Rune still courses through you. Form the darkflame."

My mind raced as I thought over all the points of the agreement. I couldn't find any loopholes, but part of me was screaming that this was a monumental mistake.

I didn't see any other way to save them. Fifty years working with her seemed a small price to pay for the lives of my family. Julien, on the other hand, would owe me big time.

I formed the darkflame and clasped her hand.

TWENTY

Pain.

The word didn't even begin to describe what I was feeling when she gripped my arm. Badb Catha transformed, her eyes becoming jet black as she morphed through her three personifications. With every change she remained staring at me with those bottomless eyes, and kept her grip on my forearm as the darkflame covered both our arms.

Violet, red, and black energy rose from her body and swirled around us in an energy tornado as she spoke ancient words I couldn't hope to understand. She closed her eyes for a few seconds, and then stared at me again.

"Prepare, Simon Strong," she said. "This will be pain."

"Will be?" I said, looking down at my arm. "What do you mean, 'will be'?"

She closed her eyes again, whispered some more words, and then gave a command. I swore it was the command to burn, because that's exactly what my arm started doing when she opened her eyes again.

The darkflame remained concentrated on my hand,

burning it, and then slowly crept up my arm, stopping at my elbow.

Every inch of skin it covered felt like it was being peeled off with a dull blade. Tears streamed down my face, but I couldn't form a scream—the pain was so intense, it robbed me of breath.

Once the darkflame stopped advancing, it moved inward. The feeling of small daggers burrowing into my skin hit me with a suddenness that shocked me. I looked down, but only saw the darkflame covering my arm.

I wanted to let go at that point, but she held me tight. Her grip was insane—it would have been easier to use Ebonsoul to remove my arm at the shoulder than to break her grip.

It moved from cutting deep to a deeper burning, like dipping my arm in a bath of fluroantimonic acid. This time, I was certain she was going to leave me either with the section of my arm—from my elbow to my hand—missing, or a gory mess that would need to be amputated when she was done.

I think I screamed then.

It was hard to tell, because my brain had checked out from the sensory overload. I realized after a few more seconds that some of the burning I was feeling was my curse working on overdrive as Badb Catha "sealed" the pact.

As she completed the sealing, a part of my brain knew I would have died if it wasn't for Kali's curse, and that Badb Catha knew it was the only way I could survive this pact.

Her conversation with Kali had been deeper than she let on.

A few seconds later, she nodded, reverting back to the version of herself she had been when she arrived. I saw the darkflame sink into my arm, slowly revealing another endless knot. This one matched the knot on my other hand, but pulsed with darkflame.

That was going to get some attention.

"This is Kali's mark," I said, examining my hand as she released my arm. "Are you saying she had something to do with this?"

"She has had something to do with your life from the moment she cursed you, Kali-marked," Badb Catha said. "I lay no claim over you without her consent. Even now, with this pact and sealing, it goes according to her designs."

"You're saying she *planned* all of this?"

"No, I'm saying she saw the opportunity for her Marked One to become more, and allowed it to occur," she said. "You have now absorbed this darkflame—a merging of the power of the stormblood and the First Elder Rune. A truly formidable weapon, greater than the sum of its parts. Very much like Mage Montague, you, and your hellhound."

"You could have killed me."

"Indeed."

"You continued anyway?"

"Yes. It was my understanding that the curse you possess would sustain you through the trial of the pact," she said. "It appears I was correct, since you are still alive."

"You took a major risk. What if you had blasted me to dust?"

She gave me another of her chilling smiles.

"Life is risk. I thought you had learned this by now, especially given the circumstances you find yourself in currently."

The realization of Kali's involvement collided into me gently, like a ten-ton truck. Kali knew Badb Catha would have to seal the pact, and she knew there was a possibility I could die in the process.

She consented anyway. I filed that thought away for the future.

It would make for an interesting topic for our conversation, the next time Kali and I spoke.

"Kali knew you would do this, didn't she?"

"It was a risk she was prepared to take," Badb Catha said. "Would you like to spend more time with the recriminations of your goddess, or shall I honor my side of our pact?"

"How exactly are you going to do that?" I asked. It was always best to get the details when dealing with gods. "Honor your end of the pact, I mean."

"It's quite simple actually. I need to unravel this impending disaster before it crosses the threshold of captured time."

"What does that even mean?"

"You pressed your mark within this plane."

"I did," I said—and then a thought hit me. "Did she know I would do that?"

"*Know* is a strong word," she said. "I would say she took an educated guess based on your past actions."

"What did pressing my mark do? Besides create a portal for you to come here, that is."

She nodded approvingly.

"Well done. Pressing your mark allowed me to pinpoint your exact location, and then it was only a matter of diverting Karma, while I took her place."

"Diverting Karma," I said, mostly to myself. "I didn't even think that was possible."

"You'll hear all about it when you speak to her next, I'm sure."

"What else did I do by pressing my mark?" I asked. "Did I break time?"

She gave me a look and shook her head.

"Aside from creating a pathway to you, it also caused a temporal paradox," she said, melting my brain further. Part of my brain wished for the simpler days, when it was only Professor Ziller and his theories that liquified my brain. "I must act before the threshold of captured time is breached."

"It would be excellent if you could explain that in words I understood."

"You stopped time in a plane of time dilation and contraction," she said, giving me a look that told me to get with the program. "We are in a pocket of captured time. The time of this plane is accelerated in comparison with your plane. Do you understand this?"

"So far I'm following you," I said, barely grasping the concepts. "Are you saying this is a conflict?"

"Of epic proportions, if I don't realign you with this plane."

"This realigning," I said, giving it a moment of thought. "How bad is the pain?"

She nodded.

"Good. You are learning, Kali-marked," she said with a smile. "It will be excruciating. Are you ready?"

"No, wait," I said. "Can I have the non-excruciating option? The one that bypasses the excruciating part?"

"No," she said. "Ironically, we have no more time. I must remove your entropic dissolution before the Archmage is undone."

I looked down at my newly enhanced darkflame arm.

"Will I be able to control this power?"

"That…depends on you," she said. "We must return now. Remain still and gird yourself."

She grabbed hold of her spear, took a step back, and thrust it straight up in the air in a two-handed move. She took a brief moment to look at me, and then brought the spear down straight at my head as if to cut me in half.

I'd like to say I stood there unwavering, but that would've been an enormous lie. I raised both hands and screamed as the blade of the spear sliced through the air, aimed at the top of my head.

It never made contact.

One moment I was looking at certain death, the next I stood in the blasted-out arena with Monty and Julien, behind a massive amount of defensive casts. I looked around, but I didn't see Badb Catha.

I felt some minor pain, but nothing like I expected.

Until she arrived.

She appeared a second later, in front of the darkflame orb, just as it had punched through the first of the silver outer walls Julien had created.

She wrapped a hand around the orb and it expanded for a few seconds. I realized it was trying to consume her energy. Her face remained impassive as she let the orb drain black energy from her.

Then she smiled while gazing at me.

I realized how fearsome she really was and how close I was to a true death. She was the goddess of death—even the death of an entropic dissolution.

As the orb tried to absorb her energy, she closed her fingers around it, forming a fist. All around her, I felt the energy vanish. It didn't just dissipate; it was gone, erased.

She stood in the center of a void of energy.

The orb began to shrink, until with a *whoosh*, it disappeared.

Seconds after that the stormblood disappeared. Even the sea grew dim and calmed. All of the violent energy of the plane had been controlled or transformed.

That's when every muscle in my body spasmed, and I fell to the ground in agony. Monty ran over to where I lay and cast a golden lattice over my body. Julien gestured as a silver cloud of energy descended on my body, taking away some of the pain.

I tried to speak, but nothing was cooperating. All I ended up making was a mix of grunts and groans.

"Don't try to speak," Julien said. "This is part of the cast.

The darkflame is receding from you, and your body is feeling the brunt of the cost."

My body flared with heat as my curse began to heal me. Badb Catha walked over to where I lay and placed a hand on my head, causing my muscles to unlock.

I was able to relax and breathe normally.

It took several minutes, but slowly the torture-fest of muscle contractions calmed down. Badb Catha gazed at me, nodded and then tapped me on the head with her spear.

A surge of energy flowed through me and I almost felt normal again. I sat up on the ground and slowly shook my head, taking stock of how I felt and making sure nothing was permanently damaged besides my ego.

These pain sessions were getting old fast.

Badb Catha then turned to Julien and Monty.

"Today your lives have been spared because of the Kali-marked's actions."

Julien mouthed *Kali-marked* to Monty, who pointed at me.

"He saved us?" Julien said, staring and pointing at me with barely contained anger. "He was the one who put us in this predicament to begin with!"

"Was he?" Badb Catha asked, looking at Julien. All the fight left him as he stared into her eyes. "*He* was the cause of your near destruction? Are you certain of that, *Archmage?*"

Julien remained silent for a few seconds, and then shook his head.

"No," he said finally. "The fault, if there is any to be placed, is mine and mine alone."

Badb Catha nodded.

"This plane is unstable, and you will need to leave it shortly," she said. "I will stabilize it in your absence." She gave me a glance. "I have given my word that this plane shall be saved, and so it will."

"Thank you," Julien said with a short nod. "It would have

been impossible to preserve everything in this plane on my own. My sect will be grateful it has been preserved."

"If you are to offer thanks, then offer them to the Kali-marked," she said, glancing at me. "I am merely fulfilling my end of the pact we have formed."

"Pact?" Monty said, his voice laced with concern as he looked my way. "What pact? You entered into a pact with her?"

"You take issue with this, Mage Montague?"

"I would like to know what the terms are, goddess," Monty said, keeping his tone respectful, even though I could tell he wasn't happy. "Some deities have been known to be less than forthright when it comes to pacts."

"Are you accusing me of deceit?"

"Never, goddess," Monty said. "I am only concerned for my bond brother. A pact with a goddess of such power as yours is no light matter."

"Well said, mage," she answered. "He is not bound to secrecy. Ask him. He will be able to tell you of the pact and of my vast generosity in acquiescing to his many excessive demands."

"I'll explain it later," I said, looking at Badb Catha as I slowly and unsteadily got to my feet. "We were here to prepare for Keeper Gault. We need to stop him."

"Do you feel unprepared to face the Keeper?" she asked.

"Right now, I feel like I've been mauled by an angry ogre," I said with a groan as I moved my body. "I couldn't even face an Arcanist in this condition, much less a Keeper."

"Yet you must…eventually."

"How?" I said. "It's not like I'm going to unleash another one of those entropic dissolving orbs at him, putting everything and everyone in danger."

"You have the darkflame." She looked down at my arm. "As well as Ebonsoul and the nullifying palm. What more can the Archmage give you that you do not currently possess?"

"The what?" I said. "The what palm? Come again?"

"The nullifying palm," Monty said. "That is the third palm."

Badb Catha glanced at Julien before speaking.

"His purpose was to help you unlock the power you had access to with the stormblood and the First Elder Rune," she said. "His methods leave much to be desired, but he did manage his objective."

"I thought Monty was supposed to access the power," I said. "He's the mage, not me."

"This is power available to you *both*," she said. "It came easier to you because you lack a mage's strict control. Mage Montague can access the darkflame and the nullifying palm; he only has to want to. You acted out of vengeance, which is why you acquired them the way you did. I would suggest some actual training now, to harness the power effectively."

"I saw no evidence of the nullifying palm," Julien said. "How did he exhibit its use?"

"I understand. You were preoccupied with your imminent demise," she said. "Think back to that moment when you buried your blade into the ground and sent a wave of energy at the Kali-marked. How was it stopped?"

I thought back to the moment.

Julien had slammed his blade into the ground, point first. A shockwave of energy exploded across the arena. I had done the first thing that came to mind: I had driven a palm into the ground, stopping the energy wave, and continued moving forward.

The only thing on my mind at that moment was ending Julien.

"He stopped it," Monty said. "He placed a palm on the ground and the energy wave stopped as if it didn't exist."

"A nullifying palm," Julien said in disbelief. "How did I miss it? I didn't teach it to him. How did he learn it?"

"In a way, you did," she said. "You drove him to the brink of madness and then pushed him past it. Now, we don't have much time. This plane is still unstable, and I would rather work uninterrupted. You will be sent back to the Archmage's home."

"How long will this plane remain unstable?" Julien asked as the ground around us began to brighten. "I will need to report this instability to my sect."

"This plane will be available to you in one day's time," she said. "Do not attempt to enter before then."

"Thank you," Julien said with a bow. "You have my gratitude."

"I do not require your thanks, Archmage," she said. "The next time you choose to use despair and rage as a catalyst, think deeply on the consequences you may face. The next time you may not be so fortunate. It may cost you...everything."

"I shall," Julien said. "Thank you for your wisdom."

"Wait!" I said, stepping away from the glowing area on the ground. "My hellhound! I can't leave here without him."

"He has been sent ahead," she said. "Search your bond and know I speak truth."

I felt for Peaches, and though I felt him through our bond, he wasn't close.

I nodded and stepped next to Monty.

"Kali-marked," Badb Catha said, looking at me. "I cast you into the jaws of danger not because I wish you harm, but because even the strongest blade must be tempered, first in the heat of the forge, and then later, on the field of battle. I shall be watching, as will others."

"What does that even—?"

A red flash blinded me as Badb Catha and the plane disappeared from sight. When the flash slowly faded away, we were in the Foundry library again, standing in front of the fireplace doorway.

We were wearing our original clothing, our training robes gone. It felt good to be in normal clothing again. I saw Monty pull on a sleeve, and then noticed something faintly glowing over the left side of his chest.

A silver fleur de lis was softly pulsing on his Zegna suit.

I was about to comment on the addition when I became victim to a major pounce by my enormous hellhound. He nearly knocked me over, and I felt that if he wanted to, he probably could.

I dropped down to the ground and gave him a massive hug, letting him slobber all over me as he rubbed his head into my face and chest.

Before the threat of drowning in hellhound slobber became a serious issue, I pushed him away and gave him a once-over. When I was certain he wasn't injured, I hugged him again, rubbing his massive head behind the ears.

<I thought I lost you, boy.>

<You can never lose me. I am your bondmate.>

<Are you okay? Are you hurt?>

<No, I have eaten much meat. Which is why I am strong. You feel stronger too. Have you been eating meat?>

He stepped close and sniffed me, then padded over to Monty and did the same. Chuffing after he had smelled Monty, he padded back to me.

<You and the angry man are both stronger. It is the same and different. What did you do?>

<Once I figure it all out, I'll let you know.>

"I think I know what the goddess meant with her words about you, Strong," Julien said. "We have company."

Claude raced into the library looking a bit worse for wear.

"Who is it?" Julien asked, maintaining his calm. "Who dares attack my home?"

"Arcanists and the Sword of the Tribunal," Claude said. "They arrived here shortly after you left."

"Together?"

"No—the Arcanists came first, and then Korin arrived with force."

"I see," Julien said, looking out into the afternoon sun through one of the windows. "And the defenses?"

"They will hold for some time but not indefinitely," Claude answered. "This Korin is formidable and unrelenting. It does not appear she will stop."

"Drop the outer defenses," Julien said. "I would have words with the emissary of the High Tribunal."

"She will attack you," Claude said. "She has not listened to reason and the Arcanists support her. It is too dangerous."

"Claude, I have had a trying two days and have nearly lost my life in the process," Julien said with an edge to his voice. "Drop the outer defenses, and please escort Mage Montague and Strong to the hidden exit on the south side. I will determine what kind of a threat Korin presents."

"Oui, seigneur," Claude said with a bow, then looked up sharply. "The south side,? But that leads to—?"

"I am aware of where it leads," Julien said. "Take them."

"He will be most displeased," Claude said. "Are you certain?"

"I've been gone, at most, an hour of your time," Julien replied, his voice calm but laced with as much warmth as an arctic winter. "You question my directives?"

"No!" Claude said with a deep bow. "I wish to see no harm befall you."

"And none will," Julien said, tapping Claude on the shoulder softly. "Drop the outer defenses and escort these honorary members of the Fleur de Lis to the south exit. They saved my life even when I threatened them with death."

Claude slowly looked at Monty and me with barely suppressed awe.

"They...saved you?" he asked. "How?"

"It was due to my own foolishness," Julien said, waving Claude's words away. "I will explain after we deal with our *guests*."

"We can fight," I said, flexing my fingers. "We can help."

Julien shook his head and gazed out of the window again as a blast of violet energy crashed into the side of the Foundry. That blast was followed by a rapid succession of smaller blasts.

"You must go," Julien said. "I will delay Korin to give you some much-needed time."

"Those blasts sounded dangerous," I said, following his gaze out of the window with my own. "We can stop her."

"You will have to, but not here and not now," Julien said. "You are one blast away from collapsing, and Mage Montague is barely standing as it is. You need to rest."

"So do you," I countered. "I know you're an Archmage, but—"

"I may be spent, but I am not powerless, especially not in my own home," Julien said and smiled. "Allow me to do this for you both. It is the least I can do for what you have given me. Go now. Please. Claude, take them."

Claude motioned, leading us out of the library at a run.

TWENTY-ONE

"Korin is attacking the Foundry?" I asked as we headed downstairs. "With Arcanists?"

"More importantly," Monty said, "we've only been gone an hour, Claude?"

"*Oui* to both," Claude said, moving fast as we descended to the lower levels of the Foundry. I could hear another series of blasts hit the building. "This way, please. Hurry!"

He led us to a long, narrow corridor. It was only wide enough for us to travel single file behind Claude. He moved quickly down the passageway, touching sections of the corridor as we ran.

"What's he doing?" I asked Monty who was running in front of me. "Why does he keep touching the walls?"

"He's disabling the defenses and making sure we're going in the right direction," Monty said. "Where does the south-side exit lead, and what are all these tunnels?"

"The exit leads to safety for you; the tunnels are for *Seigneur* Julien to explain. Faster, please."

Claude went silent and kept moving, picking up the pace.

I was thinking that the man was in amazing shape when he came to a stop before a narrow door.

The door resembled the front door of the Foundry. It was covered in silver runes that I couldn't read. I sensed familiar energy behind the door, but it was a subtle thing—like remembering a dream, only to have it fly away from your mind a second later.

Claude began touching several of the runes in sequence, leaving a silver trail on the surface of the door. A few seconds later, all of the runes he had touched pulsed a bright silver three times at once.

Claude nodded.

"The exit is ready," he said. "I must get back. Please accept our apologies for the short notice. *Seigneur* Julien will contact you at his earliest convenience. Now, you must go."

Monty opened the door into a swirling silver cloud that obscured everything beyond it. He stepped through and disappeared.

I was about to follow when Claude placed a hand on my shoulder.

"One moment," Claude said. "I will speak with you."

"Claude, I'm not really in the mood to dance with you right now," I said, turning to face him and letting my hand rest on Grim Whisper. "We can set up an appointment to pound on each other another day, but right now, I need—"

"*Merci*, Strong," he said, holding up a hand. "For saving my seigneur."

"He didn't deserve being undone, though he *did* try to kill me first."

Claude nodded.

"*Je comprends*. He can be a difficult man, but he is good"— he tapped his heart—"in here. So I say, *merci beaucoup*—thank you. I am in your debt."

When someone like Claude takes a moment to tell you

they're in your debt, you do the honorable thing and let them say their piece, adding and taking nothing from it, especially when it's someone who doesn't like you, but has acquired a grudging respect for you.

This wasn't the time to be petty, but the temptation was strong.

"I hope you never have to repay that debt, Claude," I said with a nod. "You should get back."

"And you should get going," he said. "*Adieu*, Strong."

I stepped into the silver cloud with Peaches by my side and into a room filled with armed women dressed in a skintight black-and-white checkered costume. Their faces were hidden behind black masks. Their masks were a combination of tragedy and comedy.

All of them held glowing rune covered tonfas, and all of them looked ready to strike.

I was standing in the Hellfire Club.

Specifically I was in a large recreation room with several pool tables, a large and fully stocked library that covered two entire walls, and several small tables with wingback chairs around them.

In front of one of the walls not covered by books sat a large sofa that looked comfortable enough to double as a bed.

The room was spacious, yet felt cozy at the same time. It probably had something to do with the subdued lighting and the soft music playing in the background with Sade asking me if something was a crime.

All of the Harlequins—and I counted ten of them, easily—were ready to introduce me to the tonfa tango. I raised my hand and kept Peaches close as I looked around for Erik or Monty.

"Stand down," I heard Erik's voice. "It's Strong."

All of the Harlequins eased in their stances and slowly made for the exit. I turned slowly to look at a scowling Erik.

He was wearing the usual mageiform: black suit, gray shirt, black tie and black shoes. Everything was impeccably arranged and shone with the latent power of deep violet runes.

"Hey, Erik," I said. "How are things? Is that Sade on the sound system? Good choice. Very mellow and jazzy."

"Have you lost your mind?" Erik asked.

"What are you talking about?"

"You have assassins after you and you're in here asking about the music?"

"I did start with, 'How are things?'" I said. "But you want to go from zero to sixty in 1.2 seconds. Fine. Seen any mage assassins looking to eliminate Monty and me lately? Is that better than 'How are things?'"

"How are things?" he said with a dark look. "Let me tell you what I told Tristan. What in the actual hell are you doing?"

I kept my hands in the air and glanced to the sides.

"Right now? I'm standing in your club with a mage going ballistic," I said, slowly looking around and wondering if any Harlequins had decided to hide in a corner, ready to pounce. "Is that a trick question? What do you mean what am I doing?"

"The Foundry is under attack," he said. "Do you know how serious that is? And lower your hands. I'm not going to attack you."

I lowered my hands slowly and took in the room again.

"I have an idea, but maybe you can tell me why you're so upset?" I asked, keeping my voice calm. "Where's Monty?"

"In the training area, working on something he calls the darkflame," Erik snapped. "You both look like shit, and should be strapped down in Haven."

"I know you have some interesting clientele with peculiar

tastes, but I'm not into being strapped down, not even at Haven."

"All I have to do is make one call to Haven, and Roxanne will have the both of you on lockdown so fast it would make a teleportation look positively glacial by comparison."

"That would be a bad idea," I said. "Are you serious? Do you really want Monty pissed at you for putting her and Haven in danger? You yourself said we have assassins after us. Your solution is having us tied down in Haven?"

"For that reason, and that reason alone, I'm not on a phone with her right now," he said. "The last thing I need is Tristan after me for putting her in danger."

I nodded.

"Besides, you know she can't help herself," I said. "If she finds out what kind of shape Monty is in, she will try to lock him down—and we are kind of in the middle of something."

"That *something* have anything to do with the Sword of the Tribunal attacking Julien at the Foundry, along with a small army of Arcanists?"

"Does *everyone* know this Sword of the Tribunal?" I asked. "What? Is she a famous celebrity mage? Do celebrity mages exist? Is that a thing?"

"You're not appreciating how deep in the abyss you and Tristan are," Erik answered, his voice dark. "She's not famous, she's infamous—and with good reason. Korin is an accomplished and powerful mage and assassin. She works directly for the High Tribunal."

"They're not exactly fans at the moment."

"She's also targeted you and Tristan," he said, "For capture and erasure, and not necessarily in that order."

"She targeted us, or the High Tribunal did?"

"You're not paying attention. It's the same thing," he said. "She executes the will of the Tribunal. She is their Sword. They don't quit, they don't stop, and they don't like to lose."

"Then they should've left Monty and me alone," I said, letting menace creep into my voice. "Julien sent us here—why? He must've had a reason for that. Why did he send us here to you at the Hellfire Club?"

"Because I can get you to safety," he said with sigh. "At least long enough to let you recuperate before Korin catches up with you again."

"Did we bring destruction to your home?"

"Oh, *now* you're concerned?" Erik asked. "After all this time, now that you pissed off the High Tribunal and a Keeper, *now* you want to know if you brought destruction to my home. That's really touching, really. It's hitting me in all the feels."

"Did we?" I asked again. "I'm serious, Erik."

"It's nothing I can't deal with," he said with another sigh, running his hand through his hair. "I lead the mages in the Dark Council. Verity won't act against me. It's why Julien sent you here. You're safe...for now."

"But it won't last."

"No, it won't," he said. "You need to remove one of these threats. If I were you, I'd choose Korin. The Keeper is out of your league...way out of your league."

"Speaking of the Dark Council—"

"She's fine," he said. "You should reach out to her, especially now that you've done... What exactly *have* you done to yourself?"

I explained about the merging of the stormblood and the First Elder Rune.

"You *should* be dead," he said when I had finished. "Both of you should."

"That's going to be a little difficult on my end."

He stared at me for a few seconds and shook his head.

"No one should be able to harness that much energy and not explode from the runic backlash. How are you still alive?"

"I don't think I have access to all of the energy," I said, giving it thought. "Monty must have access, too, since we share both the stormblood and the First Elder Rune."

"You're both insane," he said, shaking his head. "This is too much energy even for a Montague, much less for you."

I heard the unspoken implication and ignored him.

I knew I wasn't a mage and so did everyone else. Those who mattered in my life didn't care, and those who cared about my non-mage status didn't matter to me.

"I'm not arguing," I said. "Do you think you could get a word to Chi?"

"To Michiko, you mean? The *Director* of the *entire* Dark Council?"

"Yes, Chi," I said. "Can you get her a message?"

"Oh, but of course," he said with a deep bow. "I live to serve the amazing Simon Strong."

"No need to pour it on so thick," I said. "It's a simple message, and the chances are you'll see her before I do."

"True," he said with a nod. "By the time you see her, an army of Arcanists will be chasing you to blast you and Tristan apart, provided you live through whatever Korin has planned for you both. Leave it to you and Tristan to get those two groups to work together. The High Tribunal never works with the Keepers of the Arcana."

"Until now."

He nodded.

"Until now," he said. "I don't know if I should be impressed or if I should pity you. What is the message?"

"Tell her I think Ebonsoul is awake."

"You think Ebonsoul is awake?" he asked. "Isn't Ebonsoul your—?"

"Yes. I think it may be waking up."

"That would be a very bad thing, Strong. Are you sure of this?"

"Pretty sure, yes."

"Pretty sure?" he asked. "What does that mean?"

"I'm pretty sure it spoke to me, but I can't be certain unless it happens again."

"We don't want that to happen again," he said, raising his voice. "This is bad...bad. Fuck!"

Monty walked into the room.

TWENTY-TWO

"Did you know of this?" Erik asked, still raising his voice as it filled with frustration and anger. "Did you know his blade is speaking to him?"

"I assumed that to be the case," Monty said matter-of-factly. "That command you used on Julien was beyond your caliber of power."

"What command?" Erik asked. "What did he use? And did you just say against Julien? You faced off against Julien? *Archmage* Julien?"

"There were...extenuating circumstances," I said. "Yes, Archmage Julien."

Monty nodded.

"What was the command?" Erik said.

"Simon?" Monty said. "Would you like to share it, or should I?"

"I don't want to take the chance. You tell him."

Monty cleared his throat and slipped into professor mode.

"Simon—during the merger of the stormblood and the First Elder Rune—tapped into a deeper power, one which I can only assume is the latent power of Ebonsoul. Once he found the path to this power, Ebonsoul was able to communicate with him. Mind you, I say Ebonsoul, but I'm fairly certain it's some part of the essence of Izanami, the goddess inhabiting Darkspirit—Grey's sword."

"This just keeps getting worse," Erik almost whispered. "What was the command?"

"She must have instructed him on a variation of his magic-missile cast—*ignis vitae*," Monty said. "That cast, while powerful—"

"Can be neutralized," Erik finished, "but that wasn't the cast he used, was it?"

"No. As I said—prompted by whatever entity resides within Ebonsoul, he was given a new command, something significantly more potent."

"Tristan, I swear if you don't get to the damned point, I will blast you myself," Erik said, exasperated. "What was the command?"

"*Mors ignis*," Monty said. "He used *mors ignis*."

Erik stared at me dumbfounded.

"Impossible," he said once he recovered. "You must've misheard. That cast would have shredded him where he stood."

"You would think so," Monty said, glancing at me. "But he seems to be completely unshredded to me."

"He's nowhere near strong enough to withstand that cast," Erik said, shaking his head. "Even *I* can't execute that cast—no offense meant, Strong. Tristan must be mistaken."

"I had the same thought," Monty said. "Surely I must have been mistaken. He couldn't have possibly just used a *mors ignis*..."

"A *mors ignis* cast is the catalyst for an entropic—"

"Dissolution," Monty finished. "Yes, I am aware. Given that I never taught him this cast, nor did Julien, it stands to reason that the information arrived to him by unconventional means."

"Ebonsoul?" Erik asked. "Is it trying to *kill* him?"

"I'm sure there are more efficient ways of achieving that outcome," Monty said. "Failing to materialize when facing an enemy would be chief among them. No, Ebonsoul tapped into his rage and desire for vengeance. I know this, because I shared these same emotions with Simon. Our only goal in that moment was Julien's demise."

"You *both* faced off against an Archmage...and survived?" Erik asked, incredulous. "How?"

"We worked together and Simon, in addition to using the darkflame, managed to wield the nullifying palm," Monty said, glancing at me. "Quite effectively, I might add."

"The what?" Erik said. "I've never heard of a nullifying palm."

"That is not surprising," Monty said. "It was a cast designed by Mage Santiago—a forbidden technique."

"Can you show me this nullifying palm?" Erik asked. "Why hasn't this technique been documented?"

Monty remained silent for a few seconds.

"I will show you the outcome, but I will not share this technique, as it's too dangerous to do so," Monty said. "Can you abide by those conditions?"

"Too dangerous?" Erik scoffed. "Even for me?"

"Even for you," Monty said, serious. "Those are my terms. Yes or no?"

"Yes," Erik said with a nod. The expression on his face told me he didn't believe this technique was as dangerous as Monty made it out to be. "I would like to see this nullifying palm in action."

"You sure about this, Monty?" I asked. "You have this?"

"I do," he said. "I won't draw on the darkflame, just the palm. It will be enough to inform Erik. However, you and your creature may want to step back a bit. There could be some backlash."

"Well, now I'm concerned," Erik said with a smile. "What do you want me to do? Should I close my eyes and count to ten while you prepare?"

"What is your strongest offensive cast?" Monty asked. "The obliteration cascade?"

Erik stared hard at Monty.

"I've never told anyone that," Erik said, narrowing his eyes at Monty. "Not even my Harlequins know. How did you—?"

"I pay attention," Monty said, stepping back until there was about four feet between them. "Am I correct?"

"Yes, but I can't use that against you," Erik said. "I just told Strong I wasn't sending you to Haven. If I use the cascade, you'll be out of commission for weeks, even if you somehow manage to avoid some of the circles. It's deadly."

"Perfect," Monty said with a nod. "Use it."

"Tristan, this isn't funny," Erik warned. "You can get seriously hurt, or worse."

"I assume full responsibility for my actions," Monty said. "Simon will act as my witness and can fully attest that being of sound mind and body, I requested your strongest cast. Simon?"

"Don't know about the soundness of either your mind or body, but you did request Erik's strongest cast," I said, agreeing. "Should I get Rox on the phone just in case she needs to port in?"

"No need," Monty said and focused on Erik. "Whenever you're ready, you may cast."

"This is a bad idea," Erik said. "The cascade is lethal."

"But you're curious and a mage," Monty said with a small smile. "Use the cascade."

"I have a feeling I'm going to regret this," Erik said. "Roxanne is going to kill me."

Monty stood absolutely still as Erik focused energy into his body. As he took a barely noticeable breath, Monty moved. I realized that's what Monty was waiting for—the breath was Erik's tell he was about to cast.

Monty stepped forward and pulled a Peaches, blinking out and then blinking back in behind Erik.

Erik turned around to face Monty, but it was too late.

Monty placed a hand covered in violet-and-black energy on Erik's chest and whatever cast Erik had started then stopped cold. Erik stood in a void of energy as shock and surprise crossed his face.

As Monty stepped back, he tried to gather energy, and failed several times.

"What did you do?" Erik asked. "I can't draw energy."

"I used the nullifying palm," Monty said. "You can witness its potency and the potential risks."

"It requires contact to be effective?"

"From my understanding so far, yes," Monty said. "Which necessitates proximity."

"Is there a cast it won't work against?"

"If the cast uses energy, it should work, no matter how potent," Monty said. "Actually, if my theory is correct, the stronger the cast, the more effective it should be at nullifying it."

"And Strong knows this palm?" Erik asked, glancing in my direction. "How?"

"It's a shared cast like our stormblood," Monty answered as he gestured. "We both have access to it."

Monty stepped close to Erik and placed his hand on his chest again. I felt the flow of energy flow in and around Erik. It had been as if Monty had placed Erik in a bubble of null energy and cut him off from the flow of energy around us.

Erik breathed out in a rush as the power filled him.

"I have to admit, that cast is beyond me," Erik said. "This is not negomancy—I don't even know *what* it is. What have you two become?"

"I don't know," I said, shaking my head. "I think—"

"Together, with his hellhound, the three of us have become an Archmage," Monty said. "That's what we have become."

"This is why Verity wants to destroy you three," Erik said. "We need to get you some place safe tonight."

"We aren't staying here?" I asked. "I thought we were safe here."

"Are you insane? You three shine like a sun at midnight," Erik said. "It will only be a matter of hours before Korin traces you here. You need to be gone by then."

"She can follow us here?"

"You really don't know what you're dealing with, do you?"

I shook my head.

"Enlighten me," I said. "What makes her so dangerous?"

"Have you ever heard of Corbel, the Hound of Hades?" Erik asked.

"Yes," I said. "We've met."

"The rumors are that no one escapes the Hound of Hades. No one. He can find you wherever you go, and I mean wherever, even if it's off-plane. He *will* find you."

"What does that have to do with Korin?"

"Before she joined the High Tribunal as their Sword, she worked for Corbel," Erik said. "He trained her for the High Tribunal at Hades' request. She's almost as good as the Hound. They call her the Gray Shadow, because you can't escape her, no matter how hard you try. It would be like trying to escape—"

"Like trying to escape your own shadow," I finished. "Well, shit. That's going to be a major problem."

"Bloody hell. This complicates things," Monty said under his breath. "We must abandon finding a safe space to hide, and look for a location to make a last stand."

"I can get you out of the Hellfire, but you need to have a destination in mind, or it's going to be a futile exercise," Erik said. "You can't run forever. Sooner or later she *will* find you."

"We don't intend on running forever," Monty said. "Just long enough to find a location that works for us."

TWENTY-THREE

Erik led us to a door on the other side of the sitting room.

"Do you have a destination in mind?" Erik asked as he pressed parts of the door in sequence. I didn't see any runes, but I figured the sequence was some kind of failsafe. "Do you have somewhere you can go that will buy you some time?"

"Yes," Monty said, his voice firm. "The Montague School of Battle Magic."

"The *what?*" Erik said, surprised. "There's no such school."

"What you used to know as the sect of the Golden Circle is now the Montague School of Battle Magic," Monty said. "We will go there to wait for Korin. If what you say about her is true, she *will* find us there."

"Has your entire family gone mad?" Erik asked. "The Council of Sects has declared war against Dexter. You don't just usurp the authority of an entire sect. There are rules, protocols, and procedure. He dismissed them all."

"My uncle is a difficult person to understand, but I do know one thing: he *will* stand with us," Monty said. "Can you say the same for the Dark Council?"

Erik looked away.

"You know the Dark Council won't stand against Verity or the High Tribunal," he said. "The costs outweigh the benefits."

"Where are those benefits going to be when Gault destroys the balance of magic on this plane?" I asked. "What will the Dark Council do then?"

"What we must to survive."

"You think *this* fight with Verity and the High Tribunal is serious?" I asked. "You're missing the point. While the Dark Council sits on the sidelines, Gault is rewriting the rules of the game. There's no neutrality in the coming battle. If you aren't fighting for Gault, you are his enemy and he *will* kill you."

"You don't know that," Erik said, pressing another section of the door. "If we get involved now, civil war within the Dark Council is guaranteed. If we remain neutral, we can maintain the order. You should surrender to the Dark Council. Let us solve this."

I stared at him. The words were familiar, but they added up to gibberish.

"Even you can't be this naive," Monty said. "The Dark Council will get swept up in the coming conflict. I would hate to meet you on the battlefield as an enemy, Erik."

Erik remained silent for a few seconds.

"I will speak to the Director," he said after his brief pause. "Perhaps she will see the prudence of your words."

"If she fails to enter the conflict of her own volition, the Dark Council will be forced to act against her wishes—that much I can guarantee," Monty warned. "If that happens, I advise you to leave this plane before it's too late."

I extended a hand to Erik.

"Thanks for everything," I said. "I really hope you choose

to fight with us. Gault is trying to bring The End. Don't be part of the reason he succeeds."

Erik took my hand and looked at me in surprise as the darkflame jumped from my arm to arc in the air between us.

"I hope we never have to meet as adversaries," he said, glancing at the darkflame, then turned to Monty. "The door is keyed to you, Tristan. It will take you wherever you need to go—even what was the Golden Circle, though it will be a bumpy ride getting in. Your uncle has increased the defenses around the sect entrance."

"Thank you, Erik," Monty said. "Speak to the Director and get her to see reason. Share what you learned today, and tell her we will be standing against Gault. We could use all the help we can get."

Erik nodded and stepped back.

We stepped through the door.

For the briefest of seconds, I thought we had gotten lost and ended up back on Julien's island. Then Peanut came racing at us.

"You're back!" she said. "Are you going to stay longer this time?"

She rubbed Peaches' massive head, and my ham of a hellhound enjoyed every second of it. I didn't say anything to discourage him, because going through the trauma of losing a bondmate—even if it was an illusion—had a way of putting things in perspective.

"Hello, Peanut," Monty said. "Can you direct me to my uncle?"

"He's in the main building," she said and pointed to a large structure. "He just had a meeting with some crusty old mages who were really angry. They came here ready to get into it, then they saw Uncle Dex's weapon and Aunt Mo's—well, just Aunt Mo—and they calmed down real quick. There was no fighting."

She said that last part with a dejected voice, and I couldn't help but smile.

"I'm sorry you didn't get to demonstrate your impressive abilities," Monty said. "How about this? I have to go speak to my uncle. Simon has learned a new cast; maybe you can help him refine it in the Ascendance arena?"

Her eyes lit up and I shot daggers at Monty.

"The last time I helped a child with a cast, she punched a hole in the Moscow," I said. "This sounds like a terrible idea."

"On the contrary," Monty said. "You need to start honing the nullifying palm. This is the perfect opportunity. Besides, you aren't helping her with a technique—she's helping *you*."

"Semantics," I said as Peanut grabbed my hand and began pulling me away to the courtyard. "I'm going on the record protesting this exercise as one of your more horrible ideas."

"Peanut, please don't hurt Simon," Monty said. "He needs to practice, and we may have another angry group of guests."

Peanut stopped pulling on my hand.

"Are they coming to take our home?" she asked, suddenly serious. "Uncle Dex explained to the crusty old mages that he wasn't going to let them take our home away."

"What did they say?" I asked. "Did they agree?"

"Most of them listened, but a few of them turned real red in the face and started yelling at Uncle Dex," she answered. "They said that Uncle Dex had no right to do what he was doing. That's when they went to the stone tower with all the symbols. Uncle Dex pointed to it and explained something to them."

"Did they calm down?"

"Some of them did, but the ones that were red in the face stayed mad," she said. "I thought we were going to fight. I was so ready, but Aunt Mo said they were just making noise, that they were scared of Uncle Dex and that they would leave."

"Did they?" I asked.

"A few minutes ago," Peanut said. "Aunt Mo was right. They were just yelling, and not one of them tried to attack us. I was hoping they would."

Peanut smiled in a way that chilled me to the core.

She had definitely been spending way too much time around the Morrigan.

"I know you are powerful," Monty said. "Perhaps we can wait a few more years before you fight in battle?"

"Years?" she asked. "For real?"

"For real," Monty said with a nod, his voice gentle. "Trust me on this; enjoy being a young mage for a little while longer. The battles will come."

"And I'll be ready for them," she said, determined. "These guests of yours, will I be meeting them?"

"I'm afraid not," Monty said. "I have a feeling my uncle won't allow it. At least not yet."

She nodded and thought to herself for a few seconds.

"Are they coming here after you two?"

"Yes," Monty said with a nod. "It seems they are upset with us."

"What did you do?" she asked, curious. "Can you say or is it a secret?"

"They think we are going dark and present a potential threat to our plane."

"Are you?" she asked, her voice and expression hopeful. "Do you?"

"No, we are not going dark, and no, we do not pose a threat to our plane," Monty said with a small smile. "Like the other crusty old mages, they are scared of what we could do, not who we are."

"That happened to me, too," she said. "Are you going to let them take your power so they can feel safe? They wanted to take *my* power."

"No," Monty said, "I don't think we will be negotiating the erasure of powers today."

"Good. Kick their asses," she said with a wide grin and proceeded to pull me again. "Let's go, Mr. Strong. I'll help you train until you get a hang of your new cast."

I stared at Monty as I let her drag me away.

He conveniently looked away and coughed.

"I'll be with you shortly," he said. "I need to update my uncle on the current course of events."

"Don't take too long."

"Don't hurt him, Peanut," Monty said as he walked away. "We need him in one piece."

I glared at Monty's back as he created a small, green teleportation circle. He waved without turning and vanished from sight.

TWENTY-FOUR

"Don't be scared," Peanut said as we stepped into the courtyard. "I promise I won't hurt you."

"Peanut, really, thanks, but I don't think this is such a good idea," I said, standing outside of the circle. "The new cast I learned is dangerous and I'm not as skilled as you are. I barely have it under control."

"Then you should practice to get it under control, don't you think?"

I sensed the presence without turning.

Part of it was the spike in energy around me. The other reason was the cold clutch of fear that gripped my entire body.

The Morrigan.

"Oh, hell," I said under my breath. "This day just keeps getting better."

I turned to face her.

She was wearing a simple black gown that resembled a modest and loose-fitting sundress, if it had been dipped in the blackest ink in existence. Her gown wasn't black exactly; it was the absence of color and light.

Staring at the material for too long hurt my eyes, so I stopped and focused on her face. Her eyes gazed at me for a few seconds, and I saw death and devastation stare back at me.

I decided to look across the arena.

"When it was suggested you should seek out formal training," she said with a raised eyebrow, "this is not what was meant."

I raised a hand in surrender.

"This wasn't my idea."

"Peanut, be a dear and attend to your chores," the Morrigan said. Her voice was gentle, carefree even, but it held a core of iron. "Your room could use some attention, don't you think?"

"Sorry, Mr. Simon, I have to go," Peanut said, then stepped a little closer and lowered her voice. "Good luck."

She rubbed my hellhound's head one last time and dashed off, leaving the courtyard and disappearing around a corner.

The Morrigan glided over to one of the stone benches that sat around the courtyard. She patted the bench next to her, inviting me over.

I couldn't refuse even if I wanted to—and every cell in my body wanted to put as much distance between us as possible. I walked over reluctantly and sat down next to her.

"I hear the meeting with the Elders went well," I said. "No one was blasted out of existence; that has to be a plus."

"Tiny, scared men grasping at power wherever they can," she said with a hint of menace that made me reconsider sitting next to her. I glanced over at the bench across the courtyard, and I couldn't help thinking that I could probably still hear her from way over there. "Dexter persuaded most of them."

"Most of them?" I asked. "There were some holdouts?"

"Some of them insisted he step down and relinquish

control of the sect," she said, gazing off into the distance. She was terribly beautiful, and I could understand what Dex saw in her, but the constant aura of terror she carried would have fried my brain after one day around her. I didn't understand how Dex spent so much time with her. She must have seen something in my expression, because she smiled. "Dexter's darkness eclipses mine, which, if you think about it, is a staggering thought."

"Excuse me?"

"You were wondering how it worked," she said. "How he could be with a goddess of death, and not lose his mind to the terror you are currently feeling. Yes?"

"Yes," I said. "How does that even happen?"

"Do you fear Michiko?"

Her question threw me. It took a moment to regain my balance.

"What? No," I said. "Why would I fear her?"

"She's an ancient vampire, the leader of a large group of vampires, all highly trained to kill, and she is, after all, the Reaping Wind," she said. "That is no small matter. There are many who fear her, even within the Dark Council—*especially* within the Dark Council."

I gave her words thought.

I knew how dangerous Chi was as a fighter, and more importantly, as a person. She was a brilliant strategist and fearsome leader. Even though I had never mentioned her age —I was reckless, not suicidal—she was old enough to make it difficult for my brain to process.

But even with all of that, I didn't fear her. I did hold a healthy respect for her lethality, because I enjoyed breathing, but fear wasn't part of that equation.

"I don't fear her," I said. "I understand who and what she is. It is what it is, and it works for us."

"The same can be said for Dexter and myself," she said,

glancing at me. "I can only be myself, truly myself, around him."

That was a sentiment I understood.

"Can we stop Gault?" I asked. "I know Monty said that collectively we are as strong as an Archmage—"

"Stronger, actually, if you ever learn to enter the battle form with your hellhound." She glanced down at Peaches, who sat by my feet. "There are entities who would feel threatened by your very existence and would move to destroy you."

"Sort of like what's happening now?"

"What is happening now is preparation, Strong," she said. "What did I tell you when I sent you from the Archmage's plane?"

"So you really are a triune goddess, not three separate beings?"

"I am distinct and the same, like water."

"Like what, sorry?"

"Water has three forms: liquid, gas, and solid," she said. "All three different, yet all three are the same. If it helps, think of me like water."

"If water was terrifying and the goddess of death, I could see the similarity, sure."

"It's the simplest analogy I can present to you without touching on the divinity of other beings," she said. "Your human thinking, not your mind, is too limited, too narrow. Comprehending the totality of who and what I am would take you several centuries of study."

"Understood," I said, not understanding a word. "You—well, the other you—said you were casting me into the jaws of danger, not because you wished me harm, but because even the strongest blade must be tempered, first in the heat of the forge, and later on the field of battle."

"Do you understand this?" she asked. "What it means?"

"Facing Gault is part of the tempering?"

"A small part," she said. "There are greater threats awaiting you and Mage Montague."

"That doesn't exactly make me feel great," I said. "These threats are greater than Gault?"

"I will share a few things with you. Perhaps they will help you, or it's possible they will make things more difficult. The outcome will depend on how you choose."

"That sounds like you have bad news, worse news, and horrific news."

"Has anyone threatened to kill you because of your words?"

"Many times, actually," I said. "I figure it's one of my special skills: goading powerful beings into losing their shi—composure under pressure."

"Indeed," she said with a small laugh. "You are highly proficient in this skill."

"You wanted to share something?"

"Yes. The darkflame will eventually kill you and Tristan, if you don't manage to diminish its intensity within you both," she said. "However, the only way to confront and thwart Gault is by using the darkflame coupled with the nullifying palm."

"What about my curse?" I asked, her words hitting me like a truck. "Can't it mitigate the damage?"

"If you choose to let your curse handle the darkflame you will, in time serve Badb Catha completely, heart, mind, and soul. You will be her greatest and most terrible weapon."

"Weapon? We never discussed anything about being a weapon."

"Exactly. You expressly specified that you would not be her slave or assassin," she said. "You said nothing about becoming her weapon."

"But I made a pact with her," I said. "She didn't mention anything about becoming her weapon."

"Why would she?"

"Always read the fine print," I muttered to myself, shaking my head. "If the darkflame takes over—?"

"You will be like your Ebonsoul. A weapon to be utilized."

"She outplayed me," I said. "She knew she didn't have to say anything. I walked right into that."

Yes, I understood how surreal it was to be speaking to the Morrigan and referring to Badb Catha as another person in the same sentence.

"She didn't have to," she said. "It's implied. Why do you think she, Kali, or any god, would take an interest in *you*? Why would Hades give *you* a hellhound? Out of the goodness of his heart?"

"Why are you telling me this?" I asked as the thoughts whirled in my mind. "Why tell me this at all?"

"I would not see you become another pawn in the hands of gods," she said. "It would destroy everything that makes you...you. There is, however, a solution."

"I'm not seeing it," I said. "I'm so deep in this hole that when I look up, all I see is dirt."

"You have everything you need to extricate yourself from this situation," she said, patting me on my thigh before standing and looking down at me. "All you have to do is be who you truly are and return what is not yours."

"Can you be a bit clearer?" I asked. "My crypticspeak is rusty."

She smiled.

"When the time comes, do what only *you* can do, then you will see the path open ahead of you," she said. "For the time being, you have enemies to confront. Face them, restore the balance, and do so before the darkflame consumes you and Mage Montague."

I shook my head and looked away.

"I should've known better," I said. "When something looks too good to be true, it usually is."

I turned and realized I was speaking to myself.

The Morrigan was gone.

TWENTY-FIVE

Monty appeared in the courtyard a few minutes later.

"I have bad news and worse news. Which do you want first?"

"I spoke to my uncle. He told me about the darkflame," Monty said, looking across the arena. "There is a solution."

I told him what the Morrigan said.

"That concurs with what my uncle expressed," Monty said. "We have to return what doesn't belong to us."

"Oh, that's all," I said, exasperated. "For a second there I was all confused, but now it's totally clear. Thanks, that really helped."

"Don't get emotional," he said. "Think. What do we have that doesn't belong to us?"

"I haven't taken anything that doesn't belong to me."

"We have," he said. "We both have something we share that is not ours. Think about the casts you know."

"Every cast I know, I've learned or earned. I didn't take any from anyone."

"*Every* cast?"

The realization hit me hard.

"The First Elder Rune," I said. "It belongs to Evergreen."

Monty nodded.

"Somehow we must find a way to return it to him," he said. "However, we have other pressing matters at the moment."

"Korin," I said. "She's coming, isn't she?"

Monty nodded as he tugged on a sleeve.

"My uncle opened the pathway to allow her entry," he said. "She would have tried to brute force her way into here, causing extensive damage. He felt it was easier to open the door and invite her in."

"Is he going to giving us a hand, or psycho axe-mace?"

"No," Monty said. "My uncle, the Morrigan, and Peanut will leave the moment Korin and the Arcanists arrive, disabling the exit sequence."

"We're going to be locked in here with them?"

"No," he said, flexing his fingers. "They're going to be locked in here with us."

"Your confidence in our abilities is inspiring, but we don't even know what Korin is capable of, what abilities she has, or how powerful she really is."

"Does it matter if we possess the nullifying palm?"

"The nullifying palm requires proximity and contact, Monty," I said, stating what I thought was an obvious flaw in this plan of his. "You want us to get close enough to reach out and touch someone?"

"Not just someone. Korin," he said. "We have the advantage here. She doesn't know we have the nullifying palm, let alone the *both* of us. She will assume only I have the knowledge, being a mage, and will approach you with more conventional attacks—that will be our opening."

"I want to say that is thin, but that would be a lie," I said. "It's practically non-existent as an opportunity. Just because she doesn't think I can sling orbs around doesn't mean she's suddenly going to give me a hug."

"I know it's thin," he agreed. "I will do my best to create the opening for you. We will most likely only get one opportunity. Make it count."

"Sure, no pressure," I said. "This is worse than shooting down a two-meter-wide thermal exhaust port while traveling at speed and I have no experience hitting womp rats in my T-16. I don't even own a T-16."

"What exactly is a T-16?"

"Doesn't matter," I said, waving away his question. "The point is, I need to get close enough to touch her. If the palm works, and that's a huge *if,* I doubt she's going to be defenseless. She'll have other weapons—the non-magical kind."

"So do we," Monty said. "Our odds of success increase exponentially if we can engage her with conventional weapons. Refrain from any casts until you can use the palm. I doubt she will give you more than one opening."

"What about the Arcanists? We don't know how many Gault is sending. If I were him, I would send them all to crush us."

"He can't send them all," Monty said. "He can only send those directly under his authority."

"How many exactly is that?"

"Do you recall how many were with Tellus when we faced him in Hell?"

"You're not serious. That was at least a thousand Arcanists, *and* we had the Midnight Echelon helping us," I said. "How are the three of us supposed to stop Korin and a battalion of Arcanists?"

"We choose the battlefield," he said and began moving out of the courtyard. "My uncle has made some modifications to the sect."

"Modifications?" I asked, not following. "What modifications?"

"This entire place has been designed to allow a smaller force to withstand an onslaught of superior numbers," Monty said, gesturing. "There are traps everywhere. We can funnel the attacking party to a location of our choosing and neutralize Korin. If everything goes according to plan, it will be just us against Korin."

"Monty, it *never* goes according to plan," I said, shaking my head as we headed to the main building. "Still, it's better to have a plan than it is to wing it. How are we going to do this?"

"No plan survives first contact with the enemy."

"Wonderful, except that von Moltke isn't here to fight with us, is he?" I said as we entered the building. "What's the plan?"

"My uncle has placed runic detonators virtually everywhere. Every location, every building, every passage, and every location of interest can be destroyed."

"What the hell?" I said, surprised. "Is Dex expecting a war?"

"In a word, yes," Monty said. "He expects the elders to return and attempt to take the sect by force. He is prepared for that eventuality."

"By destroying everything?"

"No, not everything," Monty said, leading me to a small room. "By using selective destruction, you can control a larger invading force by directing the flow of their movement."

"So we're the Spartans at Thermopylae?" I asked. "Right now, I wouldn't mind three hundred mages standing with us."

"Unfortunately, we don't have three hundred mages to stand with us, but the analogy is accurate," he said. "We will be controlling a larger force with defenses designed for just that purpose. With some luck, we will whittle their numbers down to something more manageable."

"Even if we bring their numbers down to one hundred, Monty," I said, "it's still us three against one hundred mages and Korin. Have you ever faced a hundred mages on your own?"

"Yes," Monty said. "It's what battle mages are trained for. One battle mage should be able to hold his or her own against a battalion. It's not ideal, but it should be possible."

"Oh, I didn't know," I said, raising my eyebrows. "We don't usually go up against battalions of anything."

"I know. My apologies," he said. "I haven't exactly been forthcoming with my experiences from the war."

"No need to apologize," I said. "If you can face off against a battalion and walk away, we may be able pull this off."

He had never really discussed his experiences during the Supernatural War, and I had never pressed him for war stories. It was a matter of respect. My impression from the few times I had asked was that it had been a horrible experience.

I understood his reluctance to relive that part of his life.

In the same way, he had never asked about my time in Shadow Company. Some memories are best left as memories. There was no need to drag them into the present, and it's not like they would ever fade away or disappear. Warfare is hell.

"Our advantage lies in this room," Monty said, pointing to a door ahead of us. "My uncle personally modified the sect's defenses. I have to say, they are quite formidable."

He opened the door and led us inside.

Inside the room was a large, rune-covered, black-iron table with an architectural model of the entire sect. Every building was represented. Faintly glowing red runes showed which buildings were rigged to explode, while other locations were designated with violet symbols.

Every surface of the room we stood in was covered in runes.

The table legs rose from the floor, making it a part of the room. The table itself sat in the center of the floor, surrounded by three concentric rune-covered circles of black iron.

The room thrummed with power.

Monty closed the door, which was several feet thick and covered in wicked-looking runes. Even without being able to read them, I knew that trying to breach that door meant someone was going to die.

"What is this place?"

"This is the Defense Command Center for the entire school," Monty said. "Every defense can be enabled or disabled from here."

It was an impressive expression of deathly defense—and Dex was taking the security of the school to new levels of destruction.

"Did the sect have this? Back when it was the Golden Circle?"

"Something similar, but nowhere near as sophisticated," Monty said, looking at the model. "I would imagine it serves as an effective deterrent to attack. It's probably why the elders left without escalation today."

"That, and the fact that the Morrigan was here with the Harbinger of Death?" I said. "You think that may have had something to do with it too?"

Monty nodded.

"A distinct possibility," he said, placing a hand on the table and gesturing. The thrumming in the room intensified, causing the runes on the walls to become active. Violet and gold energy flowed from the symbols on the walls and traveled up the legs of the table. "The defenses are now active, leaving only one viable location."

I looked down at the other defenses in the model.

"What do the violet runes mean?"

"Implosion and collapse."

Throughout the model, I saw small green circles scattered along the streets. There were too many to count; the entire model was filled with them.

"Teleportation traps?"

Monty nodded.

"Bifurcating teleports, lethal and horrific," Monty explained. "One step and it teleports one part of you to one location and the other part to another location."

"Ouch, death by teleportation," I said, looking at the hundreds of green circles. "Can the Arcanists disable them?"

"It will slow them down for those," Monty said, pointing at the white orbs on top of every building. "Snipe orbs."

"Snipe orbs?" I asked. "What do they shoot?"

"Once the Arcanists enter the grounds or attempt to disable the teleports, the orbs are activated, and will fire the equivalent of a runic paralyzing agent," Monty said. "Think of your persuaders—just without the mess. No casting for twelve hours after getting hit by one of those."

"Can't they just fly in and avoid the teleport circles?"

"The circles have an aerial proximity trigger with a one-mile ceiling," Monty said. "Even flying over one will activate the bifurcating teleport. They are lethally efficient. I haven't seen them in use since the war."

"Okay, so that stops them from flying in," I said. "What's to stop the Arcanists or Korin from just ripping up the streets and destroying the circles? It's what I would do. That frees the ground and the air."

"If they choose to go that route, they will have to face those," Monty said, pointing at some figures at the end of a street. I looked around the model and realized these figures were situated on every street. "Any damage to the street in an effort to disable the teleports will activate them."

"They look like—"

"MSGs," Monty finished. "They operate on the basic principle of seeking and destroying anything they perceive as hostile, so we will have to avoid them as well, but they should effectively hamper the Arcanists."

"MSG? Like the spice?"

"Miniature Sentry Golems," he said with a sigh. "They function autonomously and are about twice the size of the average human. Incredibly difficult to destroy and relentless in their mission. They were a nightmare to face on final examinations."

"Final examinations?" I asked. "You had to face those things as part of an exam?"

"Yes," Monty said. "Thankfully, the ones I encountered were calibrated for student mages. These are military grade and not something I would enjoy facing, even now."

I looked around at all the defenses Dex had placed on the school grounds and shook my head. This may have been a sect, once, but it was an active fortress now, designed to repel any attack thrown at it. I almost felt sorry for Korin and the Arcanists headed our way. Most of them weren't going to make it.

"This isn't a school, this is a military testing ground," I said in shock. "What kind of students is Dex expecting in here…mage special forces?"

"Close," Monty said. "He's creating battlemages. On the field of battle, one battlemage, one Ordaurum—"

"That's what you are, right?"

He nodded.

"One Ordaurum could turn the tide of any battle," he said. "It's why we were feared—and targeted. Many battle mages were killed during the Supernatural War. I lost many companions and sectmates to targeted strikes against the Golden Circle mages."

"I'm sorry to hear that."

"Which is why my uncle is doing what he is doing: creating and teaching what has been suppressed to reestablish the school of—"

"Battle mages. It makes sense: a crazy, scary sort of sense, but sense," I said, shaking my head. "What's this one viable location you mentioned earlier?"

Monty pointed to the model of the main building. It was the building we were currently standing in. The building, which was only three stories high, was designed as a hexagon with a large empty stone plaza in the center.

I looked closer at the center and realized it was similar to the arena in the school's courtyard, where Cece petitioned Monty. This one only had three circles, though, not five. The three concentric circles pulsed with orange energy in the center of the hexagon.

"There." Monty pointed to the open plaza in the center of the hexagon. "We will wait for Korin there."

"Is that a—?"

"It's a battle arena," Monty clarified. "It's different from an ascendance arena. Battle arenas are designed to dampen abilities, not enhance them. They're used for live-training exercises to prevent needless casualties."

"Wait, that dampening effect—won't that affect us too?"

"Yes," Monty said, his voice grim. "But that's our best chance to stop Korin."

TWENTY-SIX

We stepped out of the Defense Command Center, and Monty secured the massive door, which whispered closed with a hiss. I got the impression that even if the entire building collapsed, that room would remain intact.

It felt that secure.

Part of my brain suggested we should wait for Korin in there, where it was safe. The other part—the part that knew how impossibly dumb it would be to lock yourself in a room and hope no one would attack—smacked the part of my brain that suggested hiding in the room and strangled it silent.

"What would it take to destroy the Command Center?"

"You recall the orb you created? The entropic dissolution?"

"I'm not going to forget that cast anytime soon," I said. "Yes, I recall."

"You'd need about ten of those unleashed on that room simultaneously, and you *may* have a chance of disabling the defenses of the school."

"Damn," I said. "Dex is beyond scary. Now I know why he's not here."

"He's not here because, as I understand it, he's having a conversation with the High Tribunal," Monty said. "If Korin succeeds, he will advocate for us."

"And if she fails?"

"He's there to make sure the High Tribunal acts according to the edicts," he said. "If they want to take further action, they will have to act directly against us. No more proxies."

"So we'll have High Tribunal mages after us. Why does that sound worse?"

"Because it is," he said. "They would have to instruct Verity to stand down, but they would then be free to attack us if they chose."

"Would they? Attack us, I mean."

"Unlikely. It places them at risk of being killed if they confront us directly," Monty said. "It's been my experience that groups entrenched in positions of power, are reluctant to relinquish their positions."

"Basically, if they come after us, they open themselves up to attack—not just from us, but from anyone who would see them as vulnerable and exploit the opportunity. I'm sure that list is long."

"Precisely. No one on the High Tribunal wants to sacrifice their life to apprehend and erase us. Especially if we defeat their Sword."

"So we can get them off our backs if we beat Korin?"

"Officially? Yes."

"And unofficially?"

"They won't stop until we stop them."

"I had a feeling you were going to say that."

"This way," he said and led us down a wide corridor. "The battle arena is at the end of this corridor. Are you ready?"

"Do I have a choice?"

He paused before answering.

"I like to always believe we have a choice," Monty said.

"Today, I'm not so sure. This feels like a shift in the order of things, and we are the catalysts of that shift. I want to say you always have a choice...but to be honest, no, you don't have a choice in this, just as I don't."

"They won't stop until we stop them," I said. "Today, we stop Korin."

He nodded.

"Let's go."

We headed down the corridor.

The corridor led out into an open-air plaza. Monty stopped us at the edge of the space as I felt the surge of energy flow from the three concentric circles in the center of the battle arena.

A spike in energy raced through the arena, and I felt power surround us. It reminded me of the energy of the Chateau. It rose in intensity for several seconds, and then suddenly disappeared.

"What was that?" I asked, looking around. "I felt a power increase, and then *wham*, it was gone."

"Along with my uncle, the Morrigan, and Peanut," Monty said. "If you focus, you will be able to sense the tide of the battle as Korin and the Arcanists approach."

I asked the question that had been on my mind since we arrived.

"Are we going to kill her?"

"We are not assassins, nor cold-blooded murderers," he said, much to my relief. "We will give those who make it this far an opportunity to cease and desist."

"But the traps will kill them."

"The traps have been set to warfare mode," Monty said, "which begins with a clear instruction to surrender and cease any hostilities."

"Somehow, I don't think they're going to pay attention to that instruction."

"That is followed by a clear warning that the defenses are set to deal with any potential threat with lethal force," Monty continued. "If they refrain from casting, or channeling energy, the defenses will use neutralizing attacks. Once they escalate, so will the defenses."

"Basically, a case of: don't start none, won't be none?"

"Apt and accurate, yes."

A blast of energy must've been released, followed by a thunderous response of energy we could hear from where we stood. It went silent for a few seconds.

"Maybe they listened to reason?" I said. "Is it possible—?"

That's when the screams started.

Peaches sat silently by my side and focused upward, looking into the sky above the arena. The deafening sounds of battle crashed all around us. Roars of power joined the screams of mages.

Many times, the screams would be brutally cut short while the sound of the casts continued on relentlessly. From the flow of energy, I could tell the Arcanists were losing. That didn't surprise me. Dex had designed these defenses to protect the students of the school. He would go for maximum lethality.

"Make sure your creature stays by your side," Monty said, glancing at Peaches. "If he goes out there, the defenses will view him as hostile. We can't afford to divide our attention between keeping him safe and facing Korin."

"You think any of the Arcanists will make it?"

"Yes. I assume Korin will keep some of them safe and transport them with her, here," he said. "The others will see the initial carnage and lose heart, retreating to the outskirts of the sect. If they remain outside the outer perimeter, they should be safe. Others will be hit by the snipe orbs and incapacitated. Many of them will survive this day…but not all."

More screams filled the air, and each time, the scream would be cut short.

Another blast cut through the sky, then, and a violet beam tore into the ground just outside the main building. Everything became silent for a few beats, as if everyone was holding their breath.

Then the rumbling started.

"Someone tried to destroy the teleport circles," Monty said, his voice cold. "That was a tactical error. They have just activated an army nearly twice their size, and one impervious to most damage, magical and conventional."

"Can the defenses be shut down?" I asked. "I mean, if they surrender, can they be shut down?"

"If they retreat and stop attacking for a continuous period of five minutes, the defenses will enter a standby protocol," he said, looking up into the sky. "All they have to do is stop attacking. What do you think the odds of that are?"

"Slim to none," I said as more screams reached us. "Make that closer to zero."

"You have to wonder, why attack at all?" Monty said. "There are no targets aside from the golems. We are not hiding; our energy signatures are easily discernible in this building."

"Could be they were given instructions to level the place in a scorched-earth maneuver," I said. "Destroy the school to prevent anyone from using it?"

"A scorched-earth policy means we would be doing the destroying," Monty said. "What they are doing is sending us a message: defy us and we will destroy everything you have, starting with this school."

"Is that message coming from Gault or the High Tribunal?"

"I have to assume both, but it's more likely this was instigated by the Keeper."

"He's flexing his authority?"

"It would seem so, very much like the High Tribunal sending only Korin," Monty said. "In their eyes, the threat we present doesn't warrant major attention. They sent her to put us down and remove an annoying pest."

"No matter how large or powerful the opponent, even a splinter can cause damage if left untended."

"We are that splinter, and they can no longer ignore us," Monty said. "Hence Korin paying us a visit."

"Maybe we can speak to her?" I said. "Convince her this is a bad idea and that she should leave?"

"We'll get our chance shortly. She's on her way."

I felt the power approach the far side of the building, opposite where we stood. Peaches rumbled by my side and looked in the direction of the power spike.

The walls of the building were vaporized as a figure dispersed the cloud of dust. Behind the figure, I saw a large group forming—Arcanists, judging from their clothing.

The dust settled and a woman wearing dark gray combat armor stared death at us. A small constellation of blue orbs surrounded her. Her armor was a mobile arsenal. I saw the gray hilts of knives sheathed everywhere. All of the knives were runed and gave off the same blue glow as the orbs around her.

Her black hair, which she wore loose, also had streaks of blue in it, and I realized then that this wasn't a stylistic choice —her entire body was flowing with power. Her features were young, and I wouldn't put her past her mid thirties.

She looked like she spent time training and enjoyed it. Her eyes, which held a gaze much older than her appearance, were two pools of contained fury. They flickered every few seconds with a flash of blue energy.

Korin.

The contrast was stark.

Where Korin looked ready to unleash a major pounding on us, just to warm up, the group behind her looked like fresh hell.

They had been chewed up, chomped on, spit out, and then stomped into paste, for good measure. Not one of them wore an intact set of clothing. Most of what they were wearing had been torn in several places. Some of them were missing jackets, while others had tears in their pants or shirts.

And these were the lucky ones.

Korin, on the other hand, looked fresh and relaxed, as if she had been out for an afternoon stroll, not storming a fortress of death.

Despite everything, I was impressed.

She had made it through all of the school defenses without so much as a scratch. She had managed to drag a bunch of Arcanists—I guessed these were the strongest of the group—with her to the main building, before blasting a hole through one of the walls without any apparent effort.

She was either incredibly powerful or extremely clever. Chances were, she was some combination of both.

Lucky us.

The group of Arcanists—I counted twenty—spread out behind Korin in a formation designed to eliminate crossfire. They may have looked like a ragged mess, but collectively they still wielded a massive amount of power.

"Diplomacy time?" I asked Monty as we stepped forward, but avoided stepping into the battle arena. "Do you think she'll listen?"

"I doubt it, but let's find out."

TWENTY-SEVEN

Korin stepped forward, but stayed outside of the arena too.

I had the feeling she must have sensed the energy inside the circles, and knew they would dampen her ability to cast.

"Remind me to smack Corbel the next time I see him for training her," I said, under my breath as we moved closer to the arena. "She feels dangerous."

"I doubt he had a choice, if he was instructed by Hades to train her," Monty answered and cleared his throat. "And I would say that is an accurate assessment. Her energy signature is considerable."

Monty turned to Korin. "Emissary of the High Tribunal," he said, addressing her with a slight nod. "To what do we owe the pleasure?"

She narrowed her eyes and gazed at us.

"I have been sent to render judgment upon you, dark mage Tristan Montague, and you, dark immortal Simon Strong. Together with the hellhound by your side, you three present a clear and present danger to the denizens and stability of your home plane."

"I see," Monty said without missing a beat. "What is the judgment and on whose authority do you render it?"

"Erasure, followed by death," she said, without averting her gaze. "To be executed by the authority vested in me by the High Tribunal."

The Arcanists behind her nodded in silent agreement.

"Why?" I asked. "Who died and made the High Tribunal the ultimate authority?"

She focused on me and her eyes turned a deep blue.

"Why?" she echoed. "To prevent aberrations like you. Your energy signature is abnormal."

"Did she just call me abnormal?" I asked, keeping my voice low. "Should I be offended?"

"I think she means your energy signature, not you, per se," Monty said in the same low voice. "Though, I could be wrong. I don't think she's done."

"It is evident you have no formal training," Korin continued, "yet you are bound to a hellhound, you track in power that does not correspond to you, and the fact that this bond is with a creature from Hell, indicates that you are dark. You also bear the Mark of Kali—a dark goddess of destruction—upon you." Then, turning to Monty, she said, "And you are his associate."

She gazed at Monty, her blue eyes darkening even further into the X-ray end of the spectrum.

"Looks like you're up," I said. "Brace yourself. She's probably got your entire resumé."

"I highly doubt it," Monty said. "I didn't come under the High Tribunal's scrutiny until I cast—"

"Two void vortices in a populated city, endangering all of the people within said city," Korin began. "That alone is an act worthy of erasure."

"Talk about having your past come back to bite you," I

said, still keeping my voice low. "Want to explain the extenuating circumstances?"

"It would be pointless," Monty said as the anger came off of him in waves. "The High Tribunal and those who serve them are the very definition of narrow-minded, inflexible megalomaniacs, who—while actually wielding great amounts of power—have become deluded by their own beliefs of grandeur and omnipotence because they haven't been challenged."

"I've met their kind before," I said with a short nod. "If you don't fit their preconceived notions, you don't have a right to exist and must be removed or exterminated."

Korin had gone silent and only stared at us with her glowing eyes.

"Another reason my uncle has begun this school," he said. "The High Tribunal would see a magic user like Peanut and deem her unworthy to wield power simply because they can't classify her. Where does it end?"

"Are you done?" Korin asked. "There is more."

"Of course there is," Monty said, staring back. "You would mention my use of blood runes, my appropriation of a minor elder rune, my possession of the First Elder Rune, and more completely spell out the fact that I am the known associate of the Marked of Kali as proof of my inherent darkness. Is there more?"

"You both unleashed a stormblood that took the life of Mage Edith, a respected and valued member of Verity, and endangered—again—the lives of the population of two cities."

"Edith was insane. She would have killed thousands in her play for power," I said. "You would've found out when it was too late. We did you a favor by putting her down."

"Spoken like a true psychopath," Korin said. "How do you both plead?"

"Oh, we get to plead?" I asked, noticing that the Arcanists around her had started getting twitchy. "Does it matter what we plead?"

"No," Korin said. "The High Tribunal has passed judgment."

"Then why ask?"

"So they can feel justified in this farce of meting out justice," Monty said. "Let us speak true, Gray Shadow. We are people of action, and lies do not become us. Who set you on this path?"

Korin's eyes stopped glowing blue as she glanced to her sides.

"They are here at Keeper Gault's command," she said as she focused on us again. "While I speak for the High Tribunal, the Keeper has deemed you a threat to the balance of magic, a threat to be removed permanently. You possess something that belongs to him, and he wants it back."

"The First Elder Rune belongs to Keeper Evergreen."

"Who is no longer," she said. "That rune now passes to the next Keeper."

"Which would be Keeper Ustrina," Monty said. "She is the next Keeper in line."

"She has abdicated succession."

"To Gault," Monty said, putting the pieces together faster than I could. "Don't you see what is happening, what he is doing? With two of the elder runes, he will easily take the other runes and become unstoppable."

"Gault got to Ustrina somehow—and no way is Evergreen gone," I said. "They just can't find him. This is wrong on so many levels."

She remained focused on Monty.

"Who are *you* to judge a Keeper?" she said. "How can you possibly imagine what they plan or conceive? You are like an ant wondering what a god thinks. You overstep your bounds, mage."

"How can you not see that you're being used?" I asked. "They're playing you. All you are is a weapon to them."

The Morrigan's words came back to me in that moment.

If you choose to let your curse handle the darkflame you will, in time serve Badb Catha completely, heart, mind, and soul. You will be her greatest and most terrible weapon.

I stared at Korin and realized I was staring at my future, if we didn't stop Gault.

"I only see that you have something that rightfully belongs to Keeper Gault," she said. "He wants it back, as is his right."

"He has employed your services, then," Monty said with a sense of finality. "With the Tribunal's consent, of course."

She nodded.

"He has," she said. "I promise to make the end swift. You will get no such assurance from Keeper Gault or the Tribunal. This is your last opportunity to surrender—accept this mercy."

"I make you the same offer, Korin: surrender and leave this place with your life," Monty said with death in his eyes. "It is a more generous offer than yours. I will not make the same offer again."

"I decline," she said, stepping into the battle arena, causing a wave of energy to radiate outward from the circles as the dampening effect took hold, her face was a mask of determination and duty. "The High Tribunal's judgments are law. There are no exceptions and they cannot be broken."

I shook my head slowly.

"You don't have to do this. Don't throw your life away," I said. "You can still walk away."

"You think you can beat *me*?" she answered with a small laugh. "Your arrogance is astounding. You are nothing, less than nothing. Not even the dampening field in this arena will save you. I will crush you all under my boot. You will beg for mercy before the end comes, and your pleas will fall on deaf ears."

"You have a choice," I said, trying one last attempt. "You have your own will. Use it. Think—this is wrong. Targeting people because they are different is wrong."

She stared at me with a look of contempt.

"You haven't been targeted because you are *different*," she scoffed. "You have been targeted because you are *dark*."

"You don't even know what that means, except what you've been told by the Tribunal," I countered. "You can stop this. Once you go down this path, it only leads to death."

"I know: yours."

"I don't understand how you could be so blind, so dense!"

"How could *you* understand?" she said. "My life belongs to the Tribunal. Heart, mind, and soul, I serve them completely. If this is their verdict, who am I to question them?"

"We tried," I said to Monty. "This is a waste. She's throwing her life away."

"She's operating under what she believes to be true," Monty said. "Zealots rarely see the truth until it is too late and they're staring at death."

"I try not to hate, but right now I'm really leaning into hating the High Tribunal."

"Don't expend the energy on them," he said. "We will deal with them in due time. Right now she is the priority."

"What's the plan?"

"Have your creature remove the Arcanists," Monty said. "Make sure he does it before they get a chance to react. I don't think they will step into the arena. It would render them powerless."

"Remove?" I asked. "You want him to—?"

"Remove, not *kill*," he clarified. "He can drop them

outside the outer wall. Whatever he does, he should not linger within the defenses of the school. It would be too dangerous for him."

"Oh, *that* kind of 'remove.' Got it," I said. "What are you going to do?"

"I'm going to show the Gray Shadow that blind loyalty is not always the best course of action," he said, his voice a dagger of death. "It promises to be a most painful lesson."

He formed several white orbs as he stepped into the battle arena. Another wave of energy flowed outward from the circles as I crouched down next to my hellhound.

<Hey, boy. You see those mages over there?>

<They look tired and hurt. Why are they here? Do they want to fight? They should eat meat first.>

<We're going to help them. If they fight here, they are going to get seriously hurt. Stop them from attacking and take them way outside of the school, away from danger. Can you do that?>

<Will you fight the gray lady?>

<Not until you get back. Monty is going to show her she is making a mistake.>

<She is strong. We will have a good fight.>

He rumbled and chuffed.

<I'd prefer a short fight over a good one.>

<When you become mighty like me, you will want good fights to show everyone how mighty you are.>

<Not really worried about being mighty right now. As soon as Monty and the gray lady start fighting, remove the others.>

<No ripping off arms?>

<No ripping off anything. Take them outside and drop them off. You can gently mangle them, but don't rip anything off.>

<I can do that.>

<Good. Get ready.>

I rubbed his head and drew Grim Whisper as the energy in the arena surged around us.

TWENTY-EIGHT

Korin unleashed her blue orbs.

Simultaneously, the Arcanists unleashed attacks of all kinds.

I remained outside of the arena and cast a dawnward. Korin raised an eyebrow at me, but her attention was immediately drawn to the white orbs Monty unleashed.

I knew he had said not to cast, but I wasn't going to be the Arcanists' punching bag, either. Peaches blinked out as I moved around the perimeter of the arena, remaining inside the large, violet dome of the dawnward and watching for the opening I knew was coming.

Peaches reappeared in the middle of a group of Arcanists, landing on one and knocking him unconscious when he landed on his chest. He whirled and clamped on the leg of another Arcanist who yelled in surprise as my hellhound blinked out, taking the two Arcanists with him.

Korin's blue orbs homed in on Monty.

He dodged and threw up lattices to deflect them as they tried to crash into him. As he was doing that, his orbs raced along the ground and slammed into Korin, who managed to cast a shield at the last moment.

The impact from Monty's orbs knocked her back as he turned to deflect several of the Arcanists' attacks.

I saw Korin roll, then pull out and throw several knives in one smooth motion.

"Incoming," I yelled out, as the blue blades sailed at Monty. "Knives!"

Monty nodded, in one motion turning and sweeping an arm in front of him, as he whispered words of power.

A semi-circular arc of violet energy intercepted the blades, disintegrating them as it made contact.

Surprise flitted across Korin's face as she formed more blue orbs and closed on Monty. Peaches reappeared and barreled into more of the Arcanists. They yelled in surprise, trying to blast him with orbs, but he was too fast for them.

Several of the Arcanists blasted each other in a classic, circular firing-squad action, as Peaches blinked out with three more Arcanists, leaving a gap of space where he'd stood moments earlier.

Korin closed the gap between her and Monty, unleashing more orbs and drawing two more knives, thrusting and slashing, as she tried to cut him several times.

He dodged away, unleashing a blast of energy which shoved her back and gained him some space to breathe.

"You're outclassed, mage," Korin said, circling around Monty. "You must realize this by now."

He turned slowly as she circled, keeping her in his line of sight.

"Really?" Monty said. "You haven't presented much of a threat."

"Allow me to correct that," she said, with a low voice as anger cemented in her expression. She drew two blades, lunging forward and fading from sight as she approached, becoming transparent. Monty flung a violet orb at her. It sailed through her body, crashing into the ground on the other side of the arena. She slid by him and sliced his arm with one of her blades. Once she was past him, she became solid again. "How about now, mage? Do you understand the threat you face?"

His runed Zegna protected him from the attack being worse. The blade went through the runed fabric, but missed cutting his arm. The blades Korin held were dangerous.

I was about to step into the arena when Monty gave me a look and small headshake.

Not yet.

"A gossamer cast," Monty said, glancing at his sleeve. "More a nuisance than an actual threat. You've ruined a perfectly serviceable jacket."

Monty had finally learned something after all this time. Mages had delicate egos and large buttons that were easily pushed, if you knew how.

I saw Peaches blinking in and out, and the number of Arcanists around us grew smaller each time he disappeared. I turned to focus on Monty and Korin.

"You can't stop my attacks," she said. "When I step into my shadow cast, your orbs are meaningless. Do you understand the futility of your resistance?"

"Did you actually just say resistance is futile?" I asked.

"Silence, maggot," Korin snapped. "I will dispatch you after I deal with the mage. Your turn to die will come soon enough."

"Maggot?" I said, and felt the rage build up.

"Simon," Monty warned. "Breathe and step back."

I took a deep breath and stepped back from the edge of the arena. I hadn't noticed I was about a foot away from stepping into it.

"Drop her, Monty," I said. "Or I—"

"Or you'll what?" she said. "Even now the mage tires. The arena has drained him more than he anticipated. You'll end up just like he will in a moment, dying on the ground as you watch your life flow onto the stones."

Monty fell to one knee.

"Monty!" I yelled. "Get back!"

Korin did her ghost thing again and raced at Monty, who formed the Sorrows as she approached. She was too committed to the attack to change course.

Monty let her get close. As she buried a blade in his side, and he crossed the Sorrows behind her, trapping her in his arms. She became solid instantly.

"Now!" he yelled. "Use the palm."

I raced into the arena and focused the darkflame into my hand. Monty rotated his body as I ran toward him and slammed my palm into her back.

Darkflame raced over her body and vanished.

She broke Monty's grip and kicked him back. He rolled to the side as she started laughing.

"That was it, mage?" she scoffed. "That was your plan? To hit me with some ineffectual cast by *him*?" She glanced at me with disgust. "I'll allow you to say your goodbyes before I end you as well. Take him and let him die with some modicum of dignity. It's more than either of you deserve."

The arrogance in her words washed over me, triggering a deep rage. I pulled Monty into the dawnward and glanced down at his side. His shirt was covered in blood.

"Monty, "I said, trying to control the worry in my voice. "What happened? The palm didn't work."

"She ruined my shirt, too," he said, looking down at his bloody shirt. "She doesn't know about the effect of the palm because of the dampening ability of the battle arena, but it neutralized her casting. It worked."

"Are you sure?" I asked, glancing in her direction. "She still looks plenty powerful and truly pissed."

"Trust me," he said. "It worked. I'd bet my life on it. Actually, I'm doing that now, aren't I?"

"Why aren't you making with the finger wiggles to heal yourself?"

"I'll get right on that, but I need you to focus. You have to stop her."

"You expect me to take her down?" I asked. "On my own?"

"You—we—have faced worse," he said and coughed up blood. "Bloody hell, it seems she may have punctured a lung. I hate to pressure you, but I may need medical attention."

"How," I started, slowly getting to my feet, "do I stop her?"

"She relies on her shadow cast to deliver her killing blow," he said, his voice raspy. "She's used it so often it's a reflex for her. Do what you do best. Get her to try and kill you. When she comes in to end you, don't let her. See? Simple."

"Your humor still sucks. Be right back."

"You have to wait until she tries to use her shadow cast. She drops her guard and uses a left-side approach. You'll have to use Ebonsoul and the darkflame together," he said, trying to sit up and failing as I stepped to the edge of the dawnward. "I'm just going to rest my eyes here for a moment."

He lay back on the ground inside the dawnward.

<Boy, protect Monty.>

Peaches appeared next to Monty a second later.

<No one will hurt him. Will you punish the gray lady for hurting the angry man?>

<Yes, she tried to kill Monty. I have to stop her.>

<Good.>

I drew Grim Whisper and closed on Korin.

TWENTY-NINE

She entered a defensive stance as I closed the distance.

"Is he dead yet?" she mocked. "Did you say goodbye?"

I pointed Grim Whisper and she ducked low, bringing both blades in front of her. I had no doubt she had the ability to deflect or dodge my rounds.

I dropped Grim Whisper next to my feet.

"I see," she said. "The truth has finally arrived. You understand you can't win. You comprehend—"

Silver mist raced down my arm.

Hints of gold, red, and violet could be seen in the mist. All of that color was overwhelmed by darkflame as Ebonsoul formed in my hand.

"I comprehend you talk too much."

"You *are* full of surprises," she said, with a smile. "Maybe you'll be more of a challenge than the mage."

She rushed at me.

She was impossibly fast as she slashed at me.

I jumped back and dodged to the side as she thrust forward and then reversed direction, trying to cut me. I parried another horizontal slash and had to backpedal as she drove inward with a second blade.

I unleashed a low leg kick, aiming to shatter her knee. She raised a leg and checked my attack, rotating the blade in her hand, and slamming an elbow into my temple. Stars danced in my vision as I staggered back.

She was good.

And she was toying with me.

My curse kicked in a few seconds later, and I felt better, but I didn't have time to celebrate. She slid in, dropping low and pushed off the ground to bury a kick in my chest, which launched me back. I landed hard gasping for breath.

"You know one trick, and you think you can stand against me?" she said as she closed the gap between us. "This has been entertaining, but I have a job to do. I want you to know that right after I kill you, I'm going to kill Mage Montague if he's still alive. I'll make sure his death is clean and swift. After that, I'll deal with your hellhound."

I laughed then, and she paused in her approach.

"What so funny?" she asked.

"That you think you can deal with my hellhound—on your own," I said, getting to my feet. "You're just a mindless peon. You have no will, no autonomy. You're a slave to a group of mages who think they are above everyone."

I stepped into a defensive stance, my chest burning.

"I was going to end you fast, but now, I think I'll take my time."

I laughed again as rage crossed her face.

"Stop laughing," she commanded me. "It seems death has fractured your mind. Allow me to end your miserable existence."

"Like I said, just a lackey with an overinflated ego," I said, with a chuckle as I stared at her. "No choice and no clue.

They use you and probably laugh at what an obedient pet you are. You're pathetic."

She screamed, then, and ran at me.

I focused and tapped into the darkflame, allowing it to rush throughout my body. When she was about five feet away, I moved toward her and really hoped Monty was right about the palm working.

If he was wrong, and she had her shadow cast, she was going to end this fight in the next three seconds.

"You have no chance," she said, as the rage danced in her eyes. "Time to put you out of your misery."

She started to fade out and my heart dropped.

Almost as soon as it had started, the shadow cast stopped. For a moment, she stood still, stunned at the loss of her ability. I lunged forward and plunged Ebonsoul into her chest.

"You have no power," I said. "This is for trying to kill Monty."

I unleashed the darkflame and it erupted around her.

She screamed as the flame devoured her.

It was over in seconds.

The darkflame had consumed her completely.

Yes, vessel. That was a satisfactory meal.

<Boy, you need to get Dex and bring him here now. I'm not...not feeling too good.>

The floor of the arena tilted in front of me and I pitched forward. Thankfully, the ground was there to catch me as I fell.

THIRTY

You are too entangled. You are not a suitable vessel. Your infernal bond makes you unsuitable for my purposes.

I'm not your vessel. Who are you?

You know me. You have always known me. I was the first of the blood drinkers.

I don't know you, and don't want to know you.

I can give you power beyond your imagination.

I'm all good in the power department. You know what I really want?

You need only ask.

I want you to be quiet...forever.

You have awakened me. I will not remain silent; we are bonded.

I am not your vessel. You have me confused with someone else. You are my weapon. Not the other way around.

I see. This is but a fraction of my essence. For now, it will be as you say.

For now and always, I am not your vessel.

I opened my eyes and looked up into the sky.

I still lay on the arena floor and figured I must have lost

consciousness—for how long, I had no idea. There were no sounds of battle, so that was a definite plus.

Then everything that had just happened came rushing back.

"Monty!" I said suddenly, looking around the arena floor. Monty was nowhere to be seen. "Monty!"

"Quit your screaming, boy," Dex said as he came into view. "Tristan is in the infirmary, recovering."

I tried to get up and found green bands of energy holding me in place. My wrists, legs, and even my chest were covered in thick bands of green energy, holding me down to the floor of the arena.

"What's going on?" I said, struggling against the bands. "Why am I being restrained?"

"That would be my doing," Dex said as he crouched down. "When your pup brought me here, you were both in a bad way. Tristan was the priority at that moment, what with the blood loss and the neutralizing of his power. He nearly died. Would you happen to know how that happened?"

"That's how he knew the palm had worked—it had worked on him too."

That's when I noticed Nemain resting on the ground next to Dex. The energy signatures surrounding him and his insane weapon were promising a painful death.

I could see what the Morrigan saw in him.

"Korin stabbed him and then I used the nullifying palm on her, but he was in close proximity. Actually he had her trapped in his arms. The palm must have affected him, too. That's why he didn't heal himself after she wounded him. He couldn't."

"That maneuver nearly ended him," Dex said. "I'm certain that was his plan. Get close, trap her, and then use the palm."

I nodded.

"I didn't think it worked, but he was positive it had," I said. "How bad is it?"

"Aye, we can discuss that later," he said, his voice concerned. "When I came in here, you were covered in a black cloud of flame."

"Darkflame," I said, and he nodded.

"Tristan had explained what had happened with Julien, so I had some idea. When did the blade wake up?"

"You sensed that?"

"It's why you're bound, boy," he said. "I have something of a unique perspective dealing with lethally sentient weapons." He glanced at Nemain. "When did your blade awaken?"

"When we fought Julien, after I thought he killed Peaches," I said, and searched for my hellhound. He was sitting a few feet away and guarding my body. "What's wrong with him?"

"Nothing," Dex said. "He's reinforcing your bond. Whatever was in Ebonsoul tried to sever it. He wasn't going to let that happen, it seems. I'm no expert in hellhounds, but from what I understand, only death can break your bond."

Peaches padded over and gave me a thorough tongue-lashing.

<I will heal you.>

I stared at Dex helplessly as my hellhound attempted to drown me in slobber.

"Dex, please?" I pleaded.

The green bands around me vanished, and I gently pushed my hellhound away.

<Thank you, boy. I'm good now—better, even, now that you've healed me.>

<I stopped the dark lady from trying to take you. She is quiet now.>

<Thank you, boy.>

Dex helped me to my feet and we headed over to the infirmary.

First, Dex had walked me through the school grounds, which resembled a warzone more than a school campus.

"Will you be able to fix it?" I asked, looking at the blown out buildings and torn up sidewalks. "This is major destruction."

"It will be taken care of, and once my nephew is healed, he can help with recasting some of the runic defenses," Dex said. "It was a good trial run. I especially liked the performance of the MSGs. I might have to tweak their instructions a bit, though."

"You were watching?"

"Did you really think I was going to leave you three here alone?"

"Monty said you went to speak to the Tribunal," I said. "You didn't go?"

"Oh, I went," he said with a small smile. "I delivered the remains of their assassin after you incinerated her with that darkflame."

"Oh," I said. "That could've been prevented, but she wouldn't listen to reason. I tried to get her to change her mind. We both did."

"Plenty of unreasonable people out there," he said. "She chose to live…and die, for her beliefs."

"The High Tribunal brainwashed her."

"No," Dex said, his face dark. "She never had a choice. The Sword of the Tribunal is selected from an early age and molded into a weapon. You were never going to convince her."

We entered Monty's room where Peanut was keeping watch.

"Hi, Simon," she said with a small wave. "Mr. Montague is

healing nicely, Aunt Morrigan said." She looked at Dex. "Can I go help her now?"

"No activating any of the defenses," Dex said with a growl. "Go on with you."

Peanut ran out of the room, but not before giving Peaches a thorough head rub and backscratching.

"She's helping doing what, exactly?"

"Some of the defenses still need to be disabled," Dex said, gazing out of the room in the direction Peanut had taken. "Mo is seeing to it personally, and using it as a teaching moment for Peanut, to explain how each defense can be enhanced or neutralized."

"Isn't that dangerous?"

"Of course," Dex said. "This is a school for battlemages. It's supposed to be dangerous."

"What happened to the Arcanists who survived?"

"I shipped them back to their Keeper," Dex said, shaking his head. "Most of them survived the attack. A large group wasn't lucky or smart. You have the Keeper's attention now."

"Now?" I asked, surprised. "I thought we've had it for a while now?"

"You had his interest, but now you have the First Elder Rune, and he wants it back," Dex said. "That means you now have his undivided attention. Congratulations."

"Yay us," I said, feeling terrible. "How bad is this?"

"Fairly horrible," Monty said from the bed. "About as horrible as I feel."

"Why didn't you tell me the palm was going to work on you, too?"

"Would you have done it if I had?"

"No."

"That's why," he said. "Is the Tribunal dealt with, Uncle Dex?"

"For the time being, yes," Dex said. "Don't think they

won't come after you. They will bide their time and strike when they think it's to their advantage. They won't stop—"

"Unless we stop them," I finished.

Dex nodded.

"Aye," Dex said. "Take some time—you've earned it. Gault won't try to mangle you to bloody lifeless pulps right away, not after this defeat. Besides, he knows where the First Elder Rune is now. He doesn't need to rush."

"And he lost most of his Arcanists. Between the Midnight Echelon and this place, I'd be surprised if he had any still willing to serve him."

"There are always those who pursue power," Dex said. "He will rebuild his Arcanists."

"We need to find a way to stop him from getting to the other Keepers," I said. "He already got to Keeper Ustrina."

"She's currently missing," Dex said, his expression dark. "No one knows where she is."

"We need to formulate a plan before we confront him," Monty said. "There's only one person who can help us with that."

I nodded, knowing where he was going.

"We need to find Keeper Evergreen, don't we?"

"Only if we want to survive."

"Now, with that, I think I can help you," Dex said. "I know someone who can point you in the right direction."

"Excellent," Monty said, sitting up. "We can formulate a plan and—"

"As soon as you heal up, or should I summon Roxanne?"

Monty lay back down.

"That was uncalled for," Monty said. "You know she'll never let me leave."

"Pity I contacted her, then," Dex said with a grin. "I knew you'd never listen to me."

"What did you do this time?" Roxanne said from the

doorway. "Honestly, is it too much to ask for you to go a month without inflicting some kind of injury upon yourself?"

"This was not self-inflicted," Monty protested. "Tell her, Simon."

I started backing out of the room with Dex.

"Don't you have somewhere to be?" Dex asked, glancing at me. "Right now you have to go have that blade checked. Isn't that right?"

"Absolutely, I was just on my way right now to see what may be wrong with it, if anything," I said, moving faster. "I'll leave you two alone to discuss things."

Monty glared daggers at Dex and me.

"I won't forget this," Monty said as Roxanne moved to the side to allow her small army of medical personnel to bring equipment into the room and situate themselves. "Mark my words. It will be my pleasure to return this gracious gift."

"See to it that he heals well, Director," Dex said. "We can handle things in the meantime. Your *only* priority should be Tristan. If you need anything, anything at all, don't hesitate to let me know."

Roxanne nodded, focusing on Monty.

We practically dashed from the room.

"That was a cruel and unusual punishment," I said as we stepped outside. "He's going to be impossible to deal with."

"Ach," Dex said, shaking his head. "He may complain, but that woman is his heart. Don't worry, though—I didn't want you to feel left out. Director Nakatomi will be arriving shortly."

"What?" I asked, dumbfounded. "Why would you do that?"

"Aside from the fact that your blade woke up?" Dex asked. "You're not paying attention, boy. You have Gault's *undivided* attention. Where would you strike if your enemy had something you wanted?"

"At their weaknesses."

"Which is why both Directors are currently visiting the Montague School of Battle Magic to discuss the future of this esteemed institution," Dex said. "The fact that you and my nephew happen to be visiting at the same time is pure coincidence."

"Of course it is," I said, giving him a sidelong glance. "He would really go after them?"

"In a heartbeat," Dex said. "It's what I would do. We call that leverage where I come from."

"You are a devious and dangerous man, Dex," I said. "I'm glad you're on our side."

"Aye. Things are going to get darker before we see the light," he said. "It's best to prepare now, before the bleeding starts."

"You know what I need?"

"Of course. I just had a new shipment delivered," Dex said, clapping me on the shoulder with a laugh. "Deathwish, extra-extra death. Come join me for a mug, if you dare."

"Don't have to ask me twice," I said. "Lead the way."

He gestured and created an enormous sausage for my hellhound as he led us to the cafeteria and to the promise of amazing javambrosia.

THE END

AUTHOR NOTES

Thank you for reading this story and jumping into the world of Monty & Strong with me.

Disclaimer: The Author Notes are written at the very end of the writing process. This section is not seen by the ART or my amazing Jeditor—Audrey. Any typos or errors following this disclaimer are mine and mine alone.

"Life is pain, highness. Anyone who says differently is selling something."
— **William Goldman**

This, of course, has become Simon's new mantra/philosophy.

My wife and a few other readers have commented on how Simon just goes from pain to to agony to greater pain, on his adventures through the world of magic he was shoved into.

Even I wince on occasion when I know a particularly excruciating section is coming up. I feel for Simon, I really do, but as Gibson says: Life is pain. It seems at its core this is the deeper message Kali wanted Simon to learn when she cursed him alive.

Of course, she then goes on to add to that pain with her particular brand of emphasis...I mean, she's Kali after all, she's not going to extend her Marked One a lifeline, unless it's made of razor wire, because that would *build character*.

I initially felt the opening of this story, when outlined, was going to move too slowly and that you, my amazing reader, would feel the pace drag. I have been assured by many of you, that you don't feel this to be the case, but were curious and eager to learn what would happen next.

I have to admit, after many rereads, the pace feels just right.

I may be used to the Terrible Trio's pace of explode everything in sight, fight (insert big bad boss here), escape with their lives (barely), create new situation (with imminent explosions), have a few moments to reflect, right before Big Bad Boss, known as 3B from here on, unleashes some other horror on them, causing them to run until running is no longer possible, in which case they must confront and fight and whew...I'm tired just writing that.

So it was a nice change of pace to have them dive deeper into what power means, who should have access to it, and why that may be important in the world of magic. It was also great fun to give Simon some time with the Morrigan and especially Badb Catha. I enjoyed his moments facing her and then when the fear passed, confronting her and exerting his will into the 'negotiations'.

I look forward to that conversation with Kali later, when he attempts to call her on the plans happening in the background without his knowledge. It will prove to be an informative (and of course, painful) lesson for him.

I have explained that these three books (LOST RUNES, ARCHMAGE, ENTROPY) are a smaller arc within the larger arc of the series. If these three books were taken as one book, this book, ARCHMAGE would be the squishy middle of the book. ENTROPY, the next book, promises to be a faster paced book with Gault coming after them early and exacting what he considers the right amount of pressure to their pain points.

It will be scary, exciting, funny, sad, and enlightening.

Pretty much a regular day for the Trio of Terror.

On that note, I do want to apologize.

One moment...I have heard that some of you read the Author Notes before reading the story, if that's what's happening right now, SPOILER ALERT...GO BACK and READ THE BOOK FIRST!

.
.
.
.
.

Okay, if you are still reading, I want to say, I apologize for Peaches dying. His death was a necessary event in the story. I'm still tearing up about it, but it was needed to get Simon to the next level.

It had to happen.

.
.
.

If you read that and flew into a rage about how I killed Peaches, you should have read the story first...you were warned. For those of you that DID read the story. I do apologize. It needed to happen the way it did and if you read the story you know it turned out okay.

I did, however, get plenty of messages warning me I was treading on thin ice and that it was cracking as I traversed the story. I was getting dangerously close to getting a visit from the MoB, and it wasn't going to be pretty.

You don't kill the dog...ever (I learned the lesson way back in Blood is Thicker, really I did. Trust me).

That being said, it was a hard scene to write, even when I knew it wasn't a final death. It did take a few moments (and several tries) to get it into the story the right way. So for *that* scare, I do apologize.

In ENTROPY we see Simon and Chi interacting again, and it will be awkward of course, they have both changed, Simon more than Michiko, and there is that little detail about Ebonsoul being a necrotic seraph with a few added bonus features that weren't present when Chi gave him the blade.

Let's not forget that Izanami is waking up too. That will present some particular challenges. It may require that Grey pay Simon a visit before things get out of hand, we'll see. That sounds like a fun and dangerous turn of events.

Yes, Dira is still out there and she wants what Simon has, except that Simon is considerably stronger since she last saw him. Will she take that into account and try to eliminate him anyway? Or will she bide her time, and attempt to grow stronger to face him on even footing? Either way, it will be interesting to see which path she chooses.

Verity, at least officially, is backing off from the Trio, but the High Tribunal—unofficially, will not relent, rest, or quit. They will do whatever they need to destroy them...even if that means they have to get their hands dirty to do it.

They will get their hands very dirty in the next few stories.

Of course, the main thrust of this next story will be Gault and his Dark Arcanists (or Darkanists, as Simon will call them), a group of arcanists he has imbued with heightened abilities, they will prove to be a clear and present danger, not only to the Trio, but to everyone they know.

In order to face Gault, they will have to bring in some big

guns (no, not The Ten..things aren't THAT bad...yet), but I think some of the unknown members of the Midnight Echelon will make an appearance, along with some of the known. They are always fun to have in a story.

On that note, we may not see much of Peanut in ENTROPY (sorry, she has major chores and studying to do), but she will make appearances in other stories (I think she would fit right in with the Brew & Chew Crew) and who knows, eventually she may get her own story in the future? Never say never.

There are other situations forming, just out of sight, that will be hinted at in ENTROPY. Some of them, will come to the forefront, some mages will die and some of those poor victims will seek out a certain immortal who happens to wield a necrotic blade and will be able to interact with the recently deceased.

Poor Simon, he's in for many sleepless nights in his immediate future.

Then there is the small matter of the First Elder Rune currently threatening to kill both, Monty and Simon (you thought I forgot, didn't you?) somehow that needs to be resolved by the end of ENTROPY. The solution will be... interesting, but I can't tell you that now—there's a whole book ahead for that.

So here we are, 20 books in and the series, which currently sits at 40 books outlined and countless spinoffs in the making (<cough> Treadwell Supernatural Directive being the latest<cough>) shows no sign of slowing down. I know I've said this many times before, but I honestly thought this would just be a trilogy—Monty, Simon & Peaches thought otherwise, and I'm enjoying this crazy amazing ride.

I hope you are too!

I want to sincerely thank you for joining me in this adventure, these are by far the easiest and hardest stories for me to tell, but your being there with me for each part of this adventure makes it worthwhile.

Read that last paragraph again, go ahead, I'll wait.

I may write the stories, but, as I said in a recent episode of the MoB Kaffeeklatsch, there is one character that is in every story I write—you. Every story I write is like sharing an adventure with you and I'm here for it...for all of it.

You, as the reader, are important to me and my storytelling, and I hope we can share so many more stories in the future, until we are sharing them with the next generation and the generations after them.

I do apologize for not being more transparent in these notes(some of the cryptic magespeak must be contagious), but I do promise the next book in the series is being worked on as you read these words. I'm as anxious as you are to get to the next part of the story, it promises to be an exciting ride.

So...grab a large mug of Death Wish Extra (for those of you who are brave or insane enough, or a combination of both—extra-extra), jump into the Dark Goat, (shove the Zen Meat Master of Sprawlificence over), and strap in. No, I'm serious, really, strap in. This is not a joke.

We have places to go, people to see, and buildings to explode!

As always, remembering the sage words of our resident Zen Hellhound Master...

Meat is Life!

Thank you again for jumping into this story with me!

SPECIAL MENTIONS

To Dolly: My rock, anchor, and inspiration. Thank you...always.

Larry & Tammy—The WOUF: Because even when you aren't there...you're there.

Orlando A. Sanchez
www.orlandoasanchez.com

Orlando has been writing ever since his teens when he was immersed in creating scenarios for playing Dungeons and Dragons with his friends every weekend.

The worlds of his books are urban settings with a twist of the paranormal lurking just behind the scenes and with generous doses of magic, martial arts, and mayhem.

He currently resides in Queens, NY with his wife and children.

BITTEN PEACHES PUBLISHING

Thanks for Reading

If you enjoyed this book, would you please **leave a review** at the site you purchased it from? It doesn't have to be long... just a line or two would be fantastic and it would really help me out.

Bitten Peaches Publishing offers more books by this author. From science fiction & fantasy to adventure & mystery, we bring the best stories for adults and kids alike.

www.BittenPeachesPublishing.com

More books by Orlando A. Sanchez

The Warriors of the Way

The Karashihan*•The Spiritual Warriors•The Ascendants•The Fallen Warrior•The Warrior Ascendant•The Master Warrior

John Kane

The Deepest Cut*•Blur

Sepia Blue
The Last Dance*•Rise of the Night•Sisters•Nightmare•Nameless

Chronicles of the Modern Mystics
The Dark Flame•A Dream of Ashes

Montague & Strong Detective Agency Novels
Tombyards & Butterflies•Full Moon Howl•Blood is Thicker•Silver Clouds Dirty Sky•Homecoming•Dragons & Demigods•Bullets & Blades•Hell Hath No Fury•Reaping Wind•The Golem•Dark Glass•Walking the Razor•Requiem•Divine Intervention•Storm Blood•Revenant•Blood Lessons•Broken Magic•Lost Runes•Archmage

Montague & Strong Detective Agency Stories
No God is Safe•The Date•The War Mage•A Proper Hellhound•The Perfect Cup•Saving Mr. K

Brew & Chew Adventures
Hellhound Blues

Night Warden Novels
Wander•ShadowStrut•Nocturne Melody

Division 13
The Operative•The Magekiller

Blackjack Chronicles
The Dread Warlock

The Assassin's Apprentice
The Birth of Death

Gideon Shepherd Thrillers
Sheepdog

DAMNED
Aftermath

RULE OF THE COUNCIL
Blood Ascension•Blood Betrayal•Blood Rule

NYXIA WHITE
They Bite•They Rend•They Kill

IKER THE CLEANER
Iker the Unseen•Daystrider

*Books denoted with an asterisk are **FREE** via my website
—www.orlandoasanchez.com

ART SHREDDERS

I want to take a moment to extend a special thanks to the ART SHREDDERS.

No book is the work of one person. I am fortunate enough to have an amazing team of advance readers and shredders.

Thank you for giving of your time and keen eyes to provide notes, insights, answers to the questions, and corrections (dealing wonderfully with my extreme dreaded comma allergy). You help make every book and story go from good to great. Each and every one of you helped make this book fantastic, and I couldn't do this without each of you.

THANK YOU

ART SHREDDERS

Amber, Anne Morando, Audrey Cienki
Barbara Hamm, Bethany Showell, Beverly Collie
Cam Skaggs, Cat, Chris Christman II

Dawn McQueen Mortimer, Denise King, Diane Craig, Dolly Sanchez, Donna Young Hatridge

Hal Bass, Helen Valentine

Jasmine Breeden, Jasmine Davis, Jeanette Auer, Jen Cooper, Joy Kiili, Joy Ollier, Julie Peckett

Karen Hollyhead

Larry Diaz Tushman, Laura Tallman I

Malcolm Robertson, Marcia Campbell, Mary Anne Petruska, Maryelaine Eckerle-Foster, Melissa Miller, Melody DeLoach

Paige Guido, Penny Campbell-Myhill

RC Battels, Rene Corrie

Sara Mason Branson, Sondra Massey, Stacey Stein, Susie Johnson

Tami Cowles, Ted Camer, Terri Adkisson

Vikki Brannagan

Wendy Schindler

ACKNOWLEDGEMENTS

With each book, I realize that every time I learn something about this craft, it highlights so many things I still have to learn. Each book, each creative expression, has a large group of people behind it.

This book is no different.

Even though you see one name on the cover, it is with the knowledge that I am standing on the shoulders of the literary giants that informed my youth, and am supported by my generous readers who give of their time to jump into the adventures of my overactive imagination.

I would like to take a moment to express my most sincere thanks:

To Dolly: My wife and greatest support. You make all this possible each and every day. You keep me grounded when I get lost in the forest of ideas. Thank you for asking the right questions when needed, and listening intently when I go off on tangents. Thank you for who you are and the space you create—I love you.

To my Tribe: You are the reason I have stories to tell. You cannot possibly fathom how much and how deeply I love you all.

To Lee: Because you were the first audience I ever had. I love you, sis.

To the Logsdon Family: The words *thank you* are insufficient to describe the gratitude in my heart for each of you. JL, your support always demands I bring my best, my A-game, and produce the best story I can. Both you and Lorelei (my Uber Jeditor) and now, Audrey, are the reason I am where I am today. My thank you for the notes, challenges, corrections, advice, and laughter. Your patience is truly infinite. *Arigato-gozaimasu.*

To The Montague & Strong Case Files Group—AKA The MoB (Mages of Badassery): When I wrote T&B there were fifty-five members in The MoB. As of this release, there are over one thousand five hundred members in the MoB. I am honored to be able to call you my MoB Family. Thank you for being part of this group and M&S.

You make this possible. **THANK YOU.**

To the ever-vigilant PACK: You help make the MoB...the MoB. Keeping it a safe place for us to share and just...be. Thank you for your selfless vigilance. You truly are the Sentries of Sanity.

Chris Christman II: A real-life technomancer who makes the **MoBTV LIVEvents +Kaffeeklatsch** on YouTube amazing. Thank you for your tireless work and wisdom. Everything is connected...you totally rock!

To the WTA—The Incorrigibles: JL, Ben Z., Eric QK., S.S., and Noah.

They sound like a bunch of badass misfits, because they are. My exposure to the deranged and deviant brain trust you all represent helped me be the author I am today. I have officially gone to the *dark side* thanks to all of you. I humbly give you my thanks, and...it's all your fault.

To my fellow Indie Authors: I want to thank each of you for creating a space where authors can feel listened to, and encouraged to continue on this path. A rising tide lifts all the ships indeed.

To The English Advisory: Aaron, Penny, Carrie, Davina, and all of the UK MoB. For all things English...thank you.

To DEATH WISH COFFEE: This book (and every book I write) has been fueled by generous amounts of the only coffee on the planet (and in space) strong enough to power my very twisted imagination. Is there any other coffee that can compare? I think not. DEATH WISH—thank you!

To Deranged Doctor Design: Kim, Darja, Tanja, Jovana, and Milo (Designer Extraordinaire).

If you've seen the covers of my books and been amazed, you can thank the very talented and gifted creative team at DDD. They take the rough ideas I give them, and produce incredible covers that continue to surprise and amaze me. Each time, I find myself striving to write a story worthy of the covers they produce. DDD, you embody professionalism and creativity. Thank you for the great service and spectacular covers. **YOU GUYS RULE!**

To you, the reader: I was always taught to save the best for last. I write these stories for **you**. Thank you for jumping down the rabbit holes of ***what if?*** with me. You are the reason I write the stories I do.

You keep reading...I'll keep writing.

Thank you for your support and encouragement.

CONTACT ME

I really do appreciate your feedback. You can let me know what you thought of the story by emailing me at:
orlando@orlandoasanchez.com

To get **FREE** stories please visit my page at:
www.orlandoasanchez.com

For more information on the M&S World...come join the MoB Family on Facebook!
You can find us at:
Montague & Strong Case Files

Visit our online M&S World Swag Store located at:
Emandes

If you enjoyed the book, **please leave a review**. Reviews help the book, and also help other readers find good stories to read.
THANK YOU!

Thanks for Reading

If you enjoyed this book, would you **please leave a review** at the site you purchased it from? It doesn't have to be a book report…just a line or two would be fantastic and it would really help us out!

Printed in Great Britain
by Amazon